ONLY A GAME

ONLY A GAME

J.M. Gregson

This first world edition published 2010
in Great Britain and in the USA by
SEVERN HOUSE PUBLISHERS LTD of
9–15 High Street, Sutton, Surrey, England, SM1 1DF.
Trade paperback edition published
in Great Britain and the USA 2010 by
SEVERN HOUSE PUBLISHERS LTD

British Library Cataloguing in Publication Data

Gregson, J. M.
   Only a Game. – (DCI Percy Peach mystery)
   1. Peach, Percy (Fictitious character) – Fiction.
   2. Police – England – Lancashire – Fiction. 3. Soccer
   teams – England – Lancashire – Fiction. 4. Soccer –
   Management – Fiction. 5. Detective and mystery stories.
   I. Title II. Series
   823.9'14-dc22

ISBN-13: 978-0-7278-6859-6   (cased)
ISBN-13: 978-1-84751-210-9   (trade paper)

All Severn House titles are printed on acid-free paper.

 **Mixed Sources**
Product group from well-managed
forests and other controlled sources
www.fsc.org Cert no. SA-COC-1565
© 1996 Forest Stewardship Council

Typeset by Palimpsest Book Production Ltd.,
Grangemouth, Stirlingshire, Scotland.
Printed and bound in Great Britain by
MPG Books Ltd., Bodmin, Cornwall.

To Rose,
who reads, advises and improves
as only a wife can.

ONE

'Of course, it's only a game. It's not a matter of life and death,' said Edward Lanchester.

He looked round the table, assessing the reactions of his listeners, trying to time the pay-off line perfectly. Then he said, 'Football's much more important than that!'

They all laughed, dutifully rather than convincingly, because they'd all heard the quotation before and had known what was coming. A little deference which cost them nothing was surely due to the oldest man in the room. Lanchester didn't notice the hollowness of the mirth. He grinned at his audience delightedly and said, 'Bill Shankly said that, you know!'

They did, and they knew two or three other of the great man's sayings, not only because Lanchester often quoted them but because this was a board meeting at Brunton Rovers Football Club. Everyone around the big boardroom table was a football man.

There was a little pause before the chairman said, 'A great man, Shankly.'

'The greatest football manager of all, in my opinion,' said Edward Lanchester reverently. 'Just what we could do with now, to get the enthusiasm back on the terraces.'

Jim Capstick glanced sideways at Robbie Black, the present manager of Brunton Rovers. He was gazing down at his agenda sheet with a fixed half-smile and didn't seem to have taken any offence. The chairman cleared his throat and said, 'As you say, Edward, fixing the prices for the cup tie replay is not a matter of life and death. Can we have suggestions, please?'

Black nodded, then spoke in his soft, Anglo-adjusted, Edinburgh accent. 'I'd like to fill the terraces for this match, to give my lads a bit of support and enthusiasm. I wouldn't say it in front of their directors, but Carlisle United aren't the biggest draw in the country. They'll bring a few supporters with them, because playing a Premiership team is a big night for them, but probably not more than a couple of thousand for a midweek evening match. I'd like to see us let people in for a tenner on that night!'

There was a shocked silence, as he had known there would be. Then the chairman said, 'We'd make a loss on the match.'

Black was ready for this. He said in his soft Scottish accent, 'Not if we had twenty-five thousand, rather than the ten thousand we might get at regular prices. What I don't want is a thin crowd and players not up for it and perhaps even a damaging defeat. We might draw Manchester United away in the next round, if we get through, and get our share of a huge gate at Old Trafford.'

The old argument that was dangled in front of small clubs throughout the land. The Theatre of Dreams, they called Old Trafford, and it was certainly the stuff of dreams for many an impoverished club and its desperate treasurer.

It was the chief executive of Brunton Rovers, still often referred to as a secretary in the old-fashioned world of football, who now provided their manager with an unexpected ally. Darren Pearson pursed his lips and took the plunge. 'It might get us some publicity. Good publicity, for a change.' He shot a challenging look at Black, who had recently condoned some strong-arm tactics on the field which had led to sendings-off and press headlines about 'Ruthless Rovers'. 'Cut-price seats will be a story for them, if we make the cuts dramatic enough. We could sell them the idea that it was still the people's game round here, the way it used to be in the days of Bill Shankly.'

'The days when we got regular crowds of thirty thousand and more. When we didn't need hundreds of policemen and scores of our own stewards to control them,' said Edward Lanchester, predictably.

'We should charge what the market will bear,' persisted Pearson. 'I agree with our manager. It's better to have the ground full or even two-thirds full than to have long rows of empty seats filling the television pictures. Get through this one and look for the pickings in subsequent rounds, that's my view.'

'I think we should defer to our chief executive and our manager on this one,' said the chairman. 'Let's face it, we're only talking about a thousand pounds or two either way. Scarcely a day's wages for an average striker, nowadays.' He held up his hand at Edward Lanchester, preventing the former chairman from coming in with his well-worn diatribe on how the abolition of the maximum wage forty-odd years earlier had ruined football and been the beginning of the end for the smaller clubs up and down the land. 'Are we agreed on a ten pound entry fee for this one night, then?'

They were, of course. Football clubs still have their boards, still pay lip service to democracy and consensus. But the reality in most cases is that chairmen are increasingly powerful. They usually have heavy financial stakes in the club, for a start, and any suggestion that they might walk away is usually enough to bring opponents scurrying into line. Today's chairmen are usually business men like Jim Capstick, who are used to power and unused to handling opposition. This dominance is both a strength and a weakness: it gives such men the dictator's power to achieve quick results, but if megalomania sets in it can blind them to any ideas other than their own.

Jim Capstick was a modern chairman, very different from the one Lanchester had been a generation earlier. He owned most of the shares in what was still a private company and the board would oppose his formidable will at its peril. Most of them recognized that reality.

The discussion now moved on to what should have been the most interesting part of the meeting, the one everyone in the room had been anticipating during the last hour's brisk despatch of more routine items. Even the chairman could not keep a little excitement out of his practised tones as he said, 'Item six on your agenda. Summer transfer activity.' He studied his sheet for a moment, revolving his silver ball pen slowly between his fingers. 'Perhaps I should reiterate what I'm sure we all think should be taken as read. On this item in particular, not a word of what is said within this room tonight should be repeated outside it. It should be obvious to all of us that any mention of either our financial situation or any particular targets we may have should not be leaked to the press or to anyone else. Any such leaks can only damage our manager's position in any dealings he may choose to initiate.'

There were murmurs of assent round the table, the murmurs he had known would come. The need for secrecy here was self-evident: the press and the rest of the media were expert at turning the merest whiff of smoke into tongues of flame. Capstick deliberately did not look at the manager himself: Robbie Black had been known to ferment dissent among the supporters and sympathy for himself by thinly veiled suggestions that he could not bid for the players he wanted because his hands were tied by a miserly board. Chairman and manager worked well together on the whole, but there was only room for one ego in the overall direction of the club.

Black now aired three of his targets for the summer close season, the only time when deals could now be done, except for a brief 'transfer window' in January. Two of them had already been mentioned as possibilities by a press that fed on rumour and transformed intelligent guesses into rumours when there were none to be had. The third player was a surprise and would present a major coup for a club which was very small in terms of the Premier league. The possibility surprised and delighted even the experienced heads around the table. If he could be prised away from Newcastle United, that would be an achievement in itself.

There was excitement at the thought of Brunton Rovers going for all three of these players. Everyone in this all-male gathering had football in his blood. Although their very presence here implied that they should be hard-headed realists, they knew that everything came back to what was achieved on the pitch. When eleven very fit young men from all over the world trotted out to represent the old cotton town, they might know little of the hundred and thirty years of history behind the proud old club, but they were well aware that the points they won or lost in the most competitive league in the world would settle its immediate destiny. Highly successful businessmen might be ruthless and clear-sighted in the rest of their dealings, but there had to be a strong streak of romanticism underlying any deep involvement with a team like Brunton Rovers.

There were limits, of course, and Darren Pearson saw it as his duty as secretary to keep feet on the ground and heads out of clouds and any other cliché which would prevent financial disaster. He now said reluctantly, 'We may need to sell before we can buy.'

There was a shocked silence, a mental throwing of hands in the air that the secretary's characteristically dismal reminder should puncture the balloon of optimism so soon. Edward Lanchester said, 'We've been prudent enough in the last year, surely? Our supporters expect the team to be strengthened.' His face brightened as an argument came into his mind. 'It will help season ticket sales for next year if we make some captures.' For almost half a century, Edward had used that nineteen fifties word for any new signing and he wasn't going to change now.

Pearson gave him the sour smile of a man who had heard the argument too many times. 'The evidence is that season ticket sales will vary by only a thousand or so whatever we do. The days when a club like ours could sign an Alan Shearer are long gone. Unless a billionaire with a big cheque book comes along, which won't happen for us, we need to cut our coat from the cloth we can afford. It's not what you want to hear, but I wouldn't be doing my job if I said anything else.'

The manager felt the need to recruit some backing for his cause. He said sternly, 'I went into this job with my eyes open. The chairman has always been honest with me and has always supported me to the limits of his powers.' It never did any harm to support the man with the power, so he smiled a little acknowledgement of Capstick's support towards the top of the table. 'But I'm walking a tightrope here. We need to strengthen the team whenever we have the opportunity. I need hardly remind you how important it is for us to stay in the Premier League. The bottom club there will get thirty million pounds this year. If we drop into the Championship and lose that money, not only the team but the whole club will disintegrate.'

'How much would we get if we sold Ashley Greenhalgh?' said the chairman.

There was a gasp round the table. It was the question which all of them wanted answered, but none of them had dared to ask. The twenty-one-year-old Greenhalgh was the local sensation, the young man who had grown up within five miles of the town and come through the Brunton Academy to reach the fringes of the England team. No one wanted him to leave, but most of them privately regarded it as inevitable in the glitzy modern football world.

A man who had been on the board in the days of Lanchester made the ritual protest. 'We can't afford to lose Greenhalgh. We should be building a team around him.' There were murmurs of assent from around the table, but no one spoke up to support the idea.

Instead, Jim Capstick said, 'That is what we'd all like to do, so there's no argument about it. It may be simply impossible to do it. Is the lad any nearer to signing a contract extension?'

Robbie Black shook his head. 'No. His agent has told him not to. He loves playing for Brunton but he's hoping one of the big four clubs will come in for him. You can't blame the lad: he thinks his England prospects will be improved by playing for one of the big clubs, and he's probably right.'

'Bloody agents! We shouldn't have to deal with them!' was Edward Lanchester's predictable reaction.

Black smiled wryly. 'I couldn't agree more, sir. Unfortunately, we have to. It's a fact of modern football life.' Don't put the old bastard down too firmly. He was a harmless enough survival from the old days, and he still carried clout in the town, if not in the football club he loved to the point of obsession. A football manager never knows when he might need friends.

The secretary reminded them of another unpleasant fact of football life. 'If he stays to the end of his contract, we won't get a fee at all. Ashley will be able to go where he pleases

on some vast wage, but the club will get nothing. If he won't
sign the new five-year deal we've offered him, we may need
to cash in this summer, whilst we can still get a big transfer
fee. I think we might get up to twenty million for him, if we
handle it right.' Darren Pearson voiced the unpleasant reality
they all had to confront with an air of sober resignation.

Jim Capstick allowed a moment of silence for this to hit
home before he said, 'I must stress again how important it
is that this discussion does not go beyond the walls of this
room. The press will continue to speculate, but if it gets out
that the Board may be willing to sell, it can only weaken
our position in any negotiations.'

The all-male gathering nodded sage agreement. A few
minutes later, they were filing out of the meeting and hurrying
to their cars, turning up their collars against the north wind
which reminded them that it was still only the beginning
of March, however much the bright crocuses might be
trumpeting spring.

The four people who had done most of the speaking gathered in the chairman's office and agreed that the meeting
had gone as well as could have been expected. Board meetings had long ceased to make any real decisions. Officially
they did so, but what happened nowadays was that they
rubber-stamped what the chairman had already decided. Jim
Capstick owned eighty per cent of the shares in the Brunton
Rovers Company, which had never gone public. Proceedings
were increasingly a recognition of the reality that power
was vested where the money and ownership lay. Anyone
who did not recognize that when it came to voting was
unlikely to remain on the board for long.

Edward Lanchester had once occupied this room himself.
He felt increasingly ill at ease in it now, aware that he was
invited in for a drink only because of his long association
and previous pre-eminence in the club. He didn't like what
was happening to what he still thought of as his club, but
he was enough of a realist to recognize that there wasn't
much he could do about it. He preserved his position as the
voice of decency with a few remarks about the shallow loyal-
ties of modern players, then downed his malt whisky as

quickly as he could and took his leave. Darren Pearson and Robbie Black made a few not unkindly remarks about the old dinosaur before following him out ten minutes later.

Jim Capstick stayed for a little while longer, sitting behind the big desk to conduct his own silent review of the evening. His secret was still his own; that was the most important thing. He hadn't come even near to revealing his plans for the next few months.

TWO

'We need an au pair.'
'Do we? I thought it was going to be easier for you now that they're both at school.'
'It is. But we can afford an au pair and I think we should have one.' Debbie Black put her empty cup back on its saucer beside the bed and rolled over to make sure that her request was treated seriously. She was not an easy woman to shrug off. But then not many people chose to shrug away Debbie Black's attentions.

Debbie had been the British number two at tennis, though her dark-haired beauty and willowy figure had enabled her to make more from modelling contracts than from a sporting career which had been much publicized without ever quite reaching the greatest international heights. She had enjoyed rather than endured the trappings of success and the racy tabloid lifestyle which went with it. Debbie had quickly become that vague but lucrative modern phenomenon, a 'personality'. By the time she retired from tennis at twenty-eight, she felt that there was little she did not know about life in general and sex in particular. Her early experiences on the international tennis circuit had taught her that her own gender held no physical attraction for her.

Within a year, Debbie had married Robbie Black, then a Scottish international football player. Robbie's looks and talent meant that his lifestyle had been subjected to the same sort of lurid tabloid coverage as her own. Although she was by then twenty-nine and he was thirty, it was a first marriage for both of them. Against the odds and what many had openly forecasted for them, the union had now lasted fifteen years.

Black was no fool, as Debbie had known from the start. He had played until he was thirty-five, then made a promising start on the hazardous but now handsomely paid career of football club manager. After success in the lower divisions, he was now one of the few British managers in the lucrative world of the English Premier League. The large and beautifully fitted modern house they lived in was tangible proof of his success. Debbie Black had found against her expectations that she enjoyed being out of the limelight and merely a glamorous presence in her husband's shadow. Even more to her surprise, she had grown to love the surrounding country and the blunt, friendly people of the North Lancashire area.

Robbie Black sighed theatrically as he felt her lithe body against his. 'I can't see that we need an au pair.' He was probably going to concede, he thought, but the persuasion might well be interesting.

Debbie lifted her head so that her large hazel eyes could look down into the darker brown of his, smiling the wide, half-mocking smile which was still as attractive as it had been twenty years ago. 'We may not actually *need* one, darling, but think how much more we'd enjoy life if we had one.'

He grinned back, enjoying the knowledge that they both knew they were playing a game of which only they knew the rules. 'I'm not here that much, am I? When I'm not checking up on the behaviour of my own players and watching them training, I'm sitting in the draughty stand of some God-forsaken second division or non-league team, watching the latest wonderkid and trying to pick up a bargain for Brunton Rovers.'

'You poor creature. Dedicated to his calling and going out to obey the call of duty in those long johns that no woman could resist.' She snuggled a little closer. 'It's a wonder that you retain any libido at all.' She slid a little further down the bed, checking on the evidence of that libido and allowing her loins a small anticipatory quiver of excitement.

He let his hand run down her back to the division at the base of it, stroking it expertly, preparing to enjoy the unhurried, confident enjoyment that comes from mutual physical knowledge. He began the teasing which was all part of that; the little, non-aggressive argument which would climax in the uninhibited joys of coupling. He muttered into the ear which was suddenly available, 'But suppose I get attracted to the au pair? Suppose her firm young Swedish body is thrust upon me and I am unable to resist?'

There was a small giggle, then a quick gasp of excitement as he entered her. 'What makes you think she'd be Swedish, or have a firm young body, Robbie? I'd be doing the shortlist and selection.'

'My God! A Romanian pensioner with no teeth, then.' He enjoyed her giggle as it shook her body delightfully, excitingly. There was no need to hurry, but he might not have that choice.

'There are no corn flakes and no rice crispies!' A high, childish, accusing voice from the doorway of the bedroom. She slid away from her husband, exciting a little involuntary cry of pain from him.

'All right, James. I bought some yesterday. They must be still in the boot of the car. I'll be there in a minute.' Debbie slid across and out of the big bed, pulling her nightdress down and hurrying to the door to give the boy a hug. But her son had turned indignantly away and was already halfway down the stairs, his small back a picture of righteous indignation.

Robbie Black stared at the ceiling and delivered an emphatic, 'Bugger it!' to no one in particular.

'There you are,' said his wife with triumphant female logic. 'Now you can see how desperately we need an au pair!'

Six miles away on the other side of the town, a very different woman from Debbie Black was also stirring herself into morning life. Helen Capstick was the second wife of the chairman of Brunton Rovers Football Club.

At forty-seven, she was ten years younger than Jim Capstick and she knew what she was about. It was her boast rather than her admission that she had been round the block a few times when she married him. That was her way of saying that she knew the male psyche intimately and that the men around her should be aware of it. Jim Capstick might know his way around business, might know more tricks of finance and manipulation than the other fish in the dangerous ponds in which he swam. But in choosing a wife – it was better to leave him with the illusion that he had done the choosing – he had given himself a partner who could anticipate his every sexual whim, his every social reaction to other men and women. He had better be aware of that fact; he had better take full account of it in his actions.

This streak of hardness, this capacity for clear-sighted assessment of herself and those closest to her, did not mean that Helen Capstick was without affection for her chosen mate. She looked at Jim in his underwear through the open door of the bathroom, as he stood before his shaving mirror and concentrated on his heavily lathered, deeply jowled face. He was a large man, not grossly overweight, but with the plumpness which often comes with high prosperity and the temptations of good food and wines. With his plentiful grey-white hair, still clear grey eyes, and heavy, regular features, he still scrubbed up well, she thought, even if at fifty-seven he needed to give more attention to the efforts of tailors and hair stylists than he would have done as a young man.

And Jim Capstick was still much taken with his younger wife. She was skilfully made up by the time he was fully dressed. Her hair was the exact shade of polished bronze which she had chosen to accentuate her striking blue eyes; the crows' feet around them had retreated dutifully before her cosmetic efforts. She kissed him lightly on the forehead, as she did every morning when he was at home, as if putting her invisible imprint upon him for the day.

'How did the meeting go last night?'

He smiled. 'As well as these things can go, I suppose. It was less dynamic than my business gatherings, where what I say is simply accepted. At the football club, I have to be careful that I do not look too bored.' Jim Capstick was well aware by now that power is the greatest of aphrodisiacs and he took care to remind Helen without boasting that he had it.

She grinned. 'I'd like to see you pretending to be democratic. It must be a sight worth seeing.'

Jim Capstick smiled the rare, satisfied smile of the man who knows that his ego is being massaged but has the confidence to enjoy it. 'I'm afraid you'd find it rather dull, my dear. One has to go through the motions and listen to

different views from one's own. So long as everything
eventually goes the way you want it to, that's all that really
matters.'

They breakfasted together. He enjoyed this quiet part of
the day, this pleasant, unthreatening domesticity. In your
own home, you could switch off your awareness to every
nuance of speech, you could cease wondering what motives
lay behind the words and how you should measure your
own responses and your own initiatives. Home might be
this big nineteenth century mansion, built by a cotton
magnate and now the preserve of a more modern mogul,
but it was still home, a place where you could relax.

Outside it Jim measured every word he said before he
uttered it. Now, as he spread marmalade on his last piece
of toast and poured them both fresh cups of coffee, he
surprised himself by the spontaneity of his words. 'I wish
we'd married earlier, Helen. When we'd been young enough
to have children.'

It was a kind of love-making. She knew it for that immediately. Men were sentimental creatures, even men like Jim
Capstick, but they were appealing when they dropped their
guards and made themselves vulnerable like this. Helen was
glad she had kept on her dressing gown for breakfast. It was
surprisingly elegant for such a garment, with blue silk matching
exactly the colour of her eyes, yet it gave a touch of intimacy
to the meal which had fostered this thought in him.

She reached across the table and put her hand on top of
his. 'Don't let's dwell on things that can't be, Jim. We can't
turn the clock back, so let's not try.' For a moment, Helen
wondered what it would have been like to have children. In
truth, she'd never really wanted them, hadn't felt the yearning
in her womb she was supposed to feel as her biological
clock ticked on inexorably. She couldn't see how they would
have been anything except a disaster in her complicated life.

She gave Jim the kind of smile which told him she was
grateful for what she knew had been a loving and complimentary thought. 'At least we're spared the agonies of taking
kids through their adolescence. Everyone with children seems
to find that hell. Let's make the most of what we've got,

love.' She was even using the Lancashire terms of endearment now, she noticed. She didn't mind that; indeed, she was pleased that the word had come to her lips so spontaneously.

As if moving consciously away from his moment of weakness, Jim glanced at his watch and said, 'Wally will be round with the car in a minute. I've a meeting in Birmingham at eleven thirty. What are you doing today?'

Wally Boyd was his driver, who lived in a self-contained flat over the big triple garage. Boyd was a squat man with a face which might have been cut from granite. He was also Jim Capstick's bodyguard, but that was never acknowledged, even between husband and wife. Helen said, 'I'm going over to Manchester. Meeting an old friend, Lucy Graham; I don't think you've met her. We'll have a good gossip, then maybe go into the shopping centre and hammer the plastic a bit.'

He wondered sometimes about the closed book which enclosed the years before he had known her. They chatted about it from time to time, but he never got her to reveal much. He controlled the impulse to find out what part this Graham woman had played in his wife's former life. 'Do you want Wally to drive you? I'm happy to drive the Bentley myself.'

'No need. I enjoy driving the Merc, as you know, and the parking is easy enough at Lucy's place.' She didn't want that silent, watchful presence at her side, recording her every action and passing an account back to the man who paid him. It would inhibit her freedom of movement.

The offer had been genuine, but Capstick was glad when she refused. He needed his man beside him as an insurance against any physical threat in the nation's second city. 'Enjoy your day, then.' He kissed her lovingly upon the lips. She responded, then used her paper napkin to remove the lipstick carefully from his mouth before he left her and went out into the world.

She liked being Helen Capstick, she told herself once again. She waved to Jim as he climbed heavily into the big car, then went upstairs and into her dressing-room, deciding unhurriedly on the clothes she would wear for the day.

Twenty minutes later, the big blue Bentley was on the M6 and heading rapidly south. Jim Capstick sat in the back and stared unseeingly at the papers he had taken out of his document case. In the intimacy of their marital exchanges, he had almost told Helen about what he planned for Brunton Rovers Football Club. He was surprised at himself when he realized that. On the whole, it was better that he hadn't, he decided. Yes, definitely better. Women were such natural gossips. It was better not to trust even women like Helen with his thoughts about the future.

DCI 'Percy' Peach enjoyed his day off. He had never been one for the long lie-in, but he breakfasted with unusual leisure, enjoying the ecstatic pleasure of bacon, egg, tomato and that anathema of the healthy eating lobby, a slice of white bread fried in bacon fat. His fiancée had lately introduced him to the *Guardian*. He passed hastily over the latest gay rights controversy and found the writing on the sports pages pleasantly illuminating.

When he was working in the CID section at Brunton nick, the weather rarely mattered to him. Today, he was pleased to see blue sky and high clouds, for he had arranged a golfing four-ball with friends at the North Lancs Golf Club in the afternoon. It was March now, and the sun was getting higher. He felt a little warmth in it as it shone upon his back in the hour of unaccustomed gardening he undertook to compensate for his breakfast indulgence.

He hadn't played golf for a while, and was a little wild at first. His companions said knowledgeably that his little-used golfing muscles must be stiff and he did not quibble. He was still fairly new to golf, but he had learned early that its practitioners were never short of an excuse for their eccentricities on the course. In the context of amateur golf, Percy Peach was still a young man at thirty-nine; the average age in the club was fifty-seven.

After a distinguished cricketing output as a quick-footed batsman in the Lancashire League, Percy had retired whilst many felt he was still at his peak. He had then taken up the challenge of golf. After three years, his handicap was a pleasing eight, and everyone assured him that there were possibilities of further improvement. He was stocky and compact, and his simple, powerful swing already had a consistency envied by all but the best golfers in the club.

His companion was a good golfer in the inevitable decline which age brings to any sportsman. Harry was in his seventies and had to make up for his disadvantage in length with his excellent short game around the greens. Their two companions had thought the old man the weakest of the four when they gave him to Percy Peach, but the two proved an effective combination, with old Harry coming in on the holes where Percy faltered, securing a score with his excellent chipping and putting.

This still very competitive elderly golfer was delighted when they won the modest stakes on the sixteenth green. He seemed to notice the weather for the first time, calling attention to the glorious sunset over the coast thirty miles to the west of them. As soon as they reached the clubhouse, he arranged a return match for Percy's next midweek day off, pointing out that very soon now the hour would be changed and it would be light until after seven. Spring was surely at hand; old Harry offered them that thought as he gleefully pocketed the losers' cash.

They had tea in the clubhouse. It was only then that Peach learned that Harry had been a coroner's officer for fifteen years before he retired. It was before Percy's time in Brunton CID, but it gave them a common bond. It also allowed Harry to expand on the past, as men of his age normally love to do. Even after their two companions had drunk their quota and left, the two exchanged anecdotes about bodies and villains, and the various tricks which had come to light when subjected to the rigorous procedures of the Coroner's Court.

Percy stopped drinking after his quota, as he knew he must, but his new companion came from a generation which was dangerously relaxed about the dangers of drink and driving. Harry went on enjoying his victory and his companionship well beyond the legal limit. Moreover, he was a much-loved elder of the club, a member for forty years and a winner in his prime of numerous competitions. Two of his former course companions deposited whiskies at their table, which were downed with relish by old Harry.

'You can't drive,' said Percy, when he eventually prised him out of the bar and into the cloakroom.

Harry urinated with a contented sigh and assured him with the inebriate's confidence that he would 'be all right'.

Percy wasn't having that. 'You won't. Even if you could drive, you'd be well over the limit. How would you get to the golf club if you lost your licence and couldn't drive?'

That harsh thought brought Harry up short, but by the time he left the golf club, he was still assuring his companion that he would drive carefully and wouldn't be stopped. Percy was about to offer the final argument, the one no policemen wants to use because it draws attention to his calling. He would have to tell Harry that he mustn't get into the driving seat of his car because a Detective Chief Inspector couldn't stand by and watch the law being broken.

Then fate intervened. As they went through the exit door of the clubhouse, the cold night air hit Harry and he reeled dramatically sideways until his hand fell upon the bonnet of a car and he steadied himself. 'Perhapsh you're right, Pershy,' he said, slurring his words for the first time. 'I'll get a taxi.' He swung round vaguely and almost fell over again.

'No need for that,' said Percy resignedly. 'I'll run you home. You can get your wife to bring you back to collect your car tomorrow.'

'She'll do that,' said Harry with the wide affectionate smile of the sentimental drunk. 'She'll give me a bollocking for being pished, but she'll run me up here tomorrow. She's a good woman, but don't tell her I shed so.'

Percy had led him to his own car and opened the passenger door for him. He fell laughing on to the seat and said with apparent surprise, 'You're right you know, Pershy. I am a bit pished!'

They had a mercifully quiet journey to his house. Percy realized after a couple of miles that the passenger he had fastened into his safety belt was fast asleep, with a smile on his face as innocent as a baby's. He accepted Harry's effusive thanks when he deposited him at his gate, watched his erratic progress until his wife opened the door and he lurched safely into his home.

Harry hadn't taken Peach very far out of his way, but he now had to drive back through the centre of Brunton to get to his ageing semi-detached house. He was negotiating the familiar labyrinth of the town's one-way system when he came upon the incident.

Three uniformed coppers and two gangs of youths. Whites and Asians; he knew that would be the case before he even looked at the participants, before he wound down his window and registered the shouted taunts and insults. With a rising Asian population and a recession in the economy to accentuate resentments, these confrontations were now almost a nightly Brunton occurrence.

The police were outnumbered as usual. There were just three of them against around a score of young men. Two men and a woman; you had to call them all police officers now, irrespective of gender.

Percy didn't want to stop. He was plain clothes and off duty, long past dealing with skirmishes like this. But it didn't seem long since he'd been a young copper himself, treading the beat and feeling the fear he could not show in dangerous situations like this. He could not say afterwards whether it was a fact that there was a woman in the trio which made him tread fiercely upon his brake pedal.

He climbed reluctantly out of the Focus and moved reluctantly back towards the screamed obscenities and the more measured warnings of the police. He brandished his warrant card as he arrived, well aware that the chief inspector rank would not be registered by young men intent upon a fight.

But his reputation went before him. The oldest man among the white contingent had a record and he recognized an old adversary. 'It's that bastard Peach!' he shouted to his companions, waving an arm with BNP tattoos towards the new arrival. 'Get the fuck out of it, or the bastard'll throw the fucking book at you!' With that warning, he and his British National Party companion forsook the group and raced away into the shadows.

It was a temporary relief. The group of Asian youths, whom the three police constables were holding back with linked arms, now saw an advantage in numbers. They surged forward against their ineffective cordon, so that the girl, losing her balance and her hat, almost descended beneath their advancing feet. Percy caught her involuntary cry of alarm in the same instant that he glimpsed the glint of steel in two places in the advancing horde.

Knives! The weapons the modern beat copper fears now more than anything, the deadly steel which can be suddenly evident in even minor incidents, often in the hands of young men who panic easily.

This incident was not minor. Percy flung himself upon the raised arm which held one of the knives, heard the yell of agony as he twisted it, even before he heard the clang of metal upon the pavement. 'You're nicked, sunshine!' he yelled at the top of his voice.

Peach thought that it must be his shouting of the formal words of arrest which had sobered the rest, but he should have known better. The blare of the police siren rang in his ears as he finished his warning, followed an instant later by the flashing blue lights of the car and the arrival of the much-needed police support the young coppers had summoned before his arrival.

The two rival gangs vanished as quickly as water through a colander, but the three uniformed officers who had been here from the start cut off the retreat of the two who had brandished knives and one other vociferous man, who seemed to be the leader of the Asian contingent. The three were stowed away in the police van with warnings against further resistance.

By the time a returning Helen Capstick drove her Mercedes along the same street ten minutes later, the town centre was silent and no one would have known there had been such recent drama there.

THREE

D arren Pearson was a man who did not panic easily. That was just as well, for being the secretary/chief executive of a Club like Brunton Rovers was a demanding task.

The club had clung characteristically to the old title of secretary, but in terms of the commercial enterprise every Premiership soccer team must be, their secretary was now what most companies would term a chief executive. Or general dogsbody, he sometimes thought. In the first hour of his working day, Pearson chivvied the printer about the delivery of the ten pound tickets and publicity posters for the 'bargain' FA Cup replay, negotiated with a superintendent at the police station about the number of police required for that night and the costs involved, and studied the extended contracts that were about to be offered to two of the Rovers' leading players.

Without the preparation he had promised himself, he now had to greet an official visitor from Barclays Bank, who was here to discuss the servicing and reduction of the club's banking debt. This promised to be a difficult half-hour, for banks in a recession were sensitive about debts and possible defaulters. Almost every Premiership team had substantial debts, but it was the small-town teams like Brunton Rovers who were most steadily under pressure from their bankers to reduce them.

Recession and their troubles of 2008 had made bankers jittery. The local ones were especially nervous about their soccer club. They looked at the diminishing numbers who trooped into Grafton Park as recession hit the earners of Brunton, read about the salaries which the millionaires on the pitch commanded, and sought some guarantee that debts would not only be serviced but eventually reduced.

'Unlike some other Premiership clubs, we own our ground and we have substantial assets,' Darren Pearson asserted sturdily, hoping that this latest banking luminary would not recognize an argument he had used many times before.

The woman gave him a tight smile which revealed nothing. Darren was still trying to conceal his surprise that a woman should be occupying this high position in the bank's commercial arm. Perhaps, he thought, she had been promoted not on merit but because Barclays' policy dictated that a certain number of women should occupy responsible posts. The next few minutes would destroy that hopeful conjecture. She gave him a wide smile and said, 'You had better give me some details of these assets, don't you think?'

'Well, er, there's our ground, as I said. And we own some land near the centre of the town. And of course our substantial training facilities at Drewcock Hall. We have thirty acres and some excellent permanent buildings there.' Darren realized that he must not use that word 'substantial' too often, but no other adjective would come to his racing mind.

She nodded, slipping a sheet from her briefcase and glancing at it for a few seconds before she replied. 'Full account was taken of your ground and the Drewcock Hall facilities when we extended your loan facilities in 2005. It's only fair to point out that property values have declined substantially in the last year. The values we have here should probably be revised downwards, particularly in the case of the Drewcock Hall estate.'

'These are not assets we intend to realize, so revisions are hardly relevant, are they? And I'm sure property values will recover in due course. It might take a year or two, but—'

'I'm sure you realize that banks have to live in the present, not in some hopeful and possibly illusory future, Mr Pearson.' She bathed him in a wider smile; an indulgent smile; a smile which bespoke her tolerance of his financial naivety. 'I have to say that there do not seem to be many other tangible assets to support the club's case for an extension of the period of the loan.'

Darren was stung by her knowledge as much as her attitude. 'On the contrary, we have very substantial assets, Ms Alcock. Most of them are exhibited to the public every Saturday or Sunday.'

'Ah! You mean your players.'

'The heart and soul of a football club. Without them, there would be no club and no client for your bank.'

'No bank deals with hearts, even less with souls, Mr Pearson. Those are matters for the various churches of the land – most of which seem to be in financial straits at the moment, incidentally. Your players are indeed assets, of course: you have a point, of sorts. But players are not the same kind of assets as bricks and mortar. Football players are the sort of asset which decline in value very quickly. They can even disappear overnight as assets, if they are unfortunate enough to suffer serious injury at their place of work.'

'Apart from their insurance value. All our players are insured against injury.'

Another smile, another assurance that she knew what he was about and had rehearsed these arguments many times before. 'I'm sure they are, Mr Pearson. But you must be aware as I am that insurance companies tend to have a very different view of current values than clubs have when players' careers are abruptly terminated. I can give you some examples, if they would be useful.' She opened her brief-case again, searching for a sheet of examples he was sure was there.

'That won't be necessary,' Pearson said hastily, feeling that the reassuring smile he now attempted himself was a feeble effort. He sought desperately for something to divert this chic and urbane assailant who seemed to have superior artillery. 'We may make some sales in the summer transfer period. It won't be entirely my decision of course, but it's possible that we might be able to offer you—'

'Ah, yes. What you would expect to get for Ashley Greenhalgh?'

Darren hoped his mouth hadn't dropped open, but he feared it had. 'I–I wasn't thinking of any particular player. It's not for me to—'

'Come, Mr Pearson, let's be realistic, shall we? You mustn't be surprised that a female should follow the sports pages nowadays. I'm a Manchester City supporter, as a matter of fact.' Ms Alcock leant forward confidentially.

Strictly between the two of us, I'm hoping they make a bid for Greenhalgh in the summer. He's just the sort of player we need, in my opinion.' She curbed the unprofessional enthusiasm which had broken through for a moment. 'All I'm saying is that you have in Greenhalgh a very substantial asset which could indeed be realized.'

'We were discussing the same thing in the board meeting the other night,' said Pearson, a little too eagerly. He checked himself; he too must behave professionally. 'Of course, you must treat that as highly confidential and I can offer you no guarantee that any particular player will be sold.'

'Of course. But my advice to you – strictly as a banker, you understand – is that the realization of a major asset of the club in the next few months would be welcomed by Barclays.' She beamed at him urbanely, as though they had reached an understanding. 'Is there anything else I can do for you this morning?'

Darren Pearson reflected that she had done precious little for him so far, other than to issue a Victorian treatise on the necessity for caution. Thrift hadn't yet been mentioned, but it was surely only a matter of time. He pointed out as firmly as he could, 'Interest rates are going down. It will be easier in the future for us to service our debt.'

'In the immediate future, yes. But you will be aware that no bank can guarantee interest rates in a year's time. It is our duty to remind our customers of that. Wherever possible in the present industrial climate, our advice is that debt should in fact be reduced.' She shook her head sadly and said weightily, 'I have to advise you that the director of my section, who is a member of the board and thus has a duty to implement its policies, advises me that he thinks this should be possible for football clubs.'

'And I in turn have to respond by saying that we are aware of the situation and will do our very best to conform.'

Ms Alcock slid her papers back into her briefcase with an air of satisfaction. She had been well aware when she came here that there would be no dramatic concessions on either side. They had played out their little game of backing and advancing, as if feeling their way into an old-time dance.

She had warned him that the club must come into line; Pearson had accepted the warning and said he would encourage his employers to take heed of it.

Alcock knew that it wasn't within Pearson's powers to do anything more concrete than that. She stood up and offered her hand. 'I hope that this will be the first of many fruitful meetings, Mr Pearson. It may not sound like it at this moment, but Barclays wants to help wherever it can. It's just that part of that help must sometimes be to issue warnings to those institutions which seem to be in danger of incurring too heavy a level of debt.'

'I understand that. I appreciate your comments, and I shall make sure our manager and my chairman are aware of them whenever any expenditure is contemplated.'

'We must meet again in September. I'll ring you again nearer the time to arrange a date.'

Which would be after the summer transfer deadline, when she could review the progress that had been made towards debt reduction. Both of them knew that, so there was no need to state it. She refused coffee and he showed her out.

In the end, it had gone as well as could be expected, Darren Pearson decided. He had been shaken to find how much Ms Allcock knew about football, but there had been no clear orders issued to sell players or to cut back on wages.

If only his personal finances were in such good order. He was struck again by the fact that he could be so organized and successful in his working life at the football club, yet so chaotic in the organization of his private life.

Detective Sergeant Lucy Blake was looking at wedding dresses whilst still wondering whether marriage was a good idea.

That wasn't because she had any of the doubts about her chosen man which others had expressed. Percy Peach was ten years older than her twenty-nine, divorced, bald and belligerent. On paper, he was no catch at all for a chestnut-haired girl with startling green-blue eyes and a figure which turned male heads of any age. 'No catch': that was the phrase her mother's generation would have used. And Lucy, though she had forsaken her mother's cottage for her own new and cosy flat in Brunton several years ago, was still very close to her mother.

Indeed, it was her mother's unlikely championing of Percy Peach and his virtues which had brought on this wedding. Agnes Blake yearned for grandchildren, but she loved her daughter far too much to have pressed her towards any mate of whom she did not thoroughly approve. She was a shrewd assessor of character who judged nothing by appearances, and she had approved of Percy an hour into his first visit to her home and never altered her opinion.

Agnes was a cricket fanatic, and the only person in Lucy's acquaintance who had instantly divined the significance of Peach's initials – he was D.C.S. Peach. 'Denis Charles Scott *Compton*,' Agnes had shouted with instant delight, divining immediately that Percy's long-dead father had named his son after her favourite batsman, 'the laughing cavalier of Lords' in the forties and fifties, and an unlikely hero of this doughty northern woman, who had been until the time of her marriage a weaver in a Brunton cotton mill.

And Lucy had approved of her mother's enthusiasm for the man they all called Percy. It was marriage she was doubtful about; not at some time in the future, but at this particular time, when her police career was burgeoning and she was thoroughly enjoying her post as Peach's chosen Detective Sergeant in the CID. She grimaced at herself in the small mirror of the cramped changing room, took a deep breath, and plunged into the more public arena of the dress shop, where her friend Diane was waiting to pass judgement.

Lucy gazed at herself in the full-length mirror, twirled swiftly, then turned to collect her colleague's judgement. 'Before you say anything, my bum looks too big in this one.'

'You've said that about three of the last five,' said PC Diane Warner with a touch of weariness. 'It doesn't. It looks voluptuous. I wish I curved like that. Every man in the church would be controlling the urge to whistle at you in that.' The thought evidently cheered her. 'I can think of one or two whose control might not hold out.'

'Alternatively, I might just have to accept the fact that

my bum *is* too big and try to disguise the fact. You don't
like the dress, do you? And don't say you do just to get us
out of here.'

'It's a temptation, I must admit,' admitted Diane with a
sigh. 'I do like it. The green picks up the colour of your
eyes, makes them look even bigger and even greener, you
lucky sod.'

'But you still don't approve of it.'

'How do you know that?' Diane held up her hand. 'No,
don't tell me, it shows in my face. That's why you're a DS
in CID, about to marry your boss, and I'm still a PC in
uniform. I do like the dress. It's just that somehow it doesn't
seem like a wedding dress.'

'You want white.'

'Not necessarily.'

'That's why I wouldn't let my mother come with me:
she'd have wanted white.'

'Even though you're a scarlet woman who's been living
in sin for two years before marriage.'

'We haven't been living together. But all right, we've slept
together more and more often over the last two years. I've
never made any secret of that to Mum and she's never made
any fuss about it. But she's seventy and her generation didn't
do that. If it wasn't her precious Percy who was involved,
I'm sure I'd have had more flack from her. I know it's
terribly old-fashioned, but it just doesn't feel right to me to
get married in church in white. I can just imagine Mum's
friends casting their eyes to the ancient vaulted ceiling and
tutting about modern young people's moral standards.'

'I think you're unduly sensitive. But I think I know what
you mean. What about cream or ivory then?'

'Off-white, you mean? So that those ladies can think of
me as only slightly soiled? All right, I'll try anything once.
Just promise not to laugh, that's all.'

Diane sighed. 'I won't do that. But I won't guarantee that
I won't weep, if we don't find something suitable soon.'

'Sorry! Won't be a tick!' Lucy Blake was much longer
than that. She paused in bra and pants to study the rear
quarters she had criticized in the changing cubicle mirror,

for a start. These contours always brought a predictable but gratifying low growl of sexual pleasure from Percy Peach, whenever he caught her in her underwear. She had a feeling that his judgement might not be the suitable one for a church aisle. Her curves were probably acceptable, in the right dress, she decided. When she had slid them into the full-length ivory silk creation she had selected, she thought that this might just be that dress.

Diane Warner's reaction confirmed it. 'That's the one!' she said delightedly. 'And if you won't take my word for it, ask them!' With a wide wave of her arm, she brought in the rest of the clientele of the busy shop beyond them, and Lucy Blake turned to find that four women had suspended their own deliberations to gaze admiringly at the woman with the striking dark red hair in the long silk dress. To cover her embarrassment, Lucy did a swift pirouette in front of the full length mirror beside her, which brought ragged applause from these fellow-shoppers.

She looked at the price-tag again, took a deep breath, swallowed determinedly, and walked over to the assistant who had helped her with her dress selections. 'I'll take this one!' she said firmly.

Edward Lanchester still missed the wife who had died of ovarian cancer almost two years previously.

They had been together for forty-eight years; they had grown even closer as he had stayed at her side through the painful and distressing months of her final illness. Even her last act had been one of love for Ted. She had chosen the hospice for the last fortnight, rather than the death at home she had always envisaged, because she had realized that the final care and the long pain of parting would have been too much even for such a husband.

It was the small things now which affected Edward most easily. There was no one now who called him Ted. His childhood friends were dead or vanished to distant areas; his daughters had always called him Dad; from those who dealt with him formally he elicited a respectful Mr Lanchester; even the closest of his present friends called him Edward.

Ted, he realized now, had been reserved for his dead wife, and he had liked it that way. There was a plethora too of other trivial things, which might seem unimportant to others. There was no one now to warn him about the extra drink or the extra pipe of tobacco; no one to tease him about the absurdity of his lifelong passion for Brunton Rovers.

He kept a cheerful face in public. People said he had taken it well. No one spoke of Eleanor, though after the first three months he would have welcomed any mention of her. He understood that people were frightened of being embarrassed; he had done the same thing himself, in similar circumstances. Now he wished that someone, anyone, would mention the wife he had loved; the silence about her made him feel as though he were a traitor, joining a conspiracy to forget her existence.

He felt lonely and increasingly isolated, despite his public cheerfulness And there was no one at hand to whom he could pour out his desolation in private, no one to receive his secret thoughts and comfort him, as he had comforted Eleanor when she had railed against the unfairness of the cancer in her moments of despair.

Edward Lanchester had owned men's outfitting shops in four Lancashire town centres. They had been steadily prosperous in the sixties and seventies. He had sold out to a national chain in 1974 for just over two million pounds. Perhaps he could have got more, but two million was a lot of money in 1974. He was happy enough with the deal and the leisure it gave him. It had given him enough wealth and local standing to become chairman of his beloved Brunton Rovers, nineteen years before the Premiership and Sky Television money made all such set-ups an anachronism in 1993.

You needed many millions now to have the financial clout to chair any Premiership club. Edward acknowledged that openly enough, even if he privately yearned for the old days, when players were not millionaires, with contracts which enabled them to dictate terms to their employers. He didn't expect things to be unchanging, he said publicly, any more than he expected his former shops to be filled with the sort of merchandise he had stocked; the company had wanted his town centre sites, not his business.

A week after the monthly board meeting at Brunton Rovers, Lanchester had taken a decision. Now he was driving his BMW into the town centre on market day to implement it. He was pleased to see the old town busy in this time of national recession. Edward remembered the days of the open market and the long-demolished market hall, with its huge ball on the summit which descended its pole every day as the clock beneath it struck one. As he stood for a moment with humanity of many hues hurrying around him, Edward remembered the days when he had run as an excited small boy with his hand in his father's to this spot to see that ball fall, abruptly to halfway down its pole, then more slowly, as strong springs ensured that its weight did not damage the roof of the tower beneath it.

The new market hall enabled people to shop under cover, which was much better than having rain dripping down your neck as you dodged between the old canvas-covered stalls. That was certainly an improvement, even if things never seemed to be quite as cheap. And he certainly missed the old clock and that ball.

At least the bank manager hadn't changed. He was eleven years younger than Edward. They had gone to the same local grammar school, but of course not at the same time. Although Edward was a little less sleek and a little more wrinkled than John White, the two men were dressed almost the same, in dark suits with lighter blue shirts and navy ties.

White saw it as his duty to be professionally cautious. Once the initial, rather old-fashioned courtesies had been exchanged, he said, 'These are large sums, Edward, even by today's standards. Have you discussed this decision with anyone?'

Lanchester grimaced. 'I've no one to discuss it with, now that Eleanor's no longer with me.'

The manager reddened a little, embarrassed as usual by any hint of intimacy, of private emotion in matters where cool decisions were called for. 'I was thinking rather of a financial advisor, actually.'

'Eh? Well, no. But I don't need that sort of advice, you see. My mind's made up and I'm confident I'm doing the right thing.' Lanchester cleared his throat, uncomfortable in his turn to bring sentiment into this temple of reason. 'They're good girls, my daughters, both of them. I want them to have the money now, when it will be of most use to them, rather than after my death.'

White was happier now, summoning arguments which he had used many times before. 'I'm sure that we both hope that death will be delayed for many years yet, Edward. We cannot foresee the future, but money is some sort of insurance against sickness and other misfortunes. Are you sure that you will not have need of this money in the future?'

'I am confident that I will not. And there are inheritance tax advantages in this decision, which you must surely approve.'

'There certainly are. Provided that you live for a minimum of seven years.'

'Or a proportion of that. Tax liability on gifts diminishes with each year, I believe.'

'It does indeed. I see you do not need any briefing on the financial implications of your decision. However, I would be failing in my duty if I did not point out to you that things can go wrong. I have indeed seen them do so too often for me not to see dangers and register my fears with you. I have spent my life with money, Edward, but it is a strange factor in family interchanges. It makes people behave badly. Sometimes it seems to change people's characters completely, though my own theory is that it simply excites strains which were previously latent.'

White was wondering how to go on from this well-rehearsed opening when Lanchester took pity upon him and came to his rescue. 'You mean that my daughters might simply take the money and desert me in my hour of need, should that hour ever come. Well, I must tell you first that I trust both of my girls implicitly and secondly that I consider I have retained enough to have a certain independence.'

White shrugged resignedly. He had issued the first two warnings, as duty dictated. The third one was a little easier, but perhaps the most important one of all. 'Have you considered the possibility, however remote it may seem to you at this moment, that your daughters' marriages may at some point dissolve? Modern law of settlements dictates that assets should be divided in such cases. I have seen too often the dismay on people's faces when they see their hard-earned savings going not to the children they cherished but to partners they would no longer wish to support. It is my duty to draw your attention to perhaps the most distressing aspect of—'

'I've considered this and decided there is nothing I can do about it, if it happens. I'm confident that it won't. Both of the couples involved wish to begin their own businesses. I see that as a unifying factor in their relationships. This may not be the best time for such initiatives, but neither of my sons-in-law is stupid. I want them to have the capital to move into new fields, not necessarily now, but whenever they feel the moment is right.'

John White smiled his qualified approval. 'Well, you've obviously thought this decision through, Edward. I wish all my clients gave as much thought to their financial moves. It was my duty to draw such things to your attention, but of course the decision in the end is yours. I will implement the transfers today. I shall need a signature from you to authorize them.'

They had a sherry to celebrate, a pleasantly old-fashioned way to conclude business, Lanchester thought. John White agreed. Before his old client left the room, he had informed him of his decision to take a slightly early retirement in two months time, and of the relief this had brought to him.

Edward Lanchester returned home and rang each of his daughters in turn. Both of them were well into their forties now, but they remained vulnerable and affectionate girls to him. Each of them was delighted; each of them asked if he was sure he could afford to do this, whether he had thought it through properly. 'Banker's advice!' said Edward crisply, stretching a point to make them feel easier about it.

They were good girls, he thought affectionately. Pity they were so far away, but they had to follow their husband's

work, that was the way of things. One was in Scotland, the
other in Wales. Somehow that seemed to stretch the mileage,
to make them further away than if they had just been in
different English counties. He didn't seem to see as much
of his grandchildren as when Eleanor had been alive, but
that was probably inevitable.

He made himself a mug of tea, then stretched his long
legs out in front of him in his favourite armchair. He had
the pleasant feeling of achievement which had always come
to him with decisions made and actions taken. Not many
people could give away two million pounds, even with
today's inflated values. His money would be appreciated
and put to good use, he was sure, and he had no use for it
now himself

Good girls, both of them, in their different ways. . . . He
dozed happily, whilst his tea grew cold beside him.

FOUR

C hief Superintendent Thomas Bulstrode Tucker was not enjoying his day.

His morning meeting with the chief constable had been something of a disaster. The CC had pressed him hard about the latest knife crime figures and the clear-up rates on burglaries. As usual, Tucker hadn't had the facts at his fingertips to present the most convincing accounts of the actions and reactions of the CID section for which he was responsible.

In the early afternoon, the crime reporter of the *Lancashire Telegraph*, Alf Houldsworth, had grilled him about the rise in the number of rapes in the Brunton area over the last twelve months. Houldsworth was an old hack with only one good eye, but thirty years of experience as crime writer for a national daily. He had cut through Tucker's obfuscations with contemptuous ease as he sought for a quote. The chief superintendent's assurances that enquiries were ongoing and proceeding steadily, that he was confident of an arrest or arrests in the near future, were likely to be translated into headlines about Brunton police bafflement and CID top brass being at a loss. The CC wouldn't like that. By three o'clock, Tucker felt very low.

And now Percy Peach was coming to see him.

Peach was both his bête noir and his saviour. He was a necessary evil, because it was Peach's efficiency as thief-taker and unceasing opponent of villainy which gave Tucker the crime statistics which disguised his own chronic inefficiency. But this meant he had to tolerate the sort of insolence and baiting from Peach which the strong respect for rank in the police service would normally have checked. Percy rarely took the trouble to disguise his contempt for the poseur he had long ago dubbed Tommy Bloody Tucker. His chief for the most part chose not to notice the barbs of the man who carried him.

Percy Peach had not had a good day himself. A morning in court with a defence counsel who treated his every word with amused contempt had severely tested his self-control. Emerging into a north-west wind and a slanting drizzle, he had found a traffic warden attaching a parking ticket to his car. His exchange with this jobsworth had not improved his frame of mind. Back at the station, his junior CID colleagues had scurried to find themselves with pressing tasks once they heard his voice and divined his mood. Now, as he climbed the two storeys to his chief's penthouse office at the top of the new Brunton police station, he felt that mood lightening a little. The prospect of baiting Tommy Bloody Tucker always brought a little cheer to a trying day.

'I've been waiting for hours for you to bring me up to date on things!' said Tucker aggressively. He had never come to terms with e-mails, and with only around two years between him and a fat pension, he didn't see why he should begin now.

'In the crown court all morning, sir. Trying to side-step a smart young lawyer who was hamming it up for all he was worth to a receptive jury. The verdict wasn't in when I left, but my money's against a custodial sentence for Len Jackson.'

'And they call it bloody justice!' said Tucker. For a moment, these two very different men were united in the traditional police contempt for lawyers who are concerned only with a personal victory, at whatever cost to the justice they purport to serve. It was like Christmas Day football between the trenches in 1914, thought a startled Peach.

He hastened to resume normal hostilities. 'There was another serious disturbance in the town centre last night, sir.'

'You need to get a grip on these things,' said Tucker, trying through his vagueness to sustain the hostility he thought necessary for Peach.

Percy noted the attempt at aggression with some relief. 'I try to maintain a grip, sir, even with the system stacked against me.' He waited for a reaction which did not come. 'I managed to get myself directly involved in this incident, even though it was my day off. You wouldn't care for a little direct involvement yourself, sir? A little confrontation with the thugs across the table in the interview room, for instance? See if you could abash them with your rank, sir?'

Tucker shook his head with a sudden, unaccustomed decisiveness. 'I couldn't possibly do that, Peach. It is my policy to keep an overview of things, as you know. I'm the general behind the troops, if you like.'

As far behind as a first world war general, thought Percy. He said mysteriously, 'Rather like the opening shots of the film of *West Side Story*.'

Tucker's jaw dropped an inch and a half, making him look like a slow-learning goldfish. It was a familiar phenomenon, but always a welcome one to Peach. 'Where the helicopter zooms in over New York and eventually focuses on mob violence in the poorer quarter, sir. Gets an overview of the violence, as you do. Puts it in its wider context.'

'Yes! Yes, that's what I have to do!'

'Without getting involved, sir.' Peach continued ruminatively, as if the other man had not spoken. 'Without contributing anything useful to a dangerous and deteriorating situation.'

Tucker didn't like the way this was going. 'I hope you're not trying to fob me off with old films instead of getting on with your job and sorting things out, Peach. I can't see what cameras in helicopters over New York have to do with violence in modern-day Brunton.'

'Mob violence, sir. Young men and an increasing number of young women who divide themselves into ethnic groups and threaten one another's very lives, sir.'

'Then get on with sorting it out. And don't fob me off with *West Side Story*, which has nothing to do with it.'

'You're probably right, sir. Except that apparently the starting-point for last night's little skirmish was a liaison between a white Brunton boy and an Asian girl. A Pakistani girl who went to school with him and has spent all but the first year of her life in the town. I thought there were certain parallels with the Puerto Rican girl in *West Side Story*. Or with *Romeo and Juliet*, for that matter. But I suppose I always was a hopeless romantic, sir.'

The vision of Percy Peach as a romantic would have been a startling concept to the criminal fraternity of the town or even to his juniors in the CID section. It was a totally baffling one for Thomas Bulstrode Tucker. He transformed himself from goldfish to Rottweiler by shutting his mouth and glaring balefully at his chief inspector. 'Tell me what the hell's been going on.'

'Nasty confrontation between two gangs last night, sir. Escalating when I arrived on the scene. Three of our junior uniformed constables were attempting to control the situation but were heavily outnumbered. One of them was knocked down and narrowly escaped serious injury.'

'He should have known how to handle himself. He shouldn't have got involved without—'

'Young woman, sir. Very nearly trampled underfoot.'

'A woman?' Tucker was a fish again, goggling at the existence of this mysterious creature.

'A third of constables are female, sir. On your orders, we're no longer allowed to refer to them as WPCs.'

'They shouldn't have got involved with these thugs.'

'No, sir. I'm sure you wouldn't have got involved, sir.' He paused to nod pensively. 'But inexperience leads to strange actions. I might well recommend an official commendation in this case.'

'There's no need to go over the top, you know. I'm simply pointing out that these junior officers should have followed official procedures. They should have called for back up before they went in.'

'And I should probably have continued my journey and left them to it. Fortunately, they *had* called for back-up. The cavalry arrived just when the situation was getting sticky. The prompt and courageous intervention of these young officers had prevented an escalation of violence and probable serious injuries. The arrival of the back-up they had called for not only saved our bacon but enabled us to arrest three of the ringleaders.'

Tucker realized that he'd been set up but, as usual with this adversary, couldn't quite pin down the moment. He thought again about the dressing-down he'd endured that morning from the CC and divined there might be a gleam of comfort here after all. 'You say this incident was racially motivated?'

'One gang was certainly Asian, sir. The other one was extreme right and extreme white.' He glanced at his chief to see if he appreciated this turn of phrase and then went hastily on. 'There were at least two National Front members. They recognized me from previous encounters and made themselves scarce.'

Tucker was too full of his own thoughts to pay much attention. He jutted his chin towards some invisible presence behind Peach. 'We should make an example of these thugs! I was talking to the CC only this morning about the number of such outbreaks which have gone unpunished. Percy, I want you to throw the book at these people!'

Peach usually took the use of his first name by his chief as a danger signal, but this time he scented the prospect of further mischief. 'This could be a big one, sir. They not only carried potentially lethal weapons but attempted to use them.'

'Have you a reliable witness?'

'Very reliable, sir. In my opinion, the most reliable of all. I have to confess to a little bias, but—'

'Who is this person?'

Percy resisted the temptation to take an elaborate bow and sweep his knuckles across the expensive carpet. 'It is I, sir! I am the man who arrested this dangerous ruffian who was brandishing a knife at the time. Nearly broke his arm doing it, and I was glad to hear the police siren which meant that the cavalry were arriving, but I have to say that—'

'You didn't use unreasonable force, did you?' Tucker's pusillanimous soul quailed before the vision of unwelcome headlines.

Peach, not unreasonably, looked a little hurt. A better man than Tucker might have made the safety of his officer his first thought, might even have congratulated him upon his crucial intervention in a nasty situation. But the prospect of alarming his chief was stronger in Percy than any dismay. 'Nearly broke the bugger's arm, sir. Sorry I didn't, in many ways.'

'Put such thoughts right out of your mind, Peach. I don't want to have to defend the actions of anyone in the CID section.'

'Even when an excited young thug had a knife against his throat, sir? Even when a young female officer was in danger of losing her life?'

Tucker brightened a little. 'I suppose that does put rather a different complexion on it.'

'I'm glad to hear it, sir.'

'Yes. If you can assure me that there's no serious damage, I think we can overlook the—'

'Glad to hear it, sir.' Peach was breathing rather heavily, but the man behind the big desk did not notice his struggle to retain his self-control. Percy said between clenched teeth, 'Do you wish to interrogate these suspects yourself? I think we have a cast-iron case against them.'

Irony was wasted on Thomas B. Tucker. 'No. No, I shan't interfere. You must do that yourself, Peach. You are the one who knows exactly what happened.' He sat suddenly bolt upright. 'And make sure you throw the book at them. We must stamp out violence on our patch. I'm right behind you on this!'

'Where you always are, sir. Where I knew you would be.' Then Percy allowed himself to catch some of his chief's enthusiasm. 'We'll nail them for this one, sir! They'll squirm a bit before they get out of the interview room, I can tell you. I'll let Messrs Ahktar and Malim know exactly how you feel about them!'

Tucker, who had risen to his feet to send his chief inspector away with a ringing declaration of his support, was suddenly frozen in horror. 'Aren't those – aren't they – Muslim names?'

'That's right, sir. You're on the ball as usual. I'll let these Pakistani thugs know that the Head of CID is going to throw the book at them! That Chief Superintendent Tucker simply isn't going to allow violence on our streets! Thank you, sir, for this ringing endorsement of aggressive policing!'

'But I thought you meant—'

'Meant it was our white right-wing thugs? Well, no, sir.

Not this time. It was their opponents with the blades, on this occasion. But never fear, sir, we'll have them for this. Without racial or religious prejudice, as always.'

'This racial element puts rather a different slant on things, you know,' said Tucker, subsiding weakly into his big leather chair.

But his minion was gone, carrying the bright torch of battle without fear or favour into the ranks of villainy. Percy Peach, descending the staircase with a smile, noted a little lightening of the greyness, even a tiny patch of blue sky, over the grey roofs of Brunton.

Jim Capstick enjoyed driving the Bentley himself, when the occasion demanded it, as this one certainly did.

It was nice to have a chauffeur, of course. It enabled you to do a certain amount of work whilst you travelled, to prepare yourself for meetings. It allowed you to concentrate your thoughts on those meetings, rather than on the exigencies of traffic and the idiocies of other motorists. When you employed someone with the physique and background of Wally Boyd, you also had a bodyguard, in the now quite rare situations where that was necessary. Most important of all, it impressed people when a chauffeur dropped you off and then drove away to park the Bentley. Even the hard-headed people with whom Capstick did business, who should have known much better, were impressed, sometimes unconsciously, by a man who had his own resident chauffeur.

Nevertheless, Jim Capstick still enjoyed the occasional opportunity to savour at first hand the power of the five-litre engine beneath the Bentley's sleek bonnet. He enjoyed the chance of opening up that power on the dual carriageway which skirted the western side of Brunton, though even at seventy miles an hour he could scarcely hear the engine note. He enjoyed even more the swift, effortless acceleration which took him past three vehicles on an open stretch of the A59 towards Preston, catching glimpses of the drivers' startled faces as he surged so swiftly past them. A far cry this from his days in the second-hand Austin-Healey Sprite he had thought so dashing thirty-five years ago; he smiled at the memory of those exciting but more innocent days of his youth.

The section of the M6 between Lancashire and Birmingham is now the busiest and most frustrating section of motorway in Britain, but that suited Capstick's purpose. Anonymity was essential for this mission, not just desirable. This was not the right car for anonymity, of course, but he had planned things carefully to obviate that. Moving south in darkness amidst the dense traffic of the M6, you were just another vehicle, for everything moved at the same pace towards the next hold-up, and you were lucky to average fifty mph.

It would have been frustrating if you had been driving a long distance, but Capstick could afford to be patient, for he had only forty miles of this to endure. Not far into Cheshire, he swung off the M6 and ran for a little while along an A road, which seemed very narrow after the hubbub of the motorway. The bright, squat block of the Travelodge hotel was visible for a mile before he reached the entrance. Seeing someone else drive out, he slid the Bentley into a slot which was not easily visible and yet not far from the entrance.

He had more sense than to adopt the sort of theatrical disguise which made one noticeable rather than obscure. He merely donned the navy anorak he kept as cover for such occasions, not even putting up its hood, divining correctly that this would attract rather than divert attention in a context like this. He passed quickly through the reception area of the hotel, nodding briefly at the receptionist. If you knew where you were going, people rarely challenged you; most of them assumed you had already booked in for the night.

The other man in the lift scarcely glanced at him. British reserve ensures that most people treasure their own privacy. Most of them know that attempts at social exchange are not likely to be welcomed in a place like this, where every patron is strictly transient. For his part, Capstick studied the instructions about the operation of the lift and did not even glance at its other occupant.

There was no one in the corridor. He moved swiftly and

silently over forty yards of blue carpet and rapped briefly on the door of Room 213. The man gave him a cursory greeting, then shut and locked the door carefully behind him. The room was furnished as were the other hundred and ninety rooms in this functional building. It had two single beds, built-in wardrobes, anodyne prints of flowers upon the walls, a door to the en suite bathroom. There were two small armchairs, which the occupant had moved to face each other at the end of the bed that would not be used.

The man's language was as efficient and serviceable as the room, but he had a thick Lebanese accent. He studied his visitor for a moment, gave him a quick, mirthless smile, and said, 'Is all this secrecy really necessary?'

Capstick slid off the anorak, revealing the expensive suit beneath it as if it were a gesture of confidence, a sign that he was now willing to relax and trust this man with the sallow face and very black hair. 'Probably not. I don't enjoy the cloak and dagger approach any more than you do. For my other dealings, I do not have to use it. But for both of us, it is a sensible precaution. Any disclosure of what we are about here would make any deal improbable if not impossible.'

The man took a second to digest this before he nodded. 'All right. I can understand that. It is not a problem for me; secrecy is usually important to the deals I broker.'

Capstick smiled, relaxing a little further, leaning back as far as the cramped little chair would allow. 'You have the advantage of me there. I have usually been able to be quite open in my dealings.'

The man opposite him doubted that. He knew only a little about his visitor, but that little told him that Capstick had not amassed his millions without some fairly clandestine manoeuvres. 'I should emphasize that I am not empowered to conclude any deal. My client wishes me to ascertain merely whether a deal is possible, and upon what terms.'

Jim Capstick gave him a practised, experienced smile. He was feeling more at ease with each passing minute. 'And for my part I must tell you that there can be no firm commitment from me this evening. I also am here to discuss the prospect of a deal, whether it is even possible for us to conclude such a deal, rather than to reach an agreement.'

The Lebanese was at his smoothest, his most emollient. But he was also studiously polite; there were millions in this for him if he could nudge the parties towards an agreement. 'That is what brokers are for, Mr Capstick. To discuss the feasibility of an agreement, in the early stages. And perhaps, at a later stage, to initiate a discussion of terms and bring the parties together.'

Capstick wondered if this was the way ambassadors behaved. Did they talk around a difficult subject, treating each other like chess players trying to anticipate the next move? He was quite enjoying this game. But he was used to blunt and direct dealings, with cards on the table and a take it or leave it attitude, rather than the obliqueness which seemed to be second nature to this oily operator. Well, the preliminaries were completed now, the terms of the contest were established. He did not want to spend any longer here than was strictly necessary.

He said brusquely, 'I am the majority shareholder in Brunton Rovers. It is not a public company, as many of the clubs in the English Premiership are. I can do a deal without reference to third parties, if it suits me.'

'That is a point of interest for my client. That is one reason why he would consider buying your club, when there are other, more successful clubs available.'

'It would need to be an attractive deal, for me even to consider selling the club.'

The Lebanese nodded and smiled, preparing to cloak his first harsh words of negotiation with an amiable veneer. 'You mean you want a sizeable sum for the club. My client also would need to find the deal attractive, if he is to follow up this initial interest. He would also need the confidential information about the present state of the club's finances which would enable him to decide whether to make any bid at all.'

'Of course. That will be available to him at two days' notice whenever he requires it. Provided of course that you can satisfy me tonight that this is a serious approach.'

'This is most important. Before he considers such an approach, my client will need the very full account of the debts and assets of the club which I have just mentioned.'

Jim Capstick was surprised anew to find that he was enjoying this cautious fencing, as the two opponents moved around each other in a narrowing circle. 'I understand that. I agree that no firm offer can be either made or entertained until your client has made a detailed examination of our finances. Nevertheless, I should emphasize to you at this stage that any Premiership soccer club is an attractive proposition. The Sky television fees alone will be thirty million for the bottom club in the league this year. And we do not intend that the bottom team will be Brunton Rovers.'

'Of course not, Mr Capstick. That would mean relegation, and an absence from the Premiership. My client would not be interested in any such club.'

'Of course not. But Brunton Rovers will not be in that position.' Capstick stood up, sensing correctly that no further progress could be made without the detailed financial analysis they had agreed. 'I am sure your client and his advisers will be gratified to see the sensible lines on which the club has been administered during the last few years. For my part, I am happy to state formally that I am prepared to consider a substantial offer for the club.'

The man in the other chair took his cue. '"Substantial" is an interesting word, Mr Capstick. But a vague one. What sort of sum were you envisaging?'

'Ah! I too would obviously need to give the matter considerable thought in the weeks to come. There is more than mere finance for me to consider, of course. I am attached to the club and to the town. Sporting allegiance and the sheer excitement it brings can never be measured merely in money.' Jim wondered if he should have said that. It sounded hollow, even in his own ears, and he wondered if this suave man from a different culture would even comprehend the sentiments, let alone believe them. 'But I would have to say that no figure of less than a hundred million would be of interest to me.'

He said it firmly but casually, as if he had been mentioning the sale of a second-hand car. The man opposite him said that it was much too early to discuss figures, that he would need to take an account of this very preliminary discussion back to the man he represented, that the detailed examination of the club's books they had agreed would form the basis of any offer. But he did not reject the sum of one hundred million out of hand.

Driving the Bentley back up the M6, Jim Capstick tried ineffectively to control his excitement and optimism.

FIVE

'**M**arch is supposed to come in like a lion and go out like a lamb. Some hope!' Agnes Blake drew back the curtains in the low-ceilinged bedroom of the cottage and looked accusingly at the clouds flying swiftly over the top of the long mound of Longridge Fell.

Her daughter rubbed her eyes and struggled to raise herself in the single bed. She had only dozed for the last half hour, clinging to that drowsy euphoria between sleep and full consciousness, the sensation which overtakes one when one wakes in a familiar place with pleasant associations. She had slept in this bed in this room when she was a girl, snuggling beneath the blankets as she heard the familiar voice of the father she had loved and who had loved her. That father had been dead twelve years now, but the sweet, sad memories this place held were one of the joys of sleeping here. One of the reasons why she still enjoyed spending the odd night here, even though she had long since asserted her independence and acquired her own snug modern flat in Brunton.

She looked out at the more limited view of fell and sky she could see from her bed. 'At least it's fine, Mum. Be thankful for small mercies! I might take you out for a pub lunch later, if you behave yourself.'

'Fat chance of doing anything else, at my age!' Agnes came and sat carefully on the edge of the bed, as she had been used to do when her only child was young. She poured the tea from the pot into the two china cups on the tray. 'Am I to see the wedding dress this morning?'

'Isn't there some superstition that forbids that?' teased Lucy. 'I wouldn't like to break any of your old folklore rules.'

'There's no such nonsense!' said Agnes indignantly. Then, realizing her daughter was not serious, 'The only rule about wedding dresses is that the grooms mustn't see them until the day of the wedding. And you'll not be flouting that, my girl, I'm sure.'

'I don't suppose any dire curse would fall upon me if I did, but I wasn't proposing to let the man see it before the big day, no.'

'Percy Peach wouldn't consent to look at it, anyway. He's more respect for tradition than some people,' said Agnes huffily.

She picked up her cup of tea and sipped it thoughtfully. 'The replies to the wedding invitations are coming in. It seems nearly everyone is able to make it, despite the short notice you allowed them.'

'I told you they would.'

'No thanks to you, our Lucy. If it had been left to you, we wouldn't have had a wedding at all!'

'That's not true! It wasn't that I had any doubts about marrying Percy. You know that. I just didn't see any need to rush into it so soon.'

'You'd have put it off for ever if it had been left to you. Thank goodness you're getting a husband with more sense than you have!'

Lucy was silent for a moment. She'd have to get used to that word 'husband', she supposed. She'd just about got over her surprise that she had taken Percy Peach as a lover. Now she'd have to spend the rest of her life introducing him as her husband. She found that an unexpectedly pleasing prospect.

She enjoyed a leisurely breakfast, accepting the bacon, egg and tomato she never had at any other time, drawing the line at the fried bread her mother tried to slide on to her plate. It was a luxury to linger over her toast, to savour the home-made marmalade, even to admit to her mother that she usually snatched breakfast on the move in her tiny kitchen at the flat.

She took a big mug of tea into the cosy lounge, settling into the cushions on the sofa and smiling up at the twin photographs in their silver frames upon the mantelpiece. One was a black and white one of her father in cricket gear, sweater over his shoulder, smiling shyly at the applause as he climbed the steps towards the sanctuary of the pavilion. The caption beneath, in her mother's familiar, careful print, gave the information that this was Jim Blake leaving the field after taking six wickets for thirty-three against Blackpool in the Northern League.

The coloured one beside it was of Percy Peach, taken only three years ago in front of another pavilion. He looked surprisingly young and dapper, his baldness hidden beneath a bright red cricket cap. Agnes Blake's neat black printing beneath it read: 'Denis Charles Scott Peach leaving the field after another dashing half-century for East Lancs in the Lancashire League.'

Typical of her mum to give Percy his full and proper names, thought Lucy with a smile. Then she thought of the vicar at the marriage service, enunciating those names clearly to Percy's CID colleagues who had never heard them, and the smile became much broader. Now that she had time to get accustomed to the notion, marriage was beginning to seem quite a good idea after all.

'Percy gave the game up much too early. I hope that was nothing to do with you, our Lucy.' The older woman had stolen unnoticed into the room and interrupted her daughter's reverie.

'Nothing at all. He gave cricket up before I ever met him – just before, admittedly. But he'd taken up golf by then.'

'GOLF!' Agnes produced the decisive explosion of contempt her daughter loved to hear; she would not have thought it possible to compress so much derision and indignation into a simple monosyllable. Mrs Blake did not go in for expletives, but golf was the most obscene of all the four-letter words for her. 'Percy was a fine aggressive batsman; I tell you, he should never have given up cricket so early.'

'From what I hear, he's also quite good at golf,' said Lucy provocatively.

'Game for nincompoops and people with too much time and money!' said Agnes dismissively. 'Game for the Bertie Woosters of this life, not hard-working men like Percy.'

'I think times have moved on, Mum. All sorts of people play golf now.'

'All sorts of idiots and creeps, you mean! You even hear of men losing games to their bosses deliberately, to curry favour. What sort of a game is it where men are willing to do that? What sort of boss is it who doesn't realize what's going on?'

Lucy had a secret sympathy for that point of view. She found it hard to envisage anyone deliberately throwing away a golf match, least of all Percy Peach with Tommy Bloody Tucker. So she said casually, 'I might even take up golf myself. It would give me some exercise and fresh air in my leisure time.'

'You won't have much leisure time in the next few years. Not with a home to set up and children to cope with.'

Lucy decided it wasn't the moment to discuss this. Agnes had not borne her only child until she was forty-one, and it was perfectly understandable that a woman of seventy should want grandchildren sooner rather than later. But Lucy did not want to abandon a promising CID career which was giving her much satisfaction. She could not at the moment see a way of reconciling these contrary ambitions of mother and daughter, and the situation was not helped by the fact that Percy Peach as usual favoured her mother's viewpoint.

She said hastily, 'Should we look at those replies to the wedding invitations now? Is it too early to begin thinking about a seating plan?'

The ploy worked well enough. Agnes had the box of replies and her tentative seating plans out in an instant. The pair spent a happy hour exchanging views on the various guests and who would go well with whom. After a cup of coffee, Lucy eased herself into her wedding dress – and caused a rare phenomenon. For almost a full minute, Agnes Blake was lost for words.

Lucy twirled repeatedly in what she thought would be the approved manner, looking into the long mirror they had brought in from the hall and secretly delighted with the way she looked in the ivory silk. Finally, she stood very still and looked down with concern at the small figure on the sofa. 'You don't like it, Mum, do you? It's not what you were expecting.'

'It's lovely, our Lucy!' Agnes's eyes filled with moisture. It was a few seconds before she controlled herself enough to add, 'I just wish your Dad could see you, that's all.'

They held each other tight on the sofa for a moment which seemed to stretch much longer. Then Lucy said softly, 'Perhaps he can, Mum. Perhaps he'll see us all in the church, on the day. Who knows? Who really knows?'

A little while later, she changed out of the dress into olive trousers and a dark green sweater which matched the colour of her eyes, and said, 'Now what about that pub lunch? You choose which one.'

Agnes loved going with her daughter to eat at the pub. Respectable women had not frequented public houses when she was young. Even now she would never have ventured into such a place on her own. But somehow food made such places much more respectable than if you just went there to drink. And though she would never have admitted it, she loved to show off her detective sergeant daughter to the locals, some of whom had known her since she was a child.

She looked up in admiration at the girl who was six inches taller than her, who had the striking chestnut hair to set off those remarkable eyes and a figure which turned heads wherever she ventured. 'The *Hare and Hounds*, I think. Everything there's cooked on the premises, not bought in.'

'The *Hare and Hounds* it is, then! You can guide me through the menu.'

Agnes Blake nodded happily. 'I will that, our Lucy. And whilst we're waiting for the food to come, we can talk about these bonny grandchildren you're going to produce.'

The head teacher was scrupulously polite, concerned to treat these visitors like any other parents. They had, she allowed, a certain distinction, and their presence in the school had been noted by other parents collecting their children. Neither of these things must affect her determinedly professional attitude. She tried to shut out thoughts of the eager speculation which would be going on at the school gates at this very moment.

Nevertheless, as she led Robbie and Debbie Black into

her office, she found herself irritated by her own reactions. Designer clothes would not affect her, any more than the fact that with a sport-crazy boyfriend she had watched this woman at Wimbledon and this man at Old Trafford. But a little extra excitement coursed through her veins at the prospect of an exchange with these celebrities. That was ridiculous. Didn't she constantly preach the tawdriness of the celebrity concept to staff and children? Didn't she abhor the very idea that fame should in any way influence her dealings with parents?

They must be in their forties now, these two; they were contemporaries of hers. For the first time that she could ever remember, she found herself wishing she was of an older generation, bringing the assets of age and gravitas to an exchange with parents. Yet she found herself hoping that she would be able to help with whatever problem had brought them here. She always wanted to do that, of course, she told herself firmly. But she was hoping a little more strongly than usual that she would be able to reassure this glamorous pair.

As if she read these thoughts, Debbie Black produced her familiar dazzling smile and said, 'I should say at the outset, Mrs Hurst, that we are not asking for any special consider-ation. We wish to be treated in exactly the same way as any other parents.'

'Of course. That should be taken as read.' Louise Hurst found her mouth was unusually dry and cleared her throat. 'What is the problem? People who come to see me usually have a problem.' Her little laugh sounded artificial to her.

Robbie Black smiled, trying to put the woman at ease, when in truth on her own ground she should have been in control. 'I have the same problem as a football manager. Whenever a player knocks on my door, I know they're bringing in trouble of some kind. You'd be surprised how many big-name players are no more than kids. Pampered kids, really – they've had everything done for them by their clubs, been thoroughly spoilt. You can't tell them that, of course.'

Louise realized with relief that he was talking a little too much because he too was nervous, that this was a situation Robbie Black had never been in before. She even divined correctly that like many men he had not wished to come here at all, had been hauled along only by his wife's insistence that he should show solidarity. She said more confidently, 'So what is it that is worrying you, Mr Black?'

He glanced sideways at his wife, who said, 'It may be something and nothing, but we felt we should bring it to your attention. We think Eleanor is being bullied at school.'

'Not physically knocked about, you understand,' her husband added hastily. 'It's more a matter of other girls being spiteful to her, saying nasty things about her and about us. A boy might shrug it off, but—'

Louise Hurst hastened to intervene before this gender discrimination could go any further. 'No one should have to shrug it off, Mr Black. If a child is being seriously upset, the situation needs attention.'

'It may not be a serious problem. It may be that as parents we are over-reacting,' said Debbie Black, wondering now if they should have come here, whether this was something they should have sorted out for themselves.

'And it may be that you have pinpointed a problem which needs attention,' said Mrs Hurst firmly, treating them now like any other parents with a worry over their precious progeny, reassured by this rediscovery of her professional attitude. 'Would you say the problem is in school or outside it? We often find what seems quite petty in here is pursued outside the school gates and made into something much larger.'

'We only know what Eleanor tells us. But she says not much happens when the teacher is around. They pull her hair a bit and push her around. But what really upsets her is that they say wounding things about us.'

'What sort of things?'

Debbie glanced sideways at her husband, 'Well, she came home a fortnight ago asking what a tart was. They'd been saying her mother was a tart and her Dad was a jumped-up hooligan.'

Mrs Hurst nodded. Nothing she hadn't come across before.

Routine stuff, but very upsetting for the small girl at the centre of it and the man and woman who sat before her. 'These aren't children's words and phrases, as you no doubt realize.'

'No.' Debbie Black's anxious features split into an un-expected smile as she thought of her daughter struggling to pronounce that word 'hooligan'. 'These girls can't have very nice mothers.'

Louise Hurst shrugged. 'They're probably no worse and no better than average. What you see and hear sometimes in this job could make you into a confirmed pessimist about human nature. It's the children who cheer you up and give you hope.'

Robbie Black said in his soft Scottish accent, 'D'ye think we're taking this too seriously, Mrs Hurst?' Like many parents, he found that once they'd come here and stated their concern, it seemed much more petty than it had when they were comforting a tearful little girl in her bedroom.

'Not at all. I'm glad you've voiced your concerns. I'll have a word with the teacher and we'll keep a watch on Eleanor and the way the other girls behave towards her. I don't think this is a very serious problem. Usually once children know there's an adult eye upon them the trouble stops.'

The Blacks had driven most of the short journey to their home when Debbie said, 'Do you think she thought we were over-reacting?'

Robbie was silent for a moment. He had been thinking about his very different first school, in the roughest part of a great Scottish city. He'd been small for his age. Fights had been common and he'd been in plenty of them, until his football skill gradually made him into a boyish hero. Times changed, but children were still children. 'No, not really. Mrs Hurst seemed to be taking it seriously. I don't think it will be a big thing from now on, though. I believe her when she says the school will attend to it.'

'I agree with that. It's a good school. I like it here. I want us to put down roots.'

* * *

Darren Pearson sighed wearily at the end of his day. As usual, he was the last to leave the Brunton Rovers' offices at Grafton Park. The night security officer was in his office beside the single thick wooden door which was all that was left open at nights. The ex-policeman bade a cheerful but respectful goodnight to the man who had appointed him, the man who did more than anyone else to keep the day to day navigation of the club upon an even keel.

Pearson was responsible for the non-footballing staff at the club. He knew all their first names and rarely forgot them; even the tea ladies and the part-time cleaners got a cheery word from him. He knew much about the triumphs and tragedies of their private lives and rarely forgot to comment on or enquire about whatever was most important to them. Apart from the one or two who had been around for a long time, the people who worked for him knew little about his own background and he preferred it that way. But most of them not only respected his authority but admired his bearing and his attitude.

If only they knew, thought Darren Pearson, as he pulled the door to behind him and walked away into the darkness. If only they knew how the man who seemed to them so competent and balanced plunged into a world of chaos when he left the familiar corridors of the football club.

He knew where he was going. He had nerved himself to do it many hours ago. Perhaps he had lingered a little longer within the familiar, intricate surroundings of Grafton Park to put off this moment. As usual, the coolness and space of the world outside was a surprise after the artificial lights and heating of the honeycomb of offices beneath the main stand of Brunton Rovers FC. Most people would have relaxed on re-entering this wider world, but Darren Pearson felt nothing but fear. He felt he was a man flung out from the womb, where all was safe and happy, into the wider and heavier threats of a world he could not deal with.

He started the engine, set in motion the heater fan which would soon mitigate the damp cold of the interior. But then he sat motionless for a long time behind the wheel, building up his nerve, trying to force action through the atrophy which beset his limbs. He had not had an alcoholic drink throughout the long day, but his body told his brain that he was not fit to drive, that he could not drive, that his legs and arms would not conduct the familiar, automatic movements to control the vehicle. Mere fancy, he told himself: it was the brain which directed the body, not the other way round. He heard a dry, scarcely human sound, and realized a second later that it was his own harsh laughter. He rehearsed yet again the speeches he had devised during the sleepless hours of the preceding night.

Brunton's brief rush hour was over. Darren drove competently enough, once he had forced himself to begin the process. The car was an automatic. He listened to the gears changing as he steered the Vectra through the town. If only someone would programme his own gears and his own humanity for him, would guide him smoothly and painlessly on automatic through whatever was left of his life.

He drove more slowly as he approached the place, beset by the familiar doubts, which dragged like weights on his resolution. He slid the Vectra into one of the visitors' bays in the small car park and switched off the engine. He would give himself a few seconds to compose himself; you could achieve little in any field if you were not composed, could you? He was frightened not of the meeting itself but of the rejection which must surely result from it. Then a sudden shiver shook his body and he felt the numbness in his legs: he must have been there for many minutes.

He stamped his feet before he went to the entrance to the flats; a man going out to his car looked at him curiously. The door he wanted was on the ground floor. His wife's face fell as soon as she opened the door. 'What is it you want, Darren?'

'Aren't you going to ask me in?'

'We've nothing to say to each other.' But she stood back and watched him walk past her, then shut the door behind him. Then she heard herself saying illogically, 'Do you want a cup of tea?'

He didn't know whether he did or he didn't. 'That would be nice.'

She went into the flat's small modern kitchen. He moved over to the bright new sofa and sat down. When she brought the tea, it was in a china mug which was familiar to him from years ago. Perhaps it was this single link with the past in her new home that emboldened him at last to speak. 'It's small, this place.'

'You've said that before. And I've told you before that it's big enough, now the kids have gone. It's modern. It's convenient. There's an extra bedroom, for when either of them wants to come to stay.' She wondered why she was giving him these arguments, volunteering as much as that when she had planned not to talk at all. Perhaps it was just because she wanted this over, wanted to truncate any conversation about the flat.

'There's plenty of room in our old place. I rattle around in it.'

She had been determined to keep emotion out of her face, but it creased now into a little frown. She said nothing. He was forced to say, 'I'd like you to come back, Margaret.' All the fine, persuasive phrases he had prepared last night and rehearsed during the day fled like cats into the night. He had to force out even the few words of this blunt, inadequate statement.

'We've been through all this too many times already.' She tried to banish emotion, even irritation. She did not want to show him even the small, irrational spurt of sympathy she felt for his helplessness. That would be the sort of weakness which would lead him on. 'I was right to leave you. I've begun a new life for myself here. I don't want to come back.'

'We're not divorced.'

'No. We can be, if that's what you want. Is it?'

'You know it isn't.'

'Because if it needs that to convince you that it's over, we can do it.'

'Neither of us has got anyone else.'

She looked at him sharply. 'You don't know that.'

'But you haven't, have you?'

'It's not your business whether I have or I haven't.' For

the first time, she wanted him to speak, but he didn't. 'Maybe it's a case of once bitten, twice shy. The last years we had together wouldn't encourage any woman to get into anything serious.'

'So you haven't got anyone serious.' He looked round the clean walls of the new room, at its neat, modest furnishings, and tried not to think how different it was from the uncaring shabbiness of his own house. 'It was good for us once, wasn't it? It could be good again – I know it could. I want you to come home, Margaret.'

She listened to him using her full name, ignoring the Meg or Maggy he had always used between them, and remembered that he had only used Margaret in the presence of her dead parents. With that remembrance, she felt a little, illogical surge of love for him, or was it no more than pity? Before her brain could answer that, emotion was translated into words. 'Are you very lonely, Darren?'

It was the first time she had expressed any interest in him; both of them caught that thought. He said carefully, anxious not to over-play the moment, 'I am sometimes, yes. Well, quite a lot of the time, actually. I spend as long as I can at work.'

'How's that going?' She was being drawn in, despite herself. The words might have been the polite phrase of a stranger, but they expressed an interest she had been determined to subdue.

'Well enough. I have a good staff. I get on well enough with the manager, Robbie Black: we're different beings with different jobs, but we understand each other.' He paused, staring straight ahead rather than at her, as if the intimacy of eye contact was something he must avoid. He was treating her as if she were a kitten he could approach but must not frighten. In the good days, they had always discussed his problems at work, but he must not push too hard. Then, without knowing he was going to do it, he voiced the fear he had as yet hardly dared to frame for himself. 'I feel there's something going on at Grafton Park that I should know about, but I can't pin it down.'

She told herself not to take up the carrot, not to ask the

inevitable question which simple curiosity as well as her former regard for the man demanded. It was too intimate, too much a request to rejoin that life she had abandoned and been right to abandon. Instead, she fixed on the brutal question which was the only alternative that came to mind. 'Did you join Gamblers Anonymous?'

After the moves he had felt her making towards him, it came like a blow in the face. He was silent for almost half a minute, feeling tears start to his eyes. Tears not for himself, but for her and what he had destroyed. He wanted to lie, to prove he could keep his promises, could slay the monster which had wrecked their marriage. But he said, 'No. But I will—'

'Are you still in debt?'

'A little, yes.' He stared miserably at the rug on the woodblock floor, then forced out the truth after a wince of what felt like physical pain. 'No, a lot really. More than I can cope with on my own.'

'More than when I left you?'

'Yes. I need you, Meg.' He lapsed into the old word in his desperation.

'It's not an option, Darren. I don't know how many times I've told you that.'

'If I got it right, would you come back?'

But he'd just said he couldn't get it right without her. She didn't remind him of that. 'You must join Gamblers Anonymous, as a first step.'

'I'll do that.'

'How do I know you will? You've promised to do it before.'

'I'll–I'll ring you, when I've done it. Tomorrow.'

'No. Get whoever enrols you to ring me. Give him my telephone number.'

'What if he won't do that?'

'He'll do it, believe me. They're used to people who can't be trusted.'

He saw the first wisp of hope drifting across his horizon. He was buoyed by her certainty, as he had been in the old days. 'I'll do that. I can still fight it, still beat it, if you help me.'

'You must do other things. They'll tell you about that at G.A.' She paused, knowing she was being drawn into this despite herself, reminding herself anew of the black cloud of the disaster which had driven her here. 'How long is it since you spoke to the bank manager?'

'I don't know. He's written to me once or twice, but I've—'

'It's a she now. You must ring her tomorrow.' She smiled grimly, looking into his face for the first time. 'After you've signed up with Gamblers Anonymous. That will impress her as evidence of good intent.'

'I'll do that. I'll do whatever you say, Meg. I'll do anything which will get you to come back to me.'

'You're doing this for yourself, Darren. For no one else but yourself.'

'Yes, of course. For myself.' He knew he should leave it at that, but he could not prevent himself from saying, 'But when I've got myself right, then we'll be able to consider—'

'You get yourself right, Darren. It won't be as easy as you think when you're sitting here. It will be hell and it will take time. It will take a steady resolution over many months, not just easy words as you sit here.'

'I know. I know that, I do really.'

'Then go away and do it. And don't feel on your own. There are people out there ready to help you. Use them.'

This time he held back, did not voice the cliché that Meg was the biggest help of all. She kissed him briefly on the lips and held his shoulders for a moment before he left. He resisted the impulse to take her into his arms and risk her rejection.

Hope and resolution grew in Darren Pearson's mind as he drove home. He was on top of his job, everyone thought so. There was no reason why he should not sort out the rest of his life.

SIX

PC Peter Forsyth was twenty years old. He was over six feet tall and weighed fourteen stones. He was impressively fit. His regular appearances as a prop forward for Preston Grasshoppers and various regional and national police teams ensured that.

Pete Forsyth was the man to have beside you in a pub brawl. He was the man every other constable wanted to be paired with when he or she went on street duties: the roughs of the town gave you very little trouble when you had PC Forsyth as your formidable companion. No one in the canteen ever escalated an argument with Peter Forsyth on the other side, not even those on the boxing team. He was not the sort of man you wanted as an enemy.

Today PC Forsyth felt not just like a wet rag but like a very sodden cloth indeed. He remained standing to attention, towering over the man at the desk beneath him, but he now felt he desperately needed to sit down. To slump to the ground, in fact, in some other place, any other place than where Detective Chief Inspector Peach was present.

Forsyth was on the wrong end of one of Percy Peach's legendary bollockings.

He did a right royal bollocking, did Percy Peach. Everyone said that. But as a uniformed constable, away from the rarefied realms of CID, Peter Forsyth had hitherto been insulated from close dealings with Peach. Today the uniformed inspector to whom he normally reported had called him in and told him that Peach wanted to see him. He had then shaken his head sadly, like a shepherd consigning a favourite sheepdog to be put down.

The bollocking was coming to an end, but Forsyth did not know that. It seemed to him to have gone on for a very long time indeed, and he had given up hope of any termination.

Peach's calm voice resumed. 'You're a prize fucking prat, lad. Is that agreed?'

'Yes, sir. I'm a prize fucking prat, sir.'

'That's the first sensible thing I've heard you say.' Forsyth had only muttered yes and no recently, his earlier attempts at apology having been aborted mercilessly by the man behind the desk. 'You've not just jeopardized a cast-iron case which even the Crown bloody Prosecution Service were happy to take to the Crown Court. You've shot it firmly up the arse. What have you done?'

'I've shot it firmly up the arse, sir.'

'There is no longer a case, thanks to your bloody efforts.'

'No, sir.'

Percy noted the limp exhaustion of the big man in front of him, but did not acknowledge it. He sighed the long sigh of the patient man who has been tried beyond endurance. 'What the hell were you trying to do, PC Forsyth?'

Peter Forsyth had decided some time earlier, when the Peach diatribe was peaking and his every word was being ridiculed, that the less he said the better. 'I don't quite know, sir. I was being a prize fucking prat, sir.'

'We've already established that, PC Forsyth. We're now trying to establish why you won the prize as the prat of the month.'

Forsyth shut his eyes and tried not to think of the re-action this was going to provoke. He took a deep breath and poured out his statement very quickly, fearful that he might be interrupted and derided before he had made any sense. 'The man was pissed in the pub, sir. His tongue was loosened. Muslims don't usually drink, so I thought I might gather more evidence to support our case. That he might incriminate other people as well as the ones you'd charged.'

Another sigh. Forsyth stared resolutely ahead, fearful of catching the basilisk eye of the man behind the desk. After what seemed to him a long time, Peach said, 'Did you know the man had been charged in the magistrates' court and remanded to the Crown Court?'

'Yes, sir.'

'And do you know that we have no right to question a man in such circumstances?'

'Yes, sir. I didn't think, sir. I was a fucking prat, sir.'

'Don't keep telling me that. It won't alter anything. This isn't a bloody confessional and I'm not a sodding priest.'

'No, sir.' Forsyth found that his mouth wanted to twist itself into a grin and screwed his shut eyes fiercely to prevent it. He wondered if hysteria was threatening him.

'So why did you do such a bloody stupid thing, PC Forsyth?'

The man in uniform shut his eyes and grimaced fearfully. What he was going to say would bring a ridicule more formidable than ever from the chief inspector, but his brain was too ravaged to furnish him with anything but the truth. 'I–I was trying to show initiative, sir.'

'Hah!'

The single incredulous monosyllable rocketed round the walls of the office like a fiercely struck squash ball, echoing so forcefully that Forsyth wondered whether silence would ever return. 'I–I had the idea that I might like to join CID, sir. Before this happened, that is. Before I acted like a prize f—'

'Hah!' That sound again, exploding into his ears, destroying all thought. 'Fools rush in where even fucking angels fear to tread, PC Forsyth. You should remember that, even when you've forgotten the very mild admonitions I've given you this afternoon. Do you think you will remember?'

'Yes, sir.'

'I expect you'll go back and tell your mates in uniform that DCI Peach is a soft bugger, that you can't believe how easily he went on you.'

'No, sir.'

'Oh, you will, I know. I realize that I have a reputation as a soft touch. You can go now, unless you've any further gems to offer me.'

'No, sir. Thank you, sir.'

Peter Forsyth turned, scarcely able to believe that the ordeal was concluded, and found that his legs still worked. He was reaching out for the handle of the door when Peach said, 'And PC Forsyth.'

He froze with his fingers on the handle. He should have
known he would not get away so easily with his last revela-
tions. His eyes were shut when the chief inspectorial voice
said, 'Don't give up showing initiative, lad. Just give up being
a fucking prat who acts without thinking. All right?'

'Yes, sir.'

'And don't give up any thought of ever joining CID.
There's one or two in the section who started off as prize
fucking prats and learned the error of their ways. That might
even be possible for a twat like you.'

The decision to reduce the price of tickets for the cup
replay with Carlisle United was a great success. The
progress of the FA Cup competition in this year had been
heavily affected by a fierce winter, which had frozen
grounds at the lesser clubs and played havoc with the sched-
ules for the earlier rounds of the competition. Everyone
attending tonight's much delayed, much anticipated game,
was not only anticipating better weather but full of enthusiasm
for this particular tie.

The floodlit ground was almost full, with many youngsters adding their shrill, enthusiastic voices to the clamour,
making their distinctive contribution to the vibrant atmosphere which a big crowd always brought to the famous old
ground. The visitors secured the early goal which always
sets pulses racing in this situation, raising as it does the
prospect of a success for the giant-killers. Brunton Rovers
equalized before half-time. Then a second half of steadily
mounting pressure from the home team saw young Ashley
Greenhalgh first put the Rovers ahead after an intricate team
move and then consolidate the victory with a brilliant individual goal five minutes from the end.

The three thousand away supporters had enjoyed the
excitement of leading for a time and giving the big boys a
run for their money. The home crowd filed out of the ground
buzzing with satisfaction and speculation about the next
round and the plum home draw with Aston Villa. The press
and the broadcasting media trumpeted two more goals for
the golden boy of Grafton Park.

They also nodded their heads sagely and pointed to the healthy 'gate' which the reduction in prices had brought to the match. In a time when the nation was tightening its belt through recession, this was the way forward, the pundits, economical as well as sporting, told anyone who would listen. There were even those who spoke romantically of the ten pound entry fee 'bringing the game back to the people', of making professional football once again the working man's outlet it had been in the last great recession of the nineteen thirties.

The people who ran Brunton Rovers were as pleased as everyone else with the success of the night. Ex-chairman Edward Lanchester was full of the warm glow which an emphatic Rovers victory always brought to him, basking in romantic memories of great cup ties from the club's long history. Robbie Black glowed with the relief which any manager feels when the prospect of humiliation by a lower-division club has been triumphantly banished.

Immediately after the match, he gave an up-beat interview by the pitch to the television cameras, praising the skill and work-rate of his players and their spirit after they had gone behind, insisting that this was the moment to enjoy success rather than look too far ahead to the next round and Aston Villa. The cameras had been delighted to show shots of his glamorous wife in the directors' box, with a becoming fake-fur hat and the blue and white Brunton Rovers scarf wound prominently over her celebrated bosom. With her two children beside her, Debbie Black waved enthusiastically to the crowd around her and continued to bond with the folk of Brunton.

Darren Pearson congratulated himself on the daring device of reducing ticket prices, which had swelled the crowd and brought in as much revenue as a much smaller 'gate' at normal prices. It had also attracted much welcome and highly favourable publicity to one of the smaller teams in the Premiership, and thus to the town where he had lived for all of his life. With the commercial eye which a football club secretary must always keep on finances, he saw that Ashley Greenhalgh's goals and the national publicity accorded to them would probably put another million on an already substantial transfer fee. As a supporter, he didn't really want to see the young man sold; as a secretary, he thought it might be inevitable and wanted the best possible price.

The biggest crowd of the season at Grafton Park dispersed happily and without causing any trouble to the huge number of police officers which the safety regulations had demanded. Not like the days of his boyhood, said Edward Lanchester, when four or five policemen patrolling the edge of the pitch towards full time had been all that was necessary. By ten thirty that night, the labyrinth of offices beneath the main stand of the football club was quiet once again. Darren Pearson toured the familiar corridors, switched off the odd light which had been carelessly left on, then gave his familiar good night to the night security man, who had earlier attended the match with his grandson.

Very few among the twenty-nine thousand people who had been at the match that night realized that the only notable absentees had been the chairman and his wife, Jim and Helen Capstick.

The betting shop was in Darwen, a small town some six miles from Brunton which was being even more badly affected by the present recession in the British economy. It was only four miles from Brunton Rovers football ground and no more than a short drive for the secretary of that club, Darren Pearson.

He preferred to come here, where he was fairly confident that his presence would not be remarked. Secretaries of football clubs, although very important to their efficient operation, are not high-profile figures, and not many people in his native Brunton would have noticed his presence in such a place. Nevertheless, having lived there since he was a boy, he knew that sooner or later his frequenting of betting shops would have been remarked and his addiction become more public.

Caution had become habitual to him now. That was as much a reflection of his own shame in his gambling addiction as of the need to keep these transactions private. There was a parking space near the betting shop, but Pearson parked the blue Vectra in the next side street and walked the hundred yards through slanting rain to the shop's entrance. He glanced furtively through the dusk to left and right before he went through the door. Such movements were more likely to attract than to divert attention, but this was conduct which was by no means abnormal among the patrons of betting establishments.

He nodded to the woman behind the grill he chose, but gave her no greeting: this was not the sort of place where social niceties were important. Nor was the need for any sort of conversational opening. He said bluntly, 'I want to put a bet on Supreme Nelly in the three thirty at Haydock Park tomorrow.'

It was a ridiculous, comical name, but neither of them even noticed that. She knew the absolute necessity of being accurate in everything she recorded. He was concerned only with the thought of what he might win, of alleviating his mountain of debt with one startling coup. The classic gambler's delusion; the classic unrealistic ambition which had enticed millions of others before Darren Pearson into deeper and more dangerous financial waters.

She made a note on the pad in front of her, glanced at the card of tomorrow's races beside her, and said unemotionally, 'Three to one, sir.'

'It was fives on Tuesday. Fours at lunchtime today. Seven to two when I rang half an hour ago.'

'It's three to one now, sir. Do you wish to place a bet?'

'I suppose so.' He looked at her desperately, seeking reassurance where none was to be had, voicing the naïve question which was as obvious as it was futile. 'The fact that the odds have come steadily down means it must be well fancied, doesn't it?'

She sighed inwardly, but kept her face studiously blank. The first rule of this job was not to get yourself involved with the punters and their problems. You might upset yourself if you did that; might even end up asking them if they could afford this, advising them against over-committing

themselves. You could lose your job that way, and jobs were
highly important, when your man had just been laid off.
'Do you wish to bet, sir?'

'Yes. Yes, I'll take three to one.'

'How much do wish to stake, sir?'

'Five hundred. No, a thousand, if it's only three to one.'
He gave her a small, strangely apologetic laugh, then looked
automatically round the almost deserted shop to check if
anyone had picked up the size of his bet.

'It's Mr Pearson, isn't it?' The first indication that she
had any notion of his identity, though she had known who
he was from the moment he presented himself before her.
Her enquiry was apologetic, in this place where many people
chose to be anonymous.

'That's right. I have an account with you. A thousand on
Supreme Nelly, please.'

'Just a moment, sir.' She turned and disappeared through
a door two yards behind her.

Darren Pearson tapped his fingers on the counter in front
of him, shifted his weight from foot to foot, tried not to
look conspicuous. There were only three other people in
the place, two elderly men and a much younger woman.
They had problems of their own and no interest whatsoever
in the restless figure at the desk, however much he felt this
delay was exciting their interest.

The woman came back through the door with a look of
determined regret on her face. 'I'm sorry, Mr Pearson. We
cannot accept this stake.'

The ultimate humiliation for a punter: his bet was being
refused. He had known in his heart what was going to happen
from the moment she asked him to wait at the grill, but
some instinct had made him brazen it out as best he could.
He felt that he was delivering someone else's lines, that he
was not Darren Pearson but a character in a play he was
watching. 'There must be some mistake. I'm a regular
customer here. I have an account with you, as I said.'

'Yes, sir. The manager's instructions are that until you
clear the arrears on that account, you are not to be awarded
further credit.'

'But I've been a client here for years. You've made good profits out of me.'

'I'm sorry, sir. This is not my decision.'

As if she had triggered some electronic device, a man now opened the door behind her and came forward. It seemed to Darren Pearson an additional insult, in the illogical way of these things, that he was a much younger man. This presumptuous fellow could not be more than twenty-five or twenty-six, his fevered brain told him. The man said, 'It's all right Mrs Harris, I'll deal with this. Is there a problem, Mr Pearson?'

He spoke loudly, and Darren was sure now that this exchange was the centre of attention in the shop. He was entirely sober, but he felt like a drunk lurching out of control. 'A misunderstanding rather than a problem, I hope, for your sake. I am one of your best customers, yet you are refusing a sizeable stake from me.'

The man's small, insultingly young, mouth twisted into a mirthless smile. 'Our best customers pay their bills, Mr Pearson. I'm afraid you have exhausted your credit and you owe us an unacceptably large sum.'

The man had used these phrases many times before. Because he knew it was best to be firm and impersonal, he was keeping all emotion out of his voice, speaking as evenly, even dully, as possible.

Darren saw only an over-promoted youngster who seemed to be enjoying this. 'Look here, young man, you're representing a national chain with a national reputation to preserve.'

'Indeed I am, Mr Pearson.'

'A company which made handsome profits last year.'

The young man hardened his stance a little, sounding more than ever like a machine. 'It is company policy that we should not allow people to run up more than a certain amount of debt. That is felt to be in the interest of the client as well as the company.'

Darren knew now that he had lost, that no one could win against the faceless battalions of a betting leviathan like Ladbrokes. But pride, the few traces of self-respect he had hardly known he still possessed, made him persist. 'I am not the sort of back-street gambler who does pound doubles. I am a customer of long standing, with a good income.'

'That is why you have been allowed the degree of credit you have been afforded, Mr Pearson.' He glanced quickly to right and left: the British reserve about voicing financial details ran deep, even in a place like this. 'You have owed the company over fifteen thousand pounds for almost a year now, despite written requests to clear or at least substantially reduce your debt. If we accepted this transaction, your liability to the company would be almost twenty thousand. I'm afraid we cannot allow that.'

Darren descended to personal insult, the drunk's last throw in a contest he has lost. 'You seem to forget that you're speaking for Ladbroke's, not some old-fashioned small bookie. I'm not going to accept the decision of a jumped-up skivvy. I shall take this matter further.'

The man behind the grill was young, but certainly not inexperienced. He recognized this threat to pursue the argument with his superiors as the last futile move in an unpleasant but necessary exchange. 'That of course is your prerogative, Mr Pearson. I'm sure you'll find that my decision is confirmed.'

The rain outside was falling more heavily. The March wind of the early evening was bitter now, slanting the wetness hard into his face. Darren Pearson struggled defeated to his car, the dark beast of his dejection filling his mind with wild and desperate thoughts.

SEVEN

The British newspapers hadn't arrived in Dubai yet. Jim Capstick had the result of the match, but still couldn't read about the victory of Brunton Rovers in the cup tie replay.

He hadn't brought his laptop with him and he wasn't going to pursue computer information in the room downstairs; the result was all he needed at this delicate stage in the negotiations. He didn't want to move out of his room more than was strictly necessary. The sheikh was a powerful man, with a huge staff and a taste for intrigue. Jim was sure that any actions he took, any sign that he was anxious about events at home, would be reported back to his host.

If the truth were told, Capstick had himself a taste for secrecy, having found it an aid to most of his activities. And only at this moment did he acknowledge to himself that he was not intensely interested in the progress of Brunton Rovers, now that there was a real prospect that he would be selling his investment on. Negotiations to dispose of the club were proceeding nicely; progress was more rapid since he and his mysterious buyer had got beyond the stage of dealing through a third party.

But the Rovers' victory suited him, as far as it had any importance at all. Success in the short term could only boost the value of his asset, particularly with a buyer who had the millions needed to develop it. His potential buyer seemed to have little knowledge of football and none at all of the history of the game and of the proud place of Brunton Rovers within it. In his experience, Arabs weren't much interested in history. There seemed no reason why he should enlighten him; football history could only get in the way of negotiations.

He paused for a moment and looked through the big window at the terrace outside. The area was deserted save for the sheikh and the three men who had come here with him.

None of them were speaking, even though he had left them on their own. Jim Capstick assumed the men were body-guards. He had supposed one of them might be some sort of financial adviser, but there was no evidence of conferral. He wondered if the powerful man at the centre of the group had demanded that the terrace be specially cleared for their meeting. It seemed odd that with the hotel more than half full, there should be no guests sitting or strolling here, as the sun dropped and the day moved towards its very brief twilight.

The thought of dealing with such absolute power made him uneasy. But perhaps he was imagining things. In any case, the fact that a man had such control could only make him a better prospect as a buyer, surely? Jim was used to making deals on his own ground, with support at his elbow and a detailed knowledge of the financial background of anyone who came to his negotiating table. He understood the need for secrecy – indeed, he had insisted upon it himself, from the beginning of this. But he felt at a disadvantage meeting this man, who had infinitely more wealth and power than he had, in this alien place and without any of his own supporters to balance the numbers.

Capstick took a deep breath and moved out to join the party at its table. He gave the sheikh a smile he hoped was confident but respectful. 'That's all arranged. You probably know that the process of examining confidential financial details is referred to as "due diligence" in Britain. That material will be made available to you very quickly. I shall give the orders as soon as I am back in England.' He wondered if the man would question why he had not already set the process in motion. The sheikh was accustomed to exercising absolute power and might deride people without it. He could scarcely explain that he would need to make some explanation of what he was about before he ordered the release of sensitive infor-mation, that he wanted to keep this secret until the last possible moment. But the man in the long robes merely nodded his acceptance of these arrangements.

Jim wanted to ask the man opposite him to take off his dark glasses, but knew he must not do that. He had never had to negotiate with anyone behind shades before; he was surprised how difficult it made it to see what a man was thinking when you could not see his eyes. The sheikh looked at him for a few seconds, so that Jim thought he was going to question these arrangements. Then he gave a curt nod and said, 'My representative in the UK may need to bring certain queries to you when we have perused the figures. It will speed up the process.'

'Of course. Would you like to give me his name and telephone number?' Capstick produced his diary and silver-cased ballpoint.

'That will not be necessary. He will contact you in due course if we have queries.'

'Very well. Is there anything more we can do today?'

'Nothing at this stage, Mr Capstick.' He pronounced the strange name carefully, as if it was important to him to fix it in his memory.

'Then I shall fly home tonight and give the necessary orders to my staff.'

'Excellent. You have a seat reserved?'

'Yes.'

'Very well. I look forward to doing business with you.'

'And I with you.' Capstick hesitated, then thrust forward his hand. He thought he caught a sharp intake of breath from one of the men at the table, but after a second the sheikh took his hand and shook it firmly.

He had an hour to get to the airport. He took a shower and changed his shirt for the flight, finding the one he took off wet with sweat. The shower relaxed him; he had not realized quite how tense his muscles had become. He picked up the phone and had a call put through to his home. The tone buzzed six times in his ear before it was answered.

'Brunton eight-three-seven-two-zero-five.' The voice was not that of Helen but of Wally Boyd. Calls went through to the driver's flat over the garage when they were not answered in the main house.

'It's me, Wally. I'm about to leave the hotel in Dubai. My flight is due to land at Ringway at four twenty a.m.'

'I'll be there, sir.'

'Bloody unsocial hour. I'm sorry about that.'

'Can't be helped, Mr Capstick. I was expecting it. Won't be much traffic, at that time. Let's hope you land on time.'

Jim paused for a moment, then said as casually as he could, 'Mrs Capstick out, is she?'

'Yes, sir. Left this morning, sir. Didn't give me any idea of her plans for the day.'

'Do you think she's gone to the same place?'

'Couldn't say, sir. I couldn't ask her where she was going, could I? I hoped she'd drop something casually about her destination, but she didn't.' He paused, picturing his employer's face, trying to estimate the degree of anxiety at the other end of the line. 'I could check the mileage on the Mercedes, sir. I have the figure that was on the clock when Mrs Capstick left here.'

'Do that, will you? And try to get her story about where she's been, if you can do it without raising suspicion.'

'I will, sir. It's easy to check the mileage clock, once she puts the car in the garage. And if she's in the right mood, Mrs Capstick often volunteers information about where she's been.'

Wally Boyd rang off and looked at his watch. It must be nice to be really rich, like Jim Capstick. It gave you fast cars and people to meet you at the airport in the middle of the night and a glamorous, younger wife. But it obviously brought problems with it, as well.

In Dubai, Jim Capstick was thinking grimly that his chauffeur-bodyguard could also add spy to his job description.

DCI Peach left the two young men in the separate interview rooms for fully ten minutes before he moved to interview them. 'Which of these two beauties do you prefer?' he asked DS Blake.

Lucy shrugged. 'Whichever one you recommend. I don't know either of them.'

'I'll take Ahktar, then. He's the bugger who came at me with the knife. You take Malim. Take Brendan Murphy in with you and give him a verbal bashing. You know the situation?'

'Yes. We hope they don't realize it, but there isn't going

to be a court case against them. I gather Peter Forsyth was a bit too keen for his own good and went looking for evidence where he shouldn't have.'

'He did. I gave PC Forsyth a mild rebuke about it yesterday.'

Lucy Blake, who had bought coffee for the limp and shell-shocked Forsyth in the police canteen, smiled grimly and forbore to comment. 'I'll see what Brendan and I can get out of Malim.'

'And the big lad and I will see what we can get out of Ahktar.' Peach glanced at his watch. 'Right. Let's go!'

Wasim Ahktar was as apprehensive as Peach had hoped he would be after his wait in the interview room. He looked up in nervous anticipation as the man he had attacked ten days earlier bounced like a rubber ball into the room. 'You remember me, no doubt: DCI Peach. And this is DC Northcott.' He nodded happily at the man who was sitting down beside him.

Ahktar's anxiety was doubled rather than diminished. Peach had not exaggerated when he called his companion 'the big lad'. Clyde Northcott was six feet three, tall and lean, and gave the impression that all was bone and muscle beneath a tightly stretched skin. That skin was a very deep shade of black. Ahktar, who had previously thought that if things got really tough he would play the race card, now felt that even that rather desperate option had been removed.

Peach had the air of a rather hungry lion approaching a tethered goat. 'Good of you to come into the station voluntarily to help us with our enquiries, Mr Ahktar. The cooperation of the public is always appreciated.'

'Voluntarily? I never—'

'No more than the duty of a good citizen, of course, but appreciated nevertheless. Especially from someone as deep in the doo-dah as you are.'

'Now look, I don't—'

'I always like to assist someone who recognizes his public duty and wants to help us. But there is a problem. The question I have to ask myself is whether I can do anything useful for someone who caused an affray, pulled a knife on me, and tried to cut my throat. Would you think there was anything useful, DC Northcott?'

'Nothing at all, sir, that I can see. We could perhaps visit him in prison in due course, but that wouldn't do him any good with the rest of the men in there.'

Percy shook his head in sad agreement. 'You're probably right. Nasty sort of men you get in these long-term prisons, nowadays. In that case, I wonder if we could do anything for this lad before he gets there. Whether we might even keep him out of the can altogether.'

Northcott was well used by now to being Peach's straight man. He pursed his lips thoughtfully and said doubtfully, 'I can't see how that's going to be possible, sir, with the serious charges you have detailed. I have to say that I think you're being a little too charitable in this case, sir.'

Wasim Ahktar felt both threatened and bewildered by this strange pincer movement. He said desperately, 'I didn't pull a knife on you, Mr Peach! Not on you personally. And I'd never have cut your throat!'

'Really? Well, that hasn't been fully explored in court yet, has it?'

'And I hope you'll remember you nearly broke my bloody arm on that night.' Wasim rubbed the forearm in question with the fingers of his left hand and winced at the memory.

'Did I really, Mr Ahktar? Just shows the danger I felt I was in at the time, doesn't it? Good thing for you it wasn't DC Northcott here. Just between you and me, he's a bit of a hard bastard, is DC Northcott.' He glanced sideways at his colleague, who dutifully shifted his chair a little nearer to the small square table and stared down aggressively at the brown face which was now no more than two feet from his.

Wasim said wretchedly, 'I don't see how I can be of any use to you.'

'Well, perhaps I could help you there, then.' Peach looked ruminatively towards the ceiling for a moment and then appeared to make a decision. 'We don't do plea bargaining. We leave that sort of stuff to the lawyers; I'm sure in this case those buggers will think they have a cast iron case so won't be interested in any deals.' He shook his face regretfully at this iron element in the English law. 'But it's just possible that, if you were able to offer me a little help, I'd be able to argue to my senior officer, the man in charge of this CID section, that you'd been co-operative and thus deserved lenience. Chief Superintendent Tucker is a hard and ruthless man, but I would do my very best for you.'

Clyde Northcott's lips had threatened to twist into a smile with the description of Tommy Bloody Tucker as a hard and ruthless man. He now added hastily, 'You would do well to listen to DCI Peach, if he sees any way out for you.'

Ahktar was by now thoroughly bewildered. He said dully, 'What is it that you want of me?'

Peach gave him a disarming smile. 'A little information, Mr Ahktar. In exchange for which, I shall do my very best for you.'

Wasim stared at him suspiciously. He hadn't much experience of pigs, but everyone said you shouldn't trust them an inch. 'And what can you offer me in return? We've already been remanded to the Crown Court. What are you going to do for us there?'

Percy nodded thoughtfully. 'Good point, that, Mr Ahktar. Once we're in the hands of those damned lawyers, there's very little we can do to affect the course of justice. The only real possibility would be to avoid going to court altogether, don't you think, DC Northcott?'

Northcott's stern, hitherto unrevealing features were transformed with consternation. 'We surely couldn't do that, sir, not with charges as serious as these and police witnesses lined up to attest to them.'

Percy nodded regretfully. 'DC Northcott may well be right. My impulse to help people in trouble often unhinges my judgement, I'm afraid. The penalty for even carrying a knife was recently increased to four years, Mr Ahktar. And you were not only carrying a knife. You attempted to use it against a senior police officer who was attempting to enforce the law of the land. Maybe I was wrong to raise your hopes. Maybe we should just leave things as they are.' He shut his notebook firmly in front of him, as if setting aside temptation.

'What was it you wanted? What information?'

Peach was studiously low-key. 'Details of the people who were behind this affray, I think. The people who supplied you with knives and sent you out for this rumble with the British Nationals and their supporters.'

'They had knives too, you know. And they'd threatened us.'

'I can believe that, Mr Ahktar. But we'd like the details, you see. Then perhaps we can do something about making sure you don't get yourselves into trouble again.'

The frightened young man on the other side of the table was already receptive; the mention of the British National Party was the carrot he needed. Wasim gave them the names of the ringleaders among his enemies, the men who organized violence and sent others out to do it. Then, more reluctantly and in response to a mixture of threats and cajolery, he gave them the names of his own ringleaders, most of whom had not been there on the night in question. The majority of them were names already known to the police, but there were three significant new ones, one of them a recently elected member of the Town Council.

When he was certain that he had everything that was to be had, Peach stared down uncertainly at the notes he had made. 'Well, it's not much for me to make out a case for you, Mr Ahktar. But I promised that I would try to help you, and I shall certainly attempt that. As I have told you, Chief Superintendent Tucker is a severe and ruthless man. But perhaps, if I can catch him in one of his rare benevolent moments, I can make out a case for you. Don't get your hopes up too high, but if DS Blake is able to confirm to me that Mr Malim has been equally co-operative in the room next door, I might even try to get the charges against you in the Crown Court dropped.'

'We'd be very grateful if you could do that, Mr Peach.' Ten minutes later, a bewildered Wasim Ahktar and Fazal Malim left the station full of gratitude for the tolerance and understanding of the Brunton police.

Edward Lanchester felt very old as he moved out of the house and into the light north-east wind which was ruffling the leaves of the burgeoning daffodils.

He was very stiff and the usual ache at the bottom of his back was worse today. He would have warmed up quickly if he had had something more vigorous to do in the garden, but the man who had helped him for years had done all the routine work and left the place as tidy as usual. Edward's purpose was to decide exactly where to site the new camellias they were going to plant next week. Global warming meant that you could grow camellias even in north-east Lancashire, nowadays, if you chose a sheltered spot in the garden. Global warming felt a long way away on this cold late-March day.

Edward made a couple of decisions, then gave up and drove down to the golf club, where he settled down with a warming whisky in the bar. He was cheered when Ronnie Quigley, the man who had captained the Rovers and England when he was chairman, came in after a round of golf and spotted him. Ronnie came over and sat down at Edward's table. 'Good win the other night, Mr Lanchester.' He was twelve years younger than Edward and had never been able to break the habit of giving him his 'Mister', even in the golf club, where all were ostensibly equal.

They agreed on what a fine player the local lad Ashley Greenhalgh was becoming: not many nowadays came up through the ranks from the youth teams, as Ronnie had done in his time. The academy, as it was called now. Very soon, the two men were reminiscing about the old times, the implication being that things had been so much better then. Ronnie Quigley certainly thought so, though he had been quite modestly rewarded, even as England captain. Edward was pleased when it was Ronnie who eventually put that thought into words, rather than himself. Youth lends an inevitable enchantment to the past, but neither of them acknowledged that mundane thought.

They were so deep into happy reminiscence that that they did not see the man in the maroon sweater until he spoke. 'The elders of Brunton Rovers putting things to rights at Grafton Park, are they?'

Joe Wharton, sports writer for the *Evening Telegraph*. A member of the golf club, a man who had played golf with

both of them, at different times, and had been an affable
companion on the course. But a journalist, nonetheless. A
man looking for a quote; a man who might use a quote out
of its context, to make a better story. Better stories normally
meant mischief, and both the men at the table had suffered
in the past, so they gave the newcomer only a guarded
welcome.

Wharton understood all of this, but he had long since
acquired the thick skin which was a necessary tool of his
trade. He had a second whisky in his hand for Lanchester,
having known his preferred brand for many years, but
Quigley refused another beer, took his leave of Edward, and
went and sat with the men with whom he had played golf
earlier. Joe Wharton watched the departure of the former
Rovers' captain without rancour, then sat down in the chair
he had vacated.

He was a man now approaching sixty, with a red face,
bright blue eyes, and rapidly thinning hair. He took a sip
of his drink and said, 'New chairman still behaving himself,
is he?'

'He's no longer very new and his behaviour isn't for me
to comment upon,' said Edward primly. Then, knowing
how journalists in the past had made hay with even the
most cautious and negative of his rebuffs, he added, 'I see
very little of Jim Capstick, except at matches and at board
meetings.'

'Capstick wasn't at the match on Wednesday night, was
he?'

'No.'

'Why was that, Edward?'

Lanchester, who would have welcomed the use of his
forename by Ronnie Quigley, resented it from the journalist,
who had been a young man when he had chaired the Rovers.
'I've no idea.'

'And you don't wish to speculate as to where he might
have been?'

Edward smiled at him sourly. 'I'm not going to break the
habit of a lifetime at my age, Mr Wharton.'

'It would be off the record, of course.'

'I'm sure it would. But I don't to wish to read that "An informed source refused to comment".'

Joe Wharton was not at all abashed. 'No one was ever able to kid you, Edward. You know all the tricks.'

'It's not my business to speculate on where the chairman might have been on Wednesday night.'

'No, I suppose not. But you wouldn't be human if you weren't at least a little curious. And you've always been human, Edward. I well remember your many kindnesses to me when you were chairman and I was a raw young lad.'

Outrageous flattery was one of the less damaging of the journalist's tools, thought Edward. 'I may be human, Joe. I am also old. And one of the things I learned a long time ago was to control my curiosity. And now I am going to buy you a drink.'

He hauled himself stiffly to the bar and bought Wharton another whisky, reluctantly denying himself further indulgence as he was about to drive home. It was not until he was back in the big, rambling house, rubbing some warmth back into his hands, that he thought again about what Joe Wharton had said.

The chairman's unexplained absence was a little curious, as was some of his other recent behaviour. He'd make discreet enquiries of the secretary tomorrow, and see if Darren Pearson knew what was going on.

EIGHT

Darren Pearson was having a hectic day. He was used to that and normally he would have welcomed the opportunity to immerse himself in something other than the problems of his private life.

But today was different. He had been asked to make official appointments with the manager of the club in the early afternoon and with its chairman an hour later. He saw both of these men quite often, but when they asked for formal meetings, it usually meant there was something of considerable importance to be discussed. At the moment, he could have done without that.

He spent a solid hour giving an initial briefing to the latest additions to the club's band of official stewards for first team matches at Grafton Park. If you could control the areas within and behind the stands with your own employees, you saved a fortune on policing costs. But the police reviewed internal arrangements every year to make sure they conformed to the rigorous standards put in place since the disasters in Sheffield and Bradford twenty years earlier. Your own staff had to be properly briefed, then trained in crowd control and elementary first aid before they were accepted as club stewards. Nevertheless, the savings on police overtime rates made an army of club-directed stewards essential for a club like Brunton Rovers.

Darren leavened what seemed to him to be dull stuff with humorous anecdotes of past mishaps and one or two jokes of his own about the misconceptions people brought to this job. He was surprised how he seemed to keep the largely male audience's attention; there was even a ragged round of applause when he finished his address and sent them off for coffee. He saw himself disconcertingly for a moment from the back row of his audience. From this imaginary standpoint, he marvelled at the act he was able to put on;

how little these people must suspect of the turmoil which would take over this confident instructor's mind at the end of the day.

He was trying to relax in his office with his coffee when Edward Lanchester popped his distinguished white head round the door. 'Got a minute, Darren?'

'Of course, Edward. Always a pleasure to see you!'

It was a pleasure, really, thought Darren, trying not to resent the way the old man apparently thought he never had anything important to do, so that there was never any need for an appointment. Probably things had been less hectic in his time all those years ago. Probably he'd also have had other things then than the present and future of his beloved Brunton Rovers to occupy him all day! He liked Lanchester, who had no doubt been a lion in his day. Edward was as honest and straightforward in his dealings as the day was long and surprised when others were not the same.

Darren made sure his visitor had a cup of coffee and his favourite shortbread in his hand before he said, 'What can I do for you, Edward?'

'Very probably nothing, Darren.' Lanchester leaned back and stretched his legs reflectively in front of him. He was much shrewder than many people realized, often using his age and a slightly bumbling air as cloaks for subtle probings. 'A little information. Perhaps even less than that – a little gentle speculation might be all that you feel you can offer. Off the record, as our journalistic friends always assure us. And with the assurance that it would certainly not go beyond these walls, of course.'

Pearson found himself intrigued, despite his irritation at the gentle wordiness of the request. 'I'll help you if I can, of course.'

'Maybe you will just put an old man's fevered imagination at rest. That in itself would be a service to me. I was wondering if you knew where our present chairman was on Wednesday night.'

'Wednesday? That wasn't the first match Mr Capstick has missed, by any means. He has a variety of business interests and a fortune to maintain.'

'But he doesn't miss many matches, home or away. And doesn't he usually let you know when he is going to do so?'

'I suppose he does, yes.' Darren realized that the old man's oblique approach was masking a real suspicion. One that he had entertained himself, he thought, but hadn't previously cared to voice, even to himself. 'Jim Capstick didn't say anything about why he was going to be away on Wednesday, though.'

'Odd, then. Out of kilter with his normal behaviour.'

'But not sinister. I don't think we should make too much of it.'

'I agree, probably not sinister. Just a thought, that's all. And a thought that should be kept strictly between the two of us, as I said.' Edward nibbled his way thoughtfully through a mouthful of shortbread. 'The only reason I mention it at all is that Joe Wharton was sounding me about it.'

'Thanks for the warning. If Mr Wharton gets on to me, I'll be ready for him.'

The two men paused for a moment and sipped their coffee ruminatively, united by a mutual distrust of the men and women whose business it was to make bonfires from the thinnest wisps of smoke. Then Lanchester stood up and said, 'I won't take up any more of your time then, Darren. It was probably entirely innocent and nothing to do with us, but it would be interesting to know where Mr Capstick's been over the last couple of days, don't you think?'

He left without another word, the final image he left being that of a smile which was surprisingly mischievous in one of his advanced years. Wily old bird, thought Darren admiringly. He wasted the next five minutes of his hectic day speculating exactly where the powerful and now mysterious Jim Capstick might have been on Wednesday and Thursday.

Percy Peach knew how he was going to play this. His strategy would depend entirely on his chief not detecting what he was about, but he had every confidence in Tommy Bloody Tucker's abysmal powers of detection.

'I wanted to see you about that case you were involved in, Peach.'

Percy was pleased to see that his chief was already uneasy. 'The assault on a police officer case sir? Yes, I got your message. Everything's going swimmingly. Those young ruffians Ahktar and Malim were remanded to the Crown Court by the magistrates, as we anticipated. We should get those two custodial sentences for this. As the victim and chief witness for the Prosecution, I won't let you down, sir. Well, it's a cast iron case, isn't it? Young thug sealed his fate when he came at me with a knife like that, didn't he?'

'Well, yes, I suppose he did. Percy, I wonder if you've considered . . .'

Words failed the chief superintendent, and he squirmed ingloriously upon his chair. He did a good squirm, Percy thought; he'd like to see more of it. The use of his first name was a sure sign of weakness on this occasion, he decided. 'You'd like me to make the most of my injuries, sir? Well, I can certainly do that – wring my wrist and grimace a bit, and so on – but I think you're perhaps worrying unnecessarily. They'll go down without any histrionics from me.' He knew perfectly well that they wouldn't, that PC Forsyth's over-zealous follow-up had destroyed any chance of a conviction, that no case would ever be brought to the Crown Court. But he also knew that Tommy Bloody Tucker's pusillanimous soul was about to twist his tongue towards abject retreat, so he was confident of his ground. You owe me one, young PC Peter Forsyth, if I bring this off for you and preserve your skin from top brass damage. 'I've been through the defence case, sir. They'll be silly if they don't plead guilty and beg for judicial mercy.'

'I appreciate that, Percy. But can I ask you to consider for a moment that there may be wider issues to bear in mind here?' Tucker cast his arms helplessly wide, then squirmed again at the incomprehension in his listener; Peach beamed his approval of that exercise.

'Wider issues, sir? I seem to remember you saying when I was nursing my bruises, "We should make an example of these thugs . . . I want you to throw the book at these people". Well the book has been well and truly thrown sir, in accordance with your instructions.'

Tucker looked thoroughly miserable and continued to squirm. 'Perhaps there was a misunderstanding.' He swallowed hard and made an unprecedented concession. 'Perhaps it was my fault, Percy. I'd had a very busy day. Perhaps I failed to make myself properly clear at the time.'

'Seemed clear enough to me, sir. "Make sure you throw the book at them. We must stamp out violence on our patch. I'm right behind you on this." I remember thinking at the time that you were giving commendable support to your officers. Unprecedented support!' Peach took care to keep an absolutely straight face as he stressed his final adjective.

Behind the big desk, the squirm was developing towards a writhe. 'It's – well, it's my job to take an overview, Percy.'

'As you constantly remind us workers at the crime-face, sir.'

'And on occasions, I may even have to take the risk of being unpopular with my officers.'

'A risk you undertake with frequent and impressive calmness, sir.'

'And sometimes – very rarely, I hope, but sometimes – I have to ask my officers to take these wider considerations of mine into their calculations.'

'Ask away, sir!' Percy did the magnanimous gesture rather well, he thought. He decided that a wide sweep of his arm was enough and resisted the temptation to brush the chief superintendental carpet with the back of his hand.

Tucker was so surprised that he stopped squirming and sat bolt upright between the arms of his leather chair. 'Really? Well, I must say, this is most enlightened of you, Percy, especially in view of the fact that you were the man who fearlessly disarmed this young man of his offensive weapon.'

'Oh, hardly fearlessly, sir! I have the same reaction when I see the flash of a knife as most other front-line officers. But I suppose I felt that if I shit myself it would be in a good cause.'

Tucker shut his eyes and tried to concentrate. 'This makes it all the more regrettable to me that on this occasion I am asking you to consider whether the wider issue of community relations should perhaps take precedence over the undoubted justice of your cause. I–I feel that I should certainly put you forward for a commendation.'

'You want us to drop the case, sir.' Peach spoke dully, as if trying to contend with this bombshell, as if he had not been aware from the outset where this was going.

Tucker bit the bullet and resumed squirming. 'I'd like you to consider it, Percy. Relationships with the Asian community in this town are very delicate.'

'Not so delicate that three of the buggers couldn't try to knife us, sir.'

'That is true and I know it, Percy. But public relations with the ethnic section of our community are very important. So important that I feel they should occasionally take precedence over individual concerns.'

'Like assault with knives upon a young female and a young male officer, together with a CID chief inspector, sir?'

'Well, perhaps.'

'I see, sir. And no doubt you would wish me to undertake the delicate task of explaining to the officers concerned that this case was not going to be taken to court.'

Thomas Bulstrode Tucker ran his finger round the inside of his collar, which seemed to have suddenly tightened upon his timorous neck. 'That would be the best thing, if you would do it.'

Percy sighed the long sigh of the martyr resigned to his fate. 'Perhaps it would be better if I handled it, sir. It would preserve the integrity of your overview, among other things.'

'I shan't forget this, Peach.'

Percy noted the resumption of his surname with some relief and allowed himself his first smile for many minutes. 'I shan't allow you to forget it, sir. You owe me one, sir.'

Thomas Bulstrode Tucker smiled back, acknowledging the argot of the service from which he had divorced himself for so long. He couldn't quite understand how he had managed to engineer it, but he had got his way in this. His bête noir Percy Peach had agreed to drop a cast-iron case, at his behest. He leaned forward earnestly and put both hands on the leather of the desk. 'I'm glad that you have allowed me to paint the wider picture for you, Peach. I'm sure when you look back in a few years you will see that there was wisdom in this.'

'Yes, sir. And if there isn't, you will no longer be sitting behind that desk to sort out the consequences but in happy retirement. I'll explain things as best I can to the lads and lasses downstairs. And no doubt you will explain the rationale behind the climb-down to young Malim's father at the next meeting of the Lodge.'

Tucker reddened with a pleasing swiftness. 'Freemasonry has nothing to do with this, Peach!'

'No, sir. Just a pleasing coincidence for you.'

'I'm sorry you can't accept defeat gracefully. It's one of the flaws in your make-up to which you should give attention, Peach. That will be all, thank you.'

Left alone, Thomas Bulstrode Tucker tried hard to rejoice in his unexpected victory over his chief inspector, but found it curiously hard to feel the exultation he thought appropriate. Back in his own office, Peach was thinking that perhaps against all the odds he owed that young idiot Peter Forsyth an unexpected drink.

At the same time on that Friday afternoon, Darren Pearson was planning his meeting with the chairman and owner of Brunton Rovers.

The football manager, Robbie Black, had cancelled his earlier meeting because he wanted to supervise the fitness tests being undertaken by two of the players who were doubtful starters for tomorrow's match. Darren was pleased about that, because it gave him time to plan his tactics for his meeting with Jim Capstick.

In the event, no tactics were possible. It was Jim Capstick who controlled the direction as well as the tone of the exchanges. He took Pearson through a very full account of his meeting with the bank's representative earlier in the month, exacting the full details of Miss Alcock's demands on behalf of Barclays for strict control of the club's debts.

Capstick nodded, then allowed himself the smile of relish

which the troubles of a bigger business inevitably bring to
a mogul. 'Barclays have their own problems at the moment,
of course.'

'Yes. That won't necessarily help us, though. They're
worried about bad debts, and football clubs are likely to
make any bank nervous in the present recession.'

'I can see that. We don't command much public sympathy,
when the people read about the transfer fees and wages
being paid.'

'No. And most of our assets are players, and thus in an
accountant's view intangible and unreliable. The bank would
be pleased if we cashed in on one or two of our major
assets.'

'Like Ashley Greenhalgh.'

It was Darren's turn to smile. 'His name was mentioned,
as a matter of fact. Ms Alcock happens to be a Manchester
City fan. She'd like to see them prise him away from here.
So would her bank.'

'Every player has his price.'

The old football cliché marked the end of the preliminaries for Jim Capstick. He said, 'I'm glad the books are
in order and up to date. You may have to show them to
financial experts in the near future.'

'Due diligence?'

'That is the phrase, I believe.'

'Those are the words used to acknowledge that a detailed
account of the club's present financial position, including
any previously concealed assets and liabilities, must be given
to anyone pursuing a substantial interest. In layman's terms,
that means someone interested in taking over the business.'

'Correct.'

'You're thinking of selling Brunton Rovers?'

'I'm exploring the commercial possibilities, as one would
do with any other asset. It may be the right time to capital-
ize on this particular venture, from my point of view. Of
course, I would want to be assured that whoever purchased
Brunton Rovers had the interests of the club at heart and
the funds to generate future success on the field.'

He was already rehearsing the phrases for the press

handout which would come in due course, thought Pearson.
'Is one allowed to ask who this buyer might be?'

Jim Capstick smiled. 'You are allowed to ask, but you
must not expect an answer. Not at this delicate preliminary
stage. If it all comes to nothing, it will be better for all of
us that you know as little as possible.'

Darren agreed with that. It was easier to fend off the press
and broadcasting media if you knew nothing. 'You realize
that it will be almost impossible to keep this secret?'

This time Capstick's smile was not a pleasant one. 'At
the moment you and I are the only people who know about
this. It should remain that way.'

'I shall do my very best to ensure—'

'The firm involved will be one which specializes in these
things. You must give them access to everything they ask
for. The two men who will come here on Monday will be
professional accountants who specialize in examining material of this sort. They have no axe to grind for themselves.
They will be receiving a handsome fee to provide a report
for the third party who is employing them.'

'I understand that. I understand also that you do not
wish me to know who that third party is at the moment.
I don't want to know: I agree with you that the less I know
the better, when the inevitable pack of journalists descends
on me.'

'Then you understand what is good for you and good for
the club,' said Capstick grimly.

'But I shall have to give orders to other people to release
this information. The club's official auditors, for instance,
hold much of the information at present: we're at the end
of the financial year. Even if they didn't, it is inevitable that
any firm conducting the kind of detailed analysis you indicate will wish to speak to the club's auditors.'

'I know that. I've already instructed you to give these
people access to all the information they ask to see.'

'All I'm pointing out is that many more people than me
are going to be involved. It is inevitable that one or more
of them will let something out – possibly quite unintention-
ally, possibly for financial gain.'

'You're trying to pass the buck. Trying to say that if this gets out it won't be your fault.'

'It won't. But I'm trying to—'

'How's your gambling, Mr Pearson? Still running out of control?'

Darren felt as if he had received a violent blow in the middle of his chest. It was a good thing he was sitting down, because for a second or two the room and its sparse furnishings of filing cabinets and computer swam before him. Until this moment, he had had not the slightest inkling that his chairman knew anything about his personal problems.

Eventually he managed to say weakly, 'I'm dealing with it. It doesn't affect my work here.'

'If it did, you wouldn't be behind that desk. Make sure you deal with it, or you won't stay there.'

On that, Capstick stood up. It was best to leave the man with the knowledge that you had a certain hold over him; for all the empty promises Pearson had been making, it was threats which most ensured loyalty. Jim knew he shouldn't have enjoyed the moment as much as he had: it was better to be entirely dispassionate about these things. 'I appreciate what you say about others. I just want to ensure that you muzzle them as much as is humanly possible, Darren.'

He was gone then, leaving Darren Pearson thinking of all the things he might have said. He could have maintained at least a little dignity if he had told the man loftily that it didn't need threats to ensure his discretion.

But what did dignity matter, in the face of this new threat to his world and that of those around him?

NINE

Brunton Rovers won again on the next day. As the year moved into April, the prospect of relegation from the Premiership was receding fast.

Victory cheered up everyone connected with the club. Away victories were rare and vital, so the old town celebrated on Saturday night and the feeling of well-being spread like a pleasant infection along the grimy terraced streets and out into the quiet beauty of the Ribble valley beyond them. Percy Peach felt it; the petty criminals who were his foes felt it; even Agnes Blake in her cottage in Longridge, remembering her father's tales of his great day at the Cup Final of 1928, felt it.

The happiness seemed to Darren Pearson to stretch beyond the weekend and into that most detested area of the working week, Monday morning. Even the cleaning ladies at the club, who had been at work since six and were preparing to leave when he arrived at half past eight, bade him a cheerful good morning and seemed happy with their work. People congratulated him on the victory as if he had engineered it himself.

As manager, Robbie Black had done just that. He took the children to school himself on Monday morning, trying ineffectively to keep a low profile as James and Eleanor skipped along and accepted the congratulations of their peers on Saturday's victory. He found a surprising number of men among the other parents, a reflection of changing times as well as the present recession. They all commented enthusiastically on Saturday's result; perhaps they thought that by talking to him they could assert their manhood and make themselves a part of what had been achieved. Two of them even wanted to shake his hand.

He told Debbie about it when he got home. Although he had been a Scottish international and had enjoyed hero-worship in his playing days, she was more used to handling the public aspects of celebrity than he was. British tennis success had been a rare phenomenon in her day, so that reaching a Wimbledon semi-final had brought much publicity. Debbie's glamorous looks and lifestyle had increased the public adulation, so that she had become almost a show-business personality. 'Enjoy it while you can!' was her advice to Robbie; he thought he detected a rare tinge of regret for the celebrity trappings that were gone for her.

'It's quiet for you here, isn't it?' he said, watching her stack the breakfast dishes on the drainer.

'Quiet enough,' she said, looking out of the window and smiling at the sight of next door's Labrador puppy returning bouncily from his morning walk. She came over and put her hands round Robbie's arm. 'But not too quiet. I still got up this morning and congratulated myself on the fact that I won't see a single journalist today!'

'You're right about enjoying it whilst you can,' he reflected ruefully. 'Football crowds grow more fickle and less patient every year. 'They'll be calling for my head if we lose three matches in a row.'

'Not in Brunton,' said Debbie sturdily. 'They're not so daft as not to realize when they've got a good 'un.'

He laughed at her adoption of the Lancashire phrase. 'You like it round here, don't you?'

'I love it! I love the Ribble Valley. I love having the Yorkshire Dales and the Lake District not much more than an hour's drive away. I love not having to worry about drugs at the school gates.'

'Don't you ever get bored?'

'Everyone gets bored occasionally – even Robbie Black! Don't forget I've seen you in the middle of July, when there's been no football for two months and you can't wait for pre-season training to begin!'

He grinned. 'Bred into me in Glasgow, that was. We kicked a ball about even in summer up there. Cricket was a game for English toffs. But don't you sometimes find the days dragging in winter, with the kids at school and long days to fill?'

'I might do, if I didn't have my classes and my self-improvement,' she teased. Her Open University studies had been something of a family joke, until she had produced glowing assessments and high grades. In another year, she would have her degree. 'When we get our au pair, I'll be able to take a part-time job. Something interesting and useful which fits in with the children's school hours, I think.'

He went across and kissed her, first lightly on her forehead, then more firmly upon the lips. 'You're serious about putting down roots here, aren't you?'

She gave the question a moment's thought, then nodded her agreement. 'I'm serious about life, I suppose. I want to do all the things I could have done when I was young, if I hadn't been too interested in the fripperies.'

He grinned down at her, still holding her affectionately in his arms. 'You mean if you hadn't been such a looker and hadn't been a brilliant tennis player.'

'Perhaps. Anyway, having children makes you realize that life has moved on. But at forty-three, I can still do the things I want to do. And I want to do them here.'

'Well, you're still a guy guid looker, Debbie Black!'

He kissed her again and she responded. She liked it when he dropped into the Scottish dialect for his little intimacies and compliments to her. 'Tha's a right belter thiself, when tha says things like that!' she said, in the broadest Lancashire accent she could muster. It wasn't a very good effort, but the very amateurishness of it made both of them laugh all the more. 'Nah, be off with thee and earn us some brass!'

Robbie was still chuckling inwardly when he drove into his marked parking space at Grafton Park. You needed someone like Debbie at home, when you dealt with hairy footballers all day. Half of them were foreign now, but they seemed to pick up the oaths and obscenities of English faster than anything else – not surprisingly, when you heard the phrases which most of the British lads used all the time. There were exceptions, of course, but a few GCSEs were still enough to make you an intellectual in the context of most football dressing rooms.

The first team were assigned to the gym this morning.

Whatever the level of skill, Premier League matches were ferociously fast and hard. For those who weren't nursing niggling injuries, it was largely a matter of maintaining the level of fitness which had been attained, at this late stage of the season. They would do a couple of short five-a-side matches with the football, in the early afternoon, and then finish for the day: Mondays were usually light training days after a match on the Saturday; if they had played on the Sunday instead, the players were usually given Monday off altogether.

He saw two men with briefcases following Darren Pearson up the stairs towards the board room as he moved through to the players' treatment room. Auditors, probably, at this time of the year. It reminded him of his concerns about finance for the team and the meeting he had rearranged with Pearson for midday today.

Four of his team from Saturday were in the treatment room, receiving physiotherapy for knocks they had taken or strains they had aggravated. When he had started playing football almost thirty years ago with a small Scottish second division club, the treatment room had been a tiny place which reeked of embrocation, with a single washbasin and a cupboard containing elastic bandages and aspirins.

Now the corresponding place at Grafton Park looked like a hospital treatment room, with eight massage tables, heart monitors, and a variety of expensive medical machines designed to monitor players' progress and to restore them to full fitness as quickly as possible whenever they were injured. It made good sense, when you were paying average Premiership players a million pounds a year and some of the stars more than twice as much as that. There were three players in here that might be fit for next Saturday's match. Robbie would insist on them being fully fit by Thursday to be considered; intensive treatment might just make the difference

He glanced at his watch: time for his meeting with the club's secretary. Though they were on good terms with each other and genuinely liked each other, Robbie always felt at a disadvantage in any sort of formal meeting with Darren Pearson. The secretary conducted meetings, formal and

informal, all day. Some were merely with individual
members of the non-footballing staff, who all answered to
Pearson for their work, some with outsiders. Some were
with large groups, some with tiny ones. The point as far as
Robbie was concerned was that Pearson did this sort of
thing all day, whereas for him sitting down for a formal
exchange was a rarity, a necessary evil in a working day
otherwise dominated by footballing considerations.

Among other talents he had, Pearson was an expert at
giving nothing away unless he wanted to reveal it. He wanted
to sound out Black to find whether he had heard any whis-
pers about a change of ownership at the club, but he would
do so subtly and in his own good time. Let the other man
make the running whenever you could: give yourself the
opportunity to size up the situation. In this case that was
easy, because it was Black who had asked for this meeting,
which had originally been scheduled for Friday.

'What was it you wanted to talk about, Robbie?'

Black thought how very much at ease Pearson looked
behind his desk, how uncomfortable he felt in the easy chair
which had been allotted to him. He said rather desperately,
'We're almost safe from relegation now.'

'Almost. I know that you more than anyone else won't
count your chickens too early, Robbie.'

'I want to talk about what's going to happen in the summer.'

Darren wondered in that moment whether he had heard
something about the future ownership of the club. But he
wouldn't give anything away until he was certain. 'Happen
to the team? That is surely first and foremost your concern.'

'It is. And I want to know about finance.'

'Spoken like a true Scotsman. And it gladdens the heart
of the club secretary to hear it. Some managers charge on
and take no account of the financial position of their clubs.'

'I've always been a realist. But I need all the money I
can get to do my job. It gets more difficult every year to
compete with the big boys.'

'Indeed it does. I'll do everything possible to secure you
all the funds I can. I've always done that. But I don't see
it being easy, in the midst of a world recession.' The usual

caution: Darren could hear club secretaries in all but three of the ninety-two clubs playing league football uttering similar words, in the next few months.

'Will we sell Ashley Greenhalgh?'

Darren smiled. 'I wish I had a ten-pound note for every time I've been asked that over the last six months. In some respects, you're better able to answer that question than I am. He has three years left on his contract. Will he want to go this summer?'

Robbie smiled back, so that for a moment they were friends united against a common enemy. 'He's a sensible lad, is Ashley – I wish all our other youngsters had their heads screwed on like him. The trouble is that his agent will be dangling offers in front of him, like the rest of his bloody tribe. But Ashley's got enough sense to take good advice: it won't be just a question of more money. My guess is that if one of the big four clubs comes in for him, he'll go.'

'That's your answer, then. We've already had preliminary enquiries from both the Manchester clubs and from Liverpool. So far, we've always said we're not interested in selling. But you know and I know that once a player decides he wants to go, it becomes a matter of getting the best price for Brunton Rovers.'

'I think he'll be sold.'

'I agree with you. I think Ashley will decide it's time for a move and our owner will decide it's time to cash in on his asset.'

'Will I get the money to spend on new players?'

That was the key question he had wanted to ask. That was why he had requested this meeting with Pearson and both of them knew it. 'I hope so. I'll be completely honest with you, Robbie. I don't think anyone can really answer that except Jim Capstick. And I'm not sure he'd be prepared to give you an answer at this minute.'

'Without Ashley Greenhalgh we'd have gone down this year. If he goes, I'll have to spend wisely to replace him. I don't mind that, it's part of my job to back my judgement in the transfer market. But I'll need the funds to buy: we've no young players of Ashley's quality coming through the academy at the moment. I don't think we've any young-sters who can hold down a place in the first team.'

'You may need to put these arguments to Mr Capstick, in due course.'

'I'll do it tomorrow, if he'll see me. I need answers on this, as soon as possible. There are one or two managers I can chat to, before the transfer window opens. I'd rather do that than deal with agents.'

Pearson nodded. He liked Robbie Black and found him easy to work with. If he continued to be as successful as he'd been with Brunton Rovers, one of the big city clubs would be in for him, sooner rather than later. But Darren wanted to keep him here as long as possible. 'I wouldn't speak to him yet, if I were you.'

'Why? You think he'll say we can't talk about anything until we're sure relegation isn't going to happen?'

'I'm sure he would say that. And he'd probably be right. But there's something else I think you should know. In strict confidence.'

'What's that?' Robbie's mind flew suddenly to those two suited men with briefcases he had seen with Pearson earlier. 'What's going on?'

'Maybe nothing. Nothing immediate, I'm sure. And I wouldn't want this to get to the players; we don't want them unsettled by anything now that they're on a good run. The chairman has asked me to reveal all the details of our finan-cial situation to those blokes you saw with me earlier. They're accountants operating on behalf of a third party. We have a legal duty to make this information available. It's called "due diligence". It allows anyone who is considering the purchase of a business to have access to everything they ask for, so that clever and unscrupulous operators can't hide skeletons in the cupboard.'

'He's thinking of selling the club.'

'You now know as much as I do, Robbie. Mr Capstick always plays his cards close to his chest. I expect in his position we'd do the same.'

'I wouldn't trust Jim Capstick as far as I could throw him.'

Pearson smiled grimly. He agreed with that, but he drew

the line at outright criticism of his employer. 'Nothing is going to happen quickly. Mr Capstick has assured me that any possible purchaser must have the long-term interests of the club at heart.'

'Those blokes you've locked in the board room with the books aren't football men. They don't care a damn for Brunton Rovers. But they'll settle the future of all of us.'

'They're merely gathering financial information, Robbie. It's part of their job to be dispassionate about it. They'll relay their findings to a third party. For all we know, they may not even make a recommendation: that may not be part of their brief. Or whoever is employing them may decide that the figures do not make us an attractive proposition.'

'I bet it will be someone with lots of money and fuckall knowledge of football!' Black lapsed for a bitter moment into the language of the dressing room, then strove for decency. 'This wouldn't have happened in the days of Edward Lanchester. He loved the game and loved this club.'

Darren could have reminded the Scot that in those days the manager like his players would have earned a fraction of what he was being paid now. Instead he said firmly, if with a touch of regret, 'Those days are gone, Robbie, and you know it. A smallish businessman with relatively modest means could never become chairman of his local club now-adays. Not if it's a Premiership club, anyway.'

'This will get out, you know. Not from me, but it will. The rumour factory will be busy within a week at the most.'

'You're almost certainly right. When "due diligence" is exercised, due secrecy goes to the wall. Too many people have to be consulted. Our bankers and our auditors have to know, for a start. It's impossible to keep the lid on things for long.'

'I hope Jim Capstick realizes that.'

'Our chairman and owner isn't a fool,' said Darren Pearson with a tinge of bitterness. 'He knows the score about most things.'

Tea with his future mother-in-law. A prospect calculated to fill brave men with gloom and less brave ones with fear.

Yet Percy Peach was looking forward to tea with Agnes
Blake with the happiest anticipation.

'You said just tea,' said Agnes a little nervously, as her
daughter led Percy into the cottage. I've not got you a full
meal – I've just done a bit of baking.'

Percy surveyed a table groaning under thinly cut sand-
wiches, home made scones, cherry buns, fruit cake and
Victorian sponge trifle. 'I'll let you into a secret, Mrs B.
I'm only marrying your girl to get more of your cooking,
if you want the real truth of it!'

'Get off with you!' Agnes giggled delightedly and slapped
Percy's sturdy shoulder. 'But they used to say the way to a
man's heart was through his stomach, when I was a girl,
and if you're hoping for that in our Lucy, you'll be let down.
As a cook, she's a washout.'

More hilarity, only increased by Lucy Blake's attempts
at haughty disdain. 'When you two adolescents have
finished, we're supposed to be talking about final arrangements for my wedding,' she reminded them desperately. It
wasn't a subject she usually needed to raise, with her mother
around.

'All in good time, my impetuous darling,' said Percy.
'First of all, we must do justice to the culinary efforts of
the lady of the house.' He held out his arm at shoulder height
to Agnes, who stretched her fingers to meet his and allowed
herself to be led to the table, as though embarking upon a
formal minuet at an eighteenth century ball.

Lucy Blake wondered how many years of such
pantomimes she must anticipate, though not with the fore-
boding she pretended but with a certain lightness of heart.
She would never dare to voice such sentimental slush, but
it seemed to her quite miraculous that the only two people
in the world whom she really loved should have taken to
each other so readily.

It had its disadvantages, of course. It meant that they were
able to outsmart her in too many decisions. It was this
combination which had fixed her wedding for May when
she had planned to leave it for at least another year whilst she
got on with her career. She had got used to the idea now.

She found to her surprise that she was quite looking forward to being married, though she couldn't afford to admit that to either of her companions.

What she did say, as the putative bridegroom was enthusiastically demolishing a piece of fruit cake, was, 'You still haven't fixed on your best man.'

Percy finished his cake unhurriedly, aware that Agnes was looking at him even more expectantly than her daughter. 'Not easy, for a man without real friends like me,' he said gloomily.

'Isn't there one of your cricketing friends?' said Agnes Blake hopefully. Any cricketer must to her mind be a man of suitably sterling character: she had some pleasantly old-fashioned views about the national summer game.

'No one close enough, Mrs B,' said Percy dolefully. 'At least, no one whom I'd care to release upon unsuspecting bridesmaids.'

'You have an exaggerated view of the innocence of country girls,' said Lucy. 'What about one of your golfing chums?' She timed the question to provoke an indignant splutter from her mother, as she hastily set down her teacup.

Percy shook his head. 'No one close enough as yet. Golfers haven't the style and breadth of vision for this job. They tend to question my parentage every time I hole a long putt.'

'What about a senior officer in the police force? Someone you've worked with for years?' suggested Agnes Blake hopefully.

Percy shuddered. Lucy said, 'That's a thought, Percy. Chief Superintendent Tucker would do the job beautifully. He'd add the touch of gravitas which you don't seem able to muster for yourself.'

Percy glared at her; there were limits to humour. 'Tommy Bloody Tucker couldn't even find the right church.'

'Don't exaggerate.'

Percy glanced from the young face to the older one. 'There is one bloke I might use, though. But I'd need Mrs B's approval first.'

'And who is this mysterious and courageous person?'

Percy took a deep breath. 'Clyde Northcott.'

'You're not serious!'

'I'm deadly serious.'

Agnes decided it was time to intervene. 'So who is this person whom my daughter thinks cannot be a serious candidate?'

'He's a DC who works for Percy,' said Lucy. 'One of his protégés. Clyde was once a suspect in a murder case and a user and small-time supplier of cocaine. A man whom Percy recruited, first into the police service and a couple of years later into his CID team. A hard bastard.'

'Language, our Lucy,' said Percy primly.

'That's your own phrase for him. He's a young man, mum, about twenty-four, I think. He's six feet three and as tough as they come.'

'Sounds like a hard bastard,' said Agnes Blake reflectively. 'And a reformed sinner. Well, from your description, he seems eminently well suited for the job. If he's as tall and erect as you indicate, he might even bring a touch of added distinction to our old church.'

'Oh, Clyde Northcott would stand out all right, Mrs B,' said Percy. 'He's also very black indeed.'

'Is that why you needed my approval?'

'I suppose it is.'

Agnes sighed theatrically. It was always good to shock the young. 'You disappoint me, Percy Peach. I didn't think I would ever have to say that, but now I do. He will certainly add distinction to this occasion. He will set off my daughter's pink and white complexion perfectly and probably be the star of the reception at Marton Towers.' She drew herself very erect on her chair. 'I look forward to making Mr Northcott's acquaintance.'

Percy beamed fondly at her. 'And Clyde will certainly think you are the cat's whiskers with cream on, Mrs B!'

It was confession time at Gamblers Anonymous.

Darren Pearson listened to a quiet catalogue of successes from the rest of the group with increasing dismay. They were like smug participants in a Weight Watchers group who were boasting gleefully of losing a few pounds in

weight, he thought sourly. The difference here was that the
pounds lost by gamblers were monetary and deadly serious.
It was going to be his turn soon at the end of the circle; he
willed each of the three before him to confess to some
falling by the wayside, even to the veniality of being sorely
tempted, but none of them did.

It was his turn. He stared down at the threadbare carpet,
bit back the irrelevant comment that it would have been
better removed altogether. 'I slipped up, this week. Went to
the betting shop, the one I always use.' He glanced at the
counsellor in the middle of the group. 'You're right; we
should cultivate the habit of walking past those places,
concentrating on some other shop at the end of the street.
I didn't do that. I drove there specially to use the place.'
He piled on the detail, needing to lacerate himself, to expose
the full squalor of his failure.

He paused for such a long time, sinking more deeply into
his misery, that they thought he was not going to speak
again. He was not sure where the gentle voice came from
as it said, 'How much did you stake, Darren?'

They did not use surnames here, though some of them knew
each other as friends now from long acquaintance. He smiled
a mirthless smile, staring still at the tired carpet, echoing its
defeated state in his own tone. 'I tried to stake a thousand.
They wouldn't take it. I already owed too much, they said.'

The silence was profound. The group did not know
whether to celebrate this small, negative victory, which had
been offered to him rather than won by him. Again they
thought he was not going to speak, but eventually he said,
as though the words were being wrung from him against
his will, 'It won, you know, that horse. Three to one. Supreme
Nelly, it was called. Daft name, but I'd have knocked three
thousand off my debts, if they'd taken the bet.'

It was the counsellor's voice which now said firmly, 'I'm
sorry about that, Darren. Believe me, it would have been
better if it had lost. That way it wouldn't have fostered the
absurd idea that you can get yourself out of trouble by
more betting. You know and we all know that it doesn't
work like that. The reason why all of you are here is that

you have learned that the hard way. The odd win just supports illusion. What is the thing we have to do?'

She spoke to them like children, but they were children, in this context, and they knew it. A ragged wail from three or four of them said, 'Look at the whole picture!' and the others nodded firmly, to show their endorsement of this new axiom of their existence.

'And when we look at the whole picture, we invariably find that we lose far more than we gain, that the occasional windfall never compensates for our losses during a year, that we get ourselves further and further into trouble, if we try to bail ourselves out by the very means which has scuppered us.'

There was more nodding around the circle, a murmured affirmation in which even Darren Pearson eventually joined, as the group tried to bolster their weakling by a restatement of the saving dogma, like a church congregation joining fervently into the responses of a service.

Then two or three of them recounted similar falls by the wayside to that which Darren had just related, assuring him that there was strength in numbers, that he must not be discouraged, that this place and these people would help him, that the refusal to extend his credit was a blessing in itself, a tool he must use as he fought for salvation.

The counsellor had a few words with him alone before he left, voicing the truisms he knew he must observe, insisting he should ring whenever he felt tempted.

There was nothing subtle or magical about the session, yet he went home bolstered, feeling as he had not done before he enrolled that he had the strength to fight this, that he was not unique and above all not alone. It was only as he reviewed the group and its support in the small hours of the night that their comments seemed childish and their support too puny for his fight.

TEN

Liverpool at Brunton. Always one of the games of the season, but this year more than ever so. Liverpool at the top of the Premiership in a tight race, contesting the title in the last six games of the season against Manchester United and Chelsea. Brunton Rovers at the other end of the league, clear of the bottom three places at the moment, but with a tough programme of games to end the season and relegation still a possibility.

Beautifully set up, the press and the broadcasting media had decided. The big boys going flat out for their first Premiership title of the century, the smaller team on a good run of results, with all the added spice of a Lancashire derby thrown in for good measure. The managers, players and supporters of the two teams were much too nervous to want a contest which was 'beautifully set up'. They wanted not glorious uncertainty but a match with some assurance of points, of a victory in Liverpool's case and of at least a point for a draw in that of the Rovers.

Even the directors and senior officials of the two clubs had caught the excitement and the nervousness, so that there was a brittle quality to the conversation and the laughter in the board room at Grafton Park. As owner and chairman of the home team, Jim Capstick circulated among the visitors with glass in hand, as affable as he always was on these occasions. He acknowledged his team's need for points, ruefully nodded his assent to the view that Liverpool too needed the victory, for very different reasons. He did not talk about anything beyond the end of the season in another month, but that was not required of him; with such a match beginning in less than an hour, no one cared to look beyond five o'clock today.

Helen Capstick had an abstracted air: she was watching her husband's progress around the room rather than involving herself in any demanding conversational exchange. With her hair the colour of polished bronze and her erect figure and carriage, she could never be unnoticeable, but she took the easy way out and retreated behind a façade of ignorance, maintaining that her scanty knowledge of football made her a loyal supporter but nothing more. She was here as a lady who wanted to give her husband every support but did not pretend to the knowledge or involvement which excited most of the others around her.

Robbie Black was not here, of course. The Scottish manager was in the dressing room below them, bolstering his grim-faced players for the fray, stressing the tactics for the momentous ninety minutes ahead of them. But Debbie Black, still better known to most of the visitors as the glamorous tennis player and model Debbie Palmer, was making most of the men in the room think of things other than football, even with such a match in prospect. The irony was that Debbie, despite her large hazel eyes and still compelling figure, had a knowledge of the history of the game and of Brunton Rovers which would have surprised her listeners.

Debbie reminded the visiting chairman gently that Brunton Rovers were founder members of the league and had been around much longer than Liverpool. She spoke in surprising detail about the lads from Brunton who had ventured south in the nineteenth century to win the FA Cup from the southern public school toffs who regarded it as their private competition, then pointed out the old black and white photograph in the corner of the room of those sturdy champions who had won so many cups at the end of the nineteenth century.

Edward Lanchester relished the occasion because it reminded him of so many similar great days in the past. He was delighted to find that the old friend he had known for almost forty years was still on the Liverpool board. Joe Nolan was ten years older and more stooped than Edward, with red cheeks and a cherubic appearance which clothed a wealth of harsh experience. He had fought in the 1939–45 war, remembered coming home on leave and weeping when he found the Mersey dotted with the masts of sunken ships and his mother bombed out of her house. Both men remembered a harsher world, where it had seemed impossible for two or three years that their country could survive, where for six years there had been no football save for wartime 'friendlies'. The octogenarian Scouser reminded Lanchester that football was an escape from the harsher realities of life, that no matter how passionately you felt about it, it was not life itself.

'We're relics of an age that's gone,' Joe Nolan said to the younger man, without any great bitterness. 'It's good of them to keep us on – sometimes I think they like to remind themselves of times when life was simpler and it was easier to see it for what it was.'

'You're a wise man, Joe,' said Lanchester. 'You see things as they are and don't resent it. I envy you that.' He told this man who was on the other side this afternoon about the death of his wife, confessed for the first time to this relative stranger how much he missed her presence and the way she had kept his judgements sound. Joe Nolan was more moved than he could explain to himself by the death of this woman he had never known and its effect upon his friend.

Darren Pearson sat at the side of the room with his opposite number from Liverpool. He kept an eye on the busy scene to make sure all was going well, that none of the club's visitors were being neglected, and listened to the very different problems of a club with foreign owners. Their massive investment in the club made it sound as if it was on another planet, not competing in the same league as Brunton Rovers.

The crowded room grew quieter as these privileged people looked at their watches and began to filter out towards the cloakrooms and their seats in the main stand. Darren was the last to leave, complimenting the girls coming in to clear the room on the excellence of the food, reminding them to be sure to tell Mrs Bates that the visitors had said once more that she made the finest apple pies in Britain. He marvelled again that he could function so competently on this public level whilst losing the battle in his private war.

All of these luminaries forgot their own concerns in the

compressed ninety minutes of sporting war which began at three o'clock. It was a gloomy afternoon, and the floodlights made the football battlefield even more theatrical, illuminating the two acres of grass like a massive stage, contributing their own effect to the contest, as the skies gradually darkened around the old stadium and the world disappeared, save for the vivid green expanse and the players acting out their drama upon it.

Liverpool took the game to a rather nervous Rovers side at first, a fierce shot narrowly missing the goal, to a collective gasp of relief from the home supporters and a collective groan from the visitors' enclosure. Ten minutes into the match, the veteran Rovers goalkeeper pulled off a marvellous save, flicking the ball at full stretch over the corner of his goal, then rising from the turf to berate his relieved defence for not attending earlier to the threat.

The Rovers threatened more as they settled to the task, but it was twenty minutes before the Liverpool goalie made his first save and that was a straightforward one. Liverpool were swifter and more direct, exuding the confidence which came from their position in the league and a succession of good results. The Rovers' attacks were fitful and not as sustained as they would have wished. But they defended sturdily, so that there were few clear chances of goals at either end.

Then, five minutes before the half time interval, disaster struck the home side. The star French winger, for whom Liverpool had paid a transfer fee greater than the cost of all eleven Brunton players, got clear for the first time after a dazzling piece of footwork. He moved swiftly down the Rovers right flank, leaving his full back floundering well behind him. The Rovers centre half moved swiftly to cover him, as his manager had warned him he would have to do at some time in the game. He was outpaced and he knew he was, labouring behind his fleet-footed opponent as he moved into the penalty area. The Frenchman looked up, saw his two strikers free and waiting for a pass twelve yards from goal, and prepared to make an accurate cross. Panting behind him, the Rovers' defender made a desperate sliding tackle, searching desperately for a touch of the ball, any sort of touch, with his outstretched foot.

The Gallic boots were too quick for him. The defender failed in his desperate, heroic, futile tackle, missed the ball, and caught the foot of his opponent, who fell theatrically to the turf and rolled over three times with balletic energy. 'PENALTY!' roared the visiting horde behind the goal, and they were right, despite the Oscar-worthy exaggerations of the central figure. The outstretched arm of the referee, stark and black as that of the Grim Reaper himself, pointed inexorably to the penalty spot. The Rovers hung their heads; the Liverpool players hauled their man to his feet and hugged him for his efforts.

Steven Gerrard, the Liverpool icon, as native to the city as Scouse itself or the Liver Building by the Mersey, lined up the penalty, exchanging grim smiles with the Rovers' keeper: the two had known each other and been friends for ten years and more. No place for friendship, this.

Stevie G. wouldn't miss, the men behind the goal told each other, though some of them shut their eyes as he moved to the ball. The roar told those who could not bear to watch that all was well. An unstoppable shot, high and to the goalkeeper's right, hitting the stanchion which supported the post. Red and white scarves waved in triumphant unison behind the disconsolate goalkeeper; gloomy resignation on the other three sides of the ground where the blue and white favours of Brunton floundered disconsolately.

A few minutes later, the shaken Brunton team were shut in the dressing room for the half-time interval with Robbie Black, whilst the manager wondered how he was to raise the spirits and the effort of these sweating men who had heard it all before. He did not yell at them: that would risk communicating his own dismay at events thus far. They had been outplayed, but they had given maximum effort, and he would not berate them for that.

'Man for man, you're as good as they are, for all their fancy prices and their fancy wages. So far, you haven't combined as well as a team as they have, but you're going to put that right in the second half. Get it, keep it, pass it!

The basics still apply and they always will. But you need to move the ball more quickly. That's in the hands of those of you who haven't got the ball. Front men, you must give your midfield men options. The runs you make are important, even when you never get the ball, and you know it. Every time you draw defenders after you, you're making space for someone else. David will make the passes, if you give him the options.'

Robbie glanced at his constructive midfield player, the most imaginative passer in his team, who forced a strained smile from his anxious white face. Men were reduced to boys in the extreme tensions of a match like this. Robbie turned back to the rest. 'Their defence is solid, but there's room on the wings – there always is. If you can get towards the line and pull crosses back, no defence likes that. You don't like it. And neither will they. And remember, you're as good as they are, on your own pitch. You just need to operate as a team and work like hell for each other. Once you've pulled them back, they'll be rattled.'

He forced conviction into his words, trying to excite himself as well as his players. He had no idea how much effect his words would have. It was a simple game really, and you had to keep your message simple. But that meant that there was always a danger of repeating yourself and losing effect. It was always easier to convince youngsters than the hardened pros who felt they had heard and seen it all before. He had a mixture of the two in this game. He kept his captain and central defender behind as the others trooped out of the dressing room and down the passage to the pitch for the second half. 'Don't let the lads over-stretch themselves as we attack, Colin. They'll punish us if we do.'

The veteran nodded his assent, grimaced wryly to himself as he followed his team into the tunnel. Attack, but don't take risks: there was nothing like having your cake and eating it. But the boss was right, of course. The younger lads would get carried away with the prospect of beating Liverpool, if they got a goal.

The Rovers were better, certainly, as the second forty-five minutes began. They soon had the internationals who composed the Liverpool defence looking anxious for the first time, shouting instructions to each other and beckoning their attacking colleagues to come back and help. Their goalie made his first good save, then the tall Brunton centre forward headed narrowly over the bar. The home crowd, sensing a revival, roared their team on, but for twenty minutes Liverpool kept their lead. It looked as though they had weathered the storm and were ready to reassert themselves as the Rovers tired.

Then, just when it was needed, the goal came. The ball bounced free in midfield after a stern home tackle. David Greaves pounced and slid a pass along the turf between the Liverpool central defenders. Ashley Greenhalgh was on to it in a flash, moving swiftly towards goal, flicking the ball forward as his marker slid despairingly after him. He steadied himself as the goalkeeper advanced towards him, then slid the ball low and accurately past him into the corner of the net. A massive roar greeted his effort as he wheeled away towards the corner flag and the home support, his right arm raised in triumph towards his followers.

Now the home team pressed forward, riding on the continuous encouragement of their fans like surfers on an incoming tide, feeling the heady sense of destiny which a win would bring. They had three corners in quick succession, then hit the crossbar with a snap shot from the inspired David Greaves, who was urging them forward with a series of subtle passes.

Then Robbie Black's warning to his captain was abruptly justified. Liverpool needed the win rather than the draw to sustain their run for the title, and the Rovers' assault gave them the room they needed. They broke away swiftly after the third of the Rovers' corners, and had for a vital moment three attackers against two defenders. The pass from the right wing was well timed. Their leading scorer, cutting in from the left to receive it, met the ball beautifully, so that the visiting fans were up out of their seats to applaud the goal. But the Rovers goalkeeper, moving even as his opponent shot, stretched miraculously to get his flying left hand to the ball when it seemed past him.

He had the luck which his anticipation and agility deserved. The ball was diverted just enough to hit the goalpost and rebound back into play, whence it was booted out of play with massive relief by the Rovers' toiling captain. Anguish among the visiting supporters as they sank back into their seats. Cheers for their heroic goalkeeper, then laughter with a strong element of hysteria in it from the Rovers' faithful at their reprieve.

The play was more even now, with both sides going for the win. A feeling spread that the tremendous physical efforts which the Rovers' players had made would tell against them in the closing section of the match. There were fouls on both sides by tiring players, a booking and a severe lecture from the referee to the nineteen-year-old Brunton midfield player whose enthusiasm had strayed into rashness and a desperate tackle on Steven Gerrard.

Then, with five minutes to play, the unthinkable happened. Ashley Greenhalgh was suddenly free on the right wing, his clever run seen and rewarded by a subtle pass from the man behind him. He cut in towards goal, then veered away again as two men moved to cover his run. He feinted to move back inside just enough to get the full back on the wrong foot, then dipped his shoulder and moved outside him. As the ball threatened to run away from him over the goal line, he pulled it back along the ground to around the penalty spot, where his centre forward was moving in with the speed and impetus of an express train. With the crescendo of the crowd's roar in his ears, he smashed the ball unstoppably past the despairing goalkeeper, raised both arms in brief triumph to the exulting crowd, and was then submerged under the frantic congratulations of his team-mates.

Bobble hats were flung into the air, some of them never to be retrieved. Boys danced the crazy dance of unthinking joy which would never be possible for them again, young men embraced each other in the breathy male camaraderie which would have been impossible anywhere else. Old men with rheumy eyes found that for some reason they could not stop laughing. Robbie Black leapt in manic celebration on the touchline for thirty seconds, then remembered himself, and made frantic gestures of caution towards his excited players as he pointed at his watch. Edward Lanchester, on his feet and cheering in the directors' box, lost thirty years and clasped first Helen Capstick and then Debbie Black in happy embraces, effortlessly lifting them off their feet in his happiness.

The referee's urgent whistling eventually made the Brunton team regroup for the final stages of the drama. Liverpool threw their whole team forward in frantic attack as the minutes ticked away. The crowd groaned when four minutes of stoppage time were announced, the longest and most agonising four minutes that many of them could remember. At the very end, even the Liverpool goalkeeper came up for the final corner kick, but to no avail. This like the other pressure was repulsed. And as the ball arched high away from the home goal, the three long blasts of the whistle announced that the greatest Brunton result of the season was finally secure.

Robbie Black hugged each of his players in turn as they came off the field: they were all heroes today. He gave his after-match interviews to Sky television and the BBC, taking several deep breaths before he did so to enable him to seem sober and balanced rather than happily triumphalist. He genially turned aside the inevitable probings about the future of Ashley Greenhalgh, saying reasonably enough that he wanted just to savour this moment – victories over Liverpool did not come too often to the smaller teams, and this was his first one as manager.

Robbie stayed with his players to enjoy the victory with them. The dressing room was a noisy, exultant place, filled with laughter and the clumsy male teasing which normally accompanies notable team triumphs. It was an hour and more after the conclusion of the game when Black donned his suit and climbed the stairs to the hospitality suite.

Entertaining visiting dignitaries is a strange business after a game like this. The home team's representatives are trying not to exult too publicly in their victory. The visitors are trying desperately hard to be good losers. Both sides pretend that this is after all only a sporting occasion, which should be kept in its proper perspective. Neither group is normally very successful at adopting the role required of it. There is an air of strained politeness, with brittle laughter trying to soften the raw edges of triumph and disaster. Kipling's advice to treat these twin impostors with equal contempt was an admirable admonition, but he never attended a Premiership soccer match.

The Liverpool group were sensibly looking to leave as soon as they reasonably could, to drive the short distance back to their great city and nurse their wounds in private. Edward Lanchester wrung the hand of his old friend Joe Nolan heartily enough as he took his leave, but the rest of the Brunton Rovers party were no more than decently polite. They wished their visitors well in their quest for the title, though by now they knew that Liverpool's rivals had won and today's defeat would almost certainly be crucial for them.

When the Brunton party were finally left alone, Darren Pearson made sure they all had full glasses in their hands to toast the victory. The tensions of politeness dropped away, the exultation of today's result and the manner in which it had been achieved broke out anew. The noise level rose, the laughter now was uninhibited and genuine.

Jim Capstick watched and waited. On this night of euphoria, there wasn't going to be a right moment for him to drop his bombshell, but it had to be done. He couldn't leave it any longer without rumour running rife. The Sunday papers were already on to the story. The football correspondents of the *News of the World* and the *People* had phoned him during the morning, asking for comments on what they had picked up from sources they refused to name.

He rapped his glass upon the table, waited until the startled, apprehensive silence was complete and said, 'I am sorry to interrupt our celebrations of one of the most notable victories since I took over here. This is not the right time to tell you this, but I have no choice. I had much rather that you heard this from me than from anyone else. I need to tell you that I am engaged in discussions about selling my majority interest in Brunton Rovers Football Club.'

There was a shocked silence. Then, as the excited reactions began, Edward Lanchester called over the heads of the others in the room, 'You mean a take-over.'

'I do, yes. I should stress that we are at an early stage of negotiation, but at the moment it seems that a change of ownership and direction will be in my own and the club's best interests.'

Lanchester said sourly, 'Your own interests I can appreciate. We shall need convincing that this will be in the club's best interests.'

Capstick had expected this view from this source. He had also determined to point out the facts of life before anyone in this room got ideas above their station. 'The decision to sell or not to sell is entirely in my hands, Edward. You need to realize that times have changed. I will put this as clearly as I possibly can. As far as I am concerned, Brunton Rovers is one of several business assets I possess. I need to review constantly the portfolio of those assets. We are in the midst of a recession which has considerably reduced the value of many of the businesses I control. One of the few assets which I can still sell for almost the same price as at this time last year appears to be the football club. I am therefore investigating the possibilities of doing so.'

Lanchester knew now that he would be unable to affect this, even if, as he sensed, there was support for him from the rest of the room. Nevertheless, he felt compelled to state the case he knew was hopeless. 'Rich businessmen from all over the world are interested in buying Premiership clubs. Most of them have no previous affiliation with them: they are on ego trips or simply out to make money.'

Capstick smiled. 'I shall of course make every effort to ensure that the long-term interests of Brunton Rovers are borne in mind.'

'So long as it does not affect the price you receive for it.'

Jim Capstick was at ease now, with his announcement made and the realities of power becoming more explicit with each sentence in this exchange. He felt the excitement he always felt when he knew that the power over decisions was in his hands. 'So long as it does not affect the price, as you say. I have already indicated that this is the disposal of a business asset, as far as I am concerned.'

It was Debbie Black who now unexpectedly took up the argument. 'Does an afternoon like the one we've just enjoyed mean nothing to you, Jim? Surely you can see that this affects not just you, not just the people in this room, but the whole town.'

'I expected to hear this argument, which is based purely on sentiment. You can't run a business on sentiment. To put it bluntly, the feelings of the people of Brunton are no concern of mine.'

'They are when you want them to come through the gates and support your business. Without the supporters who come through the turnstiles, there would be no afternoons like the one we have all just enjoyed. No Brunton Rovers.' This was Darren Pearson, speaking up in spite of himself, in spite of what Capstick knew about him and his addiction to gambling.

'Pure sentiment, I'm afraid. I'd expect my chief executive to be more clear-sighted than that.' He looked at the unhappy Pearson and could not resist turning the screw. 'Especially if I'm to recommend his services to the new owner in due course.'

'Who is the new owner to be?' The quietly spoken question came from his own wife. It seemed that Helen Capstick wished to assert to the other people in the room that she had had no part in this.

'I'm not at liberty to say at the moment. No one that you are acquainted with.'

Debbie Black stared at Capstick accusingly. 'Middle Eastern. That's the only place with money to throw around at the moment.'

Her husband spoke for the first time, as if anxious to support his wife. 'Someone with no knowledge of football. Someone who probably knows bugger all about Brunton and its place in the history of the game.'

Jim Capstick gave him a patronizing smile. 'History doesn't buy players. History doesn't pay the wages you and your players demand nowadays, Robbie. If the buyer can pay the price I want, that is all that concerns me.'

'Will this mysterious buyer take on the existing staff? Will my job and my coaches' jobs be safe? Will Darren's job be safe? What about the people who have worked here for years?'

Capstick shrugged his shoulders elaborately. 'I can't attach strings to any sale. You should understand that. Once I wash my hands of the club, I must allow the new owner a free hand.' He looked round at the company. 'You need time to digest this. I shall leave you now. I have things to attend to in my office.' He smiled a crooked smile. 'People in the Middle East are waiting to hear from me: I have details to prepare and some important phone calls to make.'

There was no more laughter and little conversation in the hospitality suite after Capstick left. The great victory over Liverpool felt suddenly hollow. No one felt like drinking any more.

ELEVEN

Jim Capstick poured himself a malt whisky and sat contentedly in his office for a few minutes, allowing relaxation
to flow through his body until he felt it coursing through
even the extremities of fingers and toes. It was a technique
which a physiotherapist girlfriend had taught him all of
thirty years ago. He still found it effective; it still amused
him to feel the gradual, controlled slackening of his tendons,
whilst those other bodies in the world below him were taut
with the drama of the news he had brought to them.

It was twenty minutes before he made the first of his
phone calls. The man who had supervised the examination
of the accounts and the assets of Brunton Rovers Football
Club at the beginning of the week was waiting for the pre-
arranged call in Reading. He was planning to take his wife
out for a Saturday evening meal with friends, but he was
too professional to betray his impatience when he heard the
voice he had been expecting for an hour and more.

'We beat Liverpool today,' said Capstick.

'I'm afraid I don't follow football,' said the financier coldly.

'You should, in this case,' said Capstick. 'You should
regard it as part of your professional responsibilities. A result
like this is important to the financial health of the company
you have been assessing. It is not just a sporting victory but
a financial one.'

'If you say so.'

'I do say so and I require you to take note of it. Today's
result virtually ensures that Brunton Rovers will be playing
in the Premiership next season. You would be failing in your
duty if you failed to note that fact and add it to your assessment of the present financial strength of the company you
have been reviewing.'

'I see. I take your point and will make it clear to the
people who paid for the work I and my team did in Brunton.'

'Do that, please. I shouldn't want to find that your employers in Dubai found your report in any way incomplete or inefficient.'

The man became more deferential and Capstick terminated the call. You needed people like that, even sometimes needed their approval, for there was no faking things when the financial men came in. But once you had the right sort of report from them, you could still permit yourself a certain contempt for them and the narrowness of their views on life.

He fidgeted a little after the call, had to employ the techniques of relaxation again to make his hands and his feet relax. There would be at least half an hour to wait, possibly an hour or more. He had a very good idea of the way these Saudi Arabian people operated now. They were more ruthless than British bargainers, but infinitely more reliable, once they committed themselves. They were more courteous, too. You had to put up with all kinds of little humiliations, when a British deal-maker had bigger funds than you had; they often didn't ring until two or three days after the time they had promised. The sheikh could buy and sell any man Jim Capstick had dealt with before, but if he told you he would ring at a certain time you would get the call. Jim shut his eyes and tried to wait contentedly.

Even five years earlier, he would have lit a cigar and smoked it slowly and with practised relish, watching the scented smoke rising quietly into the still air around him. But Helen had persuaded him to give up all smoking, even the occasional cigar. Sensible really, when you were fifty-seven, driven about in a Bentley by a chauffeur, and able to enjoy the best food and drink the world had to offer. He felt his body tensing a little as he thought of Helen and the problem he had to address with her. He had thought she might have come up here to speak to him by now.

Perhaps she was sulking because he hadn't given her any prior notice of the deal; it had been as much a surprise to her as to the others in the hospitality suite. But that was business: the fewer people who knew what you were up to, the better – and that included wives. She might as well get used to it. He went through and locked the outer door in his PA's office, making sure that there would be no interruptions to his next and most important phone contact.

He diverted his thoughts to the exercise he was always promising Helen he would take. He certainly wasn't going to go and waste his time at the gym with all the earnest youngsters. Perhaps he would have another go at golf, after all. Even as he forced himself into that thought, he knew he would never do it. When you ruled the roost in most of the things you did, it wasn't easy to accept your physical ineptitude as you struggled to cope with a sport.

He poured himself another whisky, but kept it deliberately small. The sheikh didn't touch alcohol at all and Jim didn't want to feel at any disadvantage when he eventually spoke to him. He tried to read the American detective novel which Helen had bought for him, but couldn't concentrate on either plot or character as he waited for the phone to ring. The cop in the book had too many scruples: they were getting in the way of his efficiency. He wasn't the sort of man Jim Capstick would have employed.

He went into the little private bathroom at the far end of his office and washed his face and hands briskly in cold water. It was somehow important to him to be as spruce and fresh when he spoke to the sheikh as he would have been in a face to face meeting, even though the man would be thousands of miles away on the end of a phone and unable to see him. He even brushed his teeth and used the mouthwash, though he told himself that he was merely filling in time. He took longer than usual to comb his hair in front of the mirror.

When the phone eventually rang, he let it shrill twice before he picked it up. Prompt but not too eager. The sheikh made the elaborate enquiry about his personal welfare which always prefaced the real business. Then he pronounced himself satisfied with the report he had received, which confirmed his impressions from the less formal investigation of the company which he and his own staff had already conducted. He congratulated the owner-chairman upon today's result, assured Capstick that he understood the importance of it to the long-term future of the asset he was acquiring. You would never have known from the tone and substance of his conversation that it was the land in the town that the club owned which was the man's main interest, Jim thought admiringly.

The lawyers should now get together and move fast on a contract, the sheikh said. The finance for the deal was not a problem: it would be available as soon as both parties were satisfied with the contract and prepared to sign the relevant documents. Jim agreed to fly out to Dubai as soon as the lawyers had ironed out the details. The sheikh was full of easy, efficient, automatic charm. 'In that case, I look forward to seeing you again quite soon, Mr Capstick. There is no longer any need for us to meet on neutral ground. My staff will pick you up at the airport and bring you here. Mr Capstick, we have a deal.'

Jim sat and looked at the phone, at the desk, at the door to his PA's empty anteroom, at the fittings of this office he would soon leave behind for ever. He needed some physical action to break the spell of his content, so he walked through the outer office and unlocked the door there. He could be available again now to these people of lesser vision, whom he had shut out for the period when he had been determining the shape of all their lives.

He could not banish his foolish smile of satisfaction at the biggest deal he had ever made. He would have another drink or two before he left – he could always ring for Wally Boyd to come and pick him up, if he needed it. But for the moment, he did not need drink or any other stimulant to sustain his high.

He was not sure how many minutes went by before his visitor came. Nor could he be certain whether there was a brief knock before the door opened or whether the person simply came in unannounced. Jim said with an attempt at his normal manner, 'I was expecting you, you know!' Whether that was true or not he had no idea. 'You must join me in a celebratory drink. I'll find you a glass.'

The owner of Brunton Rovers sat down heavily in his chair, then slid it a foot to his right to enable him to open the bottom drawer of the big desk. He was bending towards it when he felt the first touch of the cord upon his neck.

He jerked his head back, but he was permitted no breath for further words. The cable tightened steadily, biting deep into his neck, cutting through the larynx and the pipes which drew air into the heavy frame of the man in the chair. He lifted his hands to the cord in brief, hopeless resistance.

In much less than a minute, Jim Capstick was dead.

TWELVE

Daughters are still children to their mothers, even when they have reached the age of twenty-nine and are shortly to be married.

Agnes Blake enjoyed spoiling her Lucy, as she had done when she was a small child recovering from a minor illness. It was not yet eight o'clock on Sunday morning and most of the nation was planning a lie-in. But Agnes had already brewed the tea and put the hand-knitted cosy over the small china teapot she kept specially for such early-morning occasions. She was preparing to mount the narrow staircase of the old cottage to her daughter's room when a phone shrilled beside her. Lucy's mobile, which she had left on the hall table the night before.

Agnes picked it up and began to state her identity. Before she could do so, Percy Peach's voice said urgently, 'Get your arse down here pronto, DS Blake! We have a suspicious death.'

'I'll thank you not to refer to my daughter's anatomy in that way!' said Agnes haughtily, taking care that no trace of amusement crept into her voice.

'Ah, it's you, Mrs B!' said Percy, thrown out of his stride for all of half a second. 'Sorry about the language. But could you convey the request to your daughter that she stows her extremely beautiful posterior into her car and drives it down to the Brunton nick immediately, please?'

'I shall do that, Denis Charles Scott Peach. But I shall endeavour to force a little breakfast into her first. I shall also tell her to massage her considerable brain into full operation on the way.'

'You're a treasure, Mrs B. I only wish I could ask you to get your own arse down here pronto and sort out some of our management problems. But that cannot be, alas!'

In no more than fifteen minutes, Lucy was in the little

blue Corsa and hurrying her way through the deserted lanes
of a silent and very beautiful Ribble Valley as the sun rose
over Pendle Hill. The hunt was on. The beautifully formed
CID nostrils were sniffing the chase. The adrenalin which
visits any detective officer in such circumstances was
coursing through DS Blake's veins.

There were already three police vehicles outside the entrance
to Brunton Rovers Football Club. The 'meat wagon' waited
quietly at the end of the line. Presently, this grey van would
ease itself forward to the shut wooden doors which currently
opened sporadically to admit some new police presence; eventually the two men reading Sunday newspapers within the
vehicle would be permitted to remove the corpse which
was the centre of this activity to a place where it would
be cut and investigated relentlessly in the pursuit of further
evidence.

Percy Peach had supported Brunton Rovers since childhood, at first standing on the terraces and then, when all
the bigger grounds became all-seaters after the Hillsborough
and other disasters in the eighties, from the seat in the stands
he had never aspired to as a boy. But he had never before
been behind the scenes at Grafton Park. There was a labyrinth
of passages here; since the establishment of the ground at
the end of the nineteenth century, the demands of the game's
sustained popularity had resulted in an ever-growing bureau-
cracy and a honeycomb of office rooms to accommodate
its operators.

There was very little natural light available; the single
long outside wall of the ground had a few windows, but not
many of the rooms and passages beyond had any direct
connection with the world outside. There was an immediately claustrophobic effect, as if this world beneath the stand
was designed to keep its secrets. The people who worked
regularly in these rooms had an immediate advantage over
strangers struggling with the design and geography of the
piecemeal development.

The white-faced man who waited to greet Peach and Blake
seemed a natural controller of this other world, a creature

used to operating for most of the day without any knowledge of the climatic conditions in the world outside. He stepped forward without even the token smile which would have been normal and said, 'I'm Darren Pearson, secretary and chief executive of Brunton Rovers. I'm here to give you whatever help you need.'

'Thank you, Mr Pearson. I'm Detective Chief Inspector Peach and this is Detective Sergeant Blake. We'll need a room for interviews. I don't think we'll set up a murder room here. I'll be able to tell you more about our requirements by the end of the day.'

'You – you could have Mr Capstick's own office, I suppose. Once the. . . .'

'Once the corpse has been removed from it, yes. Well, at the moment, that room is a crime scene, Mr Pearson. It will need to be thoroughly investigated before it can be available for any other purpose. Who discovered the body?'

'One of our cleaners. We have them in at eight o'clock on the Sunday morning after we have had a home match on the Saturday. The hospitality area has normally been well used, as it was on this occasion. But the cleaners also take the opportunity to clean the various offices, which are rarely used on a Sunday.'

Pearson spoke quickly, grateful to have the outlet of speech to relieve his tension, happy to be on safe ground, where he knew more than his visitors and could provide harmless information. Peach said, 'Were you here when the corpse was discovered?'

'No. The lady who is in charge of the four cleaners who were working today rang me with the news. I came in immediately.'

'I take it the lady who found the body is still here?'

'Yes. She's in the kitchen area. She's–she's very shaken, as I suppose you would expect her to be. I tried to give her a brandy, but she wouldn't have it.'

'I'm glad to hear it. We don't like interviewing witnesses whose perceptions have been affected by alcohol.'

Pearson's faint smile was almost a reflection of the one

on Peach's face. 'I did slip a little whisky into her tea, I'm afraid. She was very shaken. I wanted to avoid hysterics.'

'We'll see her now. Get a brief statement from her. Then you'll be able to send her home.'

'Thank you. I'll take you to her.' He led them down a series of passages and a flight of stairs to a large kitchen, which had a welcome rectangle of natural light from a long window set high into the wall. He took them through the kitchen, back into the darker areas with fluorescent light tubes set into the high ceilings, the environment which seemed more natural for this grey-faced, shaken man. 'You'll find Mrs Hurst in there,' he said, pointing to a door which carried the words 'Catering Supervisor' on a panel slid into a holder. Then, as he turned to leave them, he added the cliché they would have expected from him at the outset, 'It's a bad business, this.'

The woman who sat alone in the room looked up apprehensively as Peach knocked on the door and immediately opened it. Lucy Blake went and sat beside her whilst Peach pulled out the chair from behind the desk and set it down opposite the woman they had come here to see. 'Very unpleasant experience for you, this. We see bodies all the time, but we don't—'

'My name's Ellen Hurst. I've never seen a body before. We could have seen my grandad in his coffin but I wanted to remember him as he had been when he was alive.'

She stared past him, as if it was necessary for her to recite these words, any words, to retain a tenuous grasp on herself and what was happening to her. She was a pretty blonde, the colouring which most naturally reflected shock. The blood had drained from cheeks normally rosy with health, strands of fair hair strayed unchecked across her face. She said, 'I've got two kids at home, only six and four. I'm glad they didn't have to see this.'

'There wasn't much danger of that, Ellen, was there?' said Lucy Blake.

'No, I suppose not.' She looked at Blake for the first time and was apparently reassured, for she gave her a little, involuntary smile. It was the first relaxation her body had allowed her since she had found this awful thing.

Peach leaned forward towards her. 'Tell me about it, in your own words, Ellen. Try not to leave anything out. That's all we need from you.'

'There were four of us. We all started work in the hospitality suite, vacuuming the floors and putting the chairs back. There used to be a lot more mess with ashtrays and stuff on the floor, when people could smoke, but it's easier now.' Perhaps she sensed a little impatience in her listeners, for she said without further prompting, 'Mrs Green said the three of them could cope easily enough there, so I should go and clean the chairman's office. I've cleaned it before, you see. Mrs Green likes the same person to do it every time, as far as we can.'

'Do you remember the time when you did this, Ellen?' asked Lucy Blake.

'Everyone here calls me Ellie. It was twenty past eight. I know because I looked at the clock in the hospitality suite when Mrs Green spoke to me.'

'I know this isn't easy for you. But just tell us exactly what happened.'

'I collected my damp cloth and my vac. And I went up the stairs to Mr Capstick's suite. There was no one in the outer room that his secretary uses, but the door of the chairman's room was shut. I wasn't expecting anyone to be in there, but I knocked first, same as I always do.' It seemed that it was suddenly important to her to convince them that she had observed the proper etiquette of her calling. 'When I opened the door, he was – well, he was slumped over his desk.' The phrase seemed very inadequate for the horror which had beset her in that moment.

When it seemed she was not going to speak again, Peach said gently. 'Did you touch him, Ellie?'

'No. I think I spoke to him, but I knew he was dead. He had – he had these marks, on his neck. I think I must have just stood there and screamed, because the next thing I remember is having people all round me.'

'It's good that you didn't touch him, Ellie. You did the right thing. Did you touch anything else in the room? Anything on the desk, for instance?'

'No. I just screamed. I was no use to anyone, was I?'

'You did what most other people would have done in your position, Ellie. And it's good that you didn't touch anything.'

She nodded, staring past him as if she could still see the scene in that other room somewhere above them. 'They brought me down here, made me a cup of tea. I think Mrs Green rang Mr Pearson then.'

'Just one other thing, Ellie. Did you see anyone else, on your way up the stairs and along the passages to get to Mr Capstick's office?'

'No.'

'And you didn't hear anything which suggested to you that there was anyone around up there? Anyone in the building apart from Mrs Green and the other cleaners?'

'No.' Her eyes filled with horror. 'Do you mean that whoever did this was still . . .' She couldn't complete the question.

'Almost certainly not, Ellie. But we have to ask the question. We don't know anything, yet, you see. You're the one who's given us the first bits of information we've had about this. You can't recall anything else that you think might be helpful for us, can you?'

She was silent for a moment as she thought. The glamour of the most serious of all crimes was gripping her, despite her shock, making her feel important through her connection with it. There was a tinge of regret that she was relinquishing her contact with murder as she said quietly, 'No. Nothing else.'

'Then I'm sure Mr Pearson will arrange for someone to take you home. Back to your husband and your children and the world outside here which has not changed.'

'Thank you, sir. If I remember anything else, I'll let you know.'

'Thank you, Ellie. You've been very sensible.'

Darren Pearson, as they had expected, was still in the kitchen. He agreed that Mrs Hurst should now be sent home, said that he would make the necessary arrangements after he had led them to the scene of the crime. Peach noticed that no one at the football ground had assumed this was anything other than a crime from the outset.

It was easy to see why that was when Blake and he climbed the stairs to Capstick's office. It was luxuriously furnished, with a huge leather-topped desk, a round-backed chair and excellent prints of modern art on the walls. There was a livid black-red mark on the neck of the man in the chair which left little room for doubt as to the cause of death.

Peach had seen many deaths now, but he was struck as always by how completely death diminished humanity. Capstick had been a powerful man, owner as well as chairman of the club and with other businesses as well, a man who had controlled the destiny of hundreds, perhaps thousands, of people only yesterday. Now the thing in the chair seemed to have lost all connection with humanity and power, to be as finished and inconsequential as a cat in the gutter which had been hit by a passing vehicle.

The man who had years ago worked alongside Percy Peach as Sergeant Jack Chadwick had been a civilian for three months now, but he was still the best and most experienced scene of crime officer in the Brunton area. He knew Lucy Blake from previous cases; Chadwick was old-fashioned enough to think that her prettiness struck a jarring note in this grim arena with its macabre central figure at the desk. He nodded to the CID officers and said, 'The pathologist's on his way. It's as obvious to me as it will be to you what's happened. The only question is whether we can pick up any clues as to who did this.'

The photographer had already finished his work, but two of Chadwick's assistants were on all fours, methodically gathering stray hairs, fibres of clothing, even indeterminate blobs of fluff which might just give some indication of an alien presence in the dead man's office. Peach, looking like an alien himself in the white plastic bags he had slipped over his shoes and the plastic covering for his clothing, walked carefully over an area the woman on the floor had already searched to move close to the corpse in its chair.

'When did he die?'

'Last night,' said Chadwick without hesitation. 'The p.m. examination of stomach contents will give you a time of death, but I'd stake my reputation on the fact that this man's been here overnight.'

Peach nodded. 'Pity some bugger didn't discover the poor sod last night, then. Would have made our job a bit easier if they had.'

'They don't pay you for doing easy jobs,' said Jack Chadwick. His wry smile held no rancour. He might have had the CID career which his friend Percy had had if he hadn't been wounded in a bank raid all those years ago, but he had long since thought himself out of bitterness about might-have-beens.

The scene of crime officer looked again at the lifeless hulk in the expensive chair. 'I've never been this close to the celebrated Jim Capstick before. From what I've heard of him, I should think he had quite a lot of enemies.'

THIRTEEN

They passed the pathologist on their way back down the stairs. He promised them that they would have his report quickly. He had two road crash fatalities to deal with, but suspicious deaths still demanded a certain priority in the investigation of human remains.

Darren Pearson did not see them at first. They stood quietly outside the kitchen area whilst he issued guidance to the staff who had been cleaning all the areas used on the previous day. He warned the women that they would have tiresome contacts from the press, advised them to say as little as possible and preferably nothing. They listened to him carefully and asked a few questions about this situation which was new to all of them. He smiled. 'I deal with journalists all the time. They have a job to do, but it probably won't be in your interests to talk to them. I don't think it will happen, but if they offer you money, you should ask yourself just what you are getting yourself into. If you want any advice, don't be afraid to ring me. I'll be here for another couple of hours today and from eight thirty tomorrow morning if you wish to speak to me.'

It was obvious that the cleaners not only respected the chief executive of Brunton Rovers but liked him. He connected easily with these part-time workers, who were at the other end of the working hierarchy from him, appreciating their very different problems and genuinely anxious to help. A likeable and a highly competent man, Lucy Blake decided. In her short CID career, she had already met a couple of murderers who had both of those qualities.

It was at this moment that Pearson saw them waiting and came over to speak to them. 'I thought you might wish to talk to me when you'd finished upstairs, so I stayed on the premises.'

'Thoughtful of you, Mr Pearson. We normally like to

speak to the widow of the deceased as soon as possible in circumstances like this, but I think in this case it would be useful to have your views first.' Peach studied him unashamedly, a CID habit which members of the public often found unnerving.

Despite his obvious abilities, Darren Pearson looked shaken beneath the outward composure, particularly now that he was about to become the man at the centre of the questioning rather than the director of affairs he normally was in this place. He looked older than his forty-five years, principally because of the lack of any colour in his cheeks and the worry lines around his eyes, which were grey and watchful. He had plentiful hair, cut fairly short and with a conventional parting. But a tuft on the crown of his head stood up obstinately, making the general effect unruly. He wore the dark tie and the suit appropriate for the death of his employer, but a missing button on his shirt destroyed the formal effect.

He took them into his own office and sat behind his desk. Then, as if recognizing that the set-up was wrong when he was to be the questioned rather than the questioner, he brought his chair round the desk and sat down awkwardly opposite them. He found that murder had altered his thinking and destroyed his normal control here.

Peach said, 'When did you learn of this death, Mr Pearson?'

He glanced at his watch. 'One hour and forty minutes ago. I was still in bed when I received a phone call at my home from the lady directing the cleaning operations, Mrs Green.'

'We shall await the report from the pathologist before making any formal declaration about this crime: until then it will remain a suspicious death.'

'But you think Mr Capstick was murdered.'

Peach allowed himself a small, sad smile. 'I have no doubt of it. Neither have DS Blake and the scene of crime officer.'

Pearson nodded. 'That is what I supposed.'

'Again we await formal confirmation, but I will tell you that we are privately certain that the victim died last night.'

'That again is what I expected to hear.'

'Had you any reason to think Mr Capstick was in danger?'

The man who was used to controlling things here sat awkwardly on the chair with his knees together and pursed his lips. Pearson was clearly anxious to pick his words carefully, but that was probably a usual trait for a man who dealt daily with questions from the media. Caution about what he said was probably a habit he had developed with his occupation. 'Not in danger of his life, no. And yet I have to say that what has happened is not entirely a surprise to me.'

Peach would have preferred a man who was more emotional, less careful of his replies. Unguarded reactions were normally more useful to him at this stage. This man would eventually make a good witness in court, if he were needed. Of course, it was at this moment possible that he might be appearing in the dock rather than as a prosecution witness. 'When did you last see Mr Capstick alive?'

'At seven ten last night.' It was a reply which had been waiting for the expected question. He watched Lucy Blake making a note of it with her gold ball-pen and then said, 'That is also the last time when a whole gathering of people saw him. The exception will be the person who killed him. But I don't expect that information will be volunteered to you.'

Peach felt more at ease now. He found to his surprise that he was almost enjoying the preliminary fencing with this man who had clearly prepared exactly what he was going to release to them. He said, 'I think you had better put us in the picture about this. In other words, tell us exactly what went on before this time of seven ten about which you are so definite.'

'I'm sure that would be useful to you. You will no doubt be speaking to the other people who were there. If I give you the facts, you can gather other people's impressions in due course.'

'The facts are always a useful starting point, I find. We shall also require your impressions, as well as those of others. The way in which people's impressions of what happened vary is often revealing.'

It sounded like a warning, but if he registered it as such, Pearson showed no discomfort. He embarked carefully on phrases he seemed to have prepared. 'Mr Capstick was a powerful man, as I'm sure you already know. He was a considerate employer, so long as you operated efficiently.' He paused for a moment. 'He had his own agenda, which wasn't always going to be acceptable to the people he worked with.'

'You mean he was ruthless in the pursuit of his own interests.'

'Yes, I suppose I do. I'm not saying that—'

'It's not unusual for successful tycoons to be ruthless. I presume you would agree that your late employer was a tycoon?'

'Yes, he was certainly that.'

'Then I think you should press on and tell us what recent action of his it was which seemed to you particularly ruthless.'

Pearson was a little ruffled to be shaken out of his measured revelation, as Peach had intended him to be. He said bluntly, almost resentfully, 'He was planning to sell the club.'

Peach glanced at Blake, who took up the questioning smoothly but less aggressively, 'How long had you known about this, Mr Pearson?'

'Mr Capstick gave me the first intimation of it just over a week ago. I had to know that a change of ownership was in the offing, you see, because I had to give instructions for confidential information about the finances of the club to be released to the representatives of the putative purchaser.'

'How many other people knew about this?'

For the first time, Pearson did not have his reply ready. He gave every appearance of trying to be as honest and informative as possible. 'No one except me, officially, until last night.'

'Officially?' Lucy Blake raised the eyebrows beneath the dark red hair beguilingly and brought the first, vestigial smile from her now apprehensive informant. 'It's almost impossible to keep these things completely confidential, once the operation of what is called "due diligence" begins. Our chairman of thirty years ago, Edward Lanchester, had picked up a rumour from somewhere and quizzed me about it. He's a shrewd old bird, Mr Lanchester,' Pearson added, with what seemed genuine affection.

It was at this stage that Percy Peach, black moustache bristling suspiciously beneath the shining bald head, took up the questioning again. 'And who else had picked up on rumours?'

'Robbie Black, our manager, saw the financial men in here last week. He sensed something was in the wind, but he knew nothing definite, any more than the rest of us, until last night.'

'And what happened then?'

Pearson paused, making himself take his time, wary of making a mistake in this key revelation. He knew other people were going to be questioned about this. It was important to him that he now conveyed every impression of honesty. 'It was a strange occasion. Everyone connected with the club was euphoric about the victory over Liverpool yesterday afternoon.'

Percy remembered his own almost childish delight, as he had lingered in his seat after the final whistle to savour the triumph. 'You mean even level-headed people like the chief executive of the club?'

This time Darren Pearson's grin was genuine, a recognition of the delight of a fellow-supporter. 'Particularly the chief executive, Detective Chief Inspector Peach.' He was amused for a moment by the parallel titles. 'I am Brunton born and bred, so I'm always elated by a victory, especially over someone like Liverpool. If you want a more rational, hard-headed explanation, yesterday's victory almost guarantees our continued participation in the Premiership, which as you know means many millions of pounds to us.'

'So everyone was very excited. Hardly the right moment for Jim Capstick to throw a spanner into the works, was it?'

Darren Pearson was silent for a moment. 'It wasn't, but I don't blame Mr Capstick for that. Rumours were already circulating and in those circumstances all sorts of wild stories gain currency. It was better to have the facts out in the open, however unpalatable they might be for some of us.'

Lucy Blake looked up from her notes. 'You had better tell us exactly what happened. Remember that we know nothing at the moment, either about the detail of these events or the people involved.'

'I'm not sure I wish to comment on other people's feelings. I was concerned with the way the announcement was going to affect me personally at the time, not with what others thought.'

Peach said sternly, 'Within a few hours of revealing this news, Jim Capstick was dead. Almost certainly murdered. It must surely have occurred to you that the two events might be connected.'

'I'm not sure I've done much thinking. I dressed and rushed down here as soon as I got the news. Since then, I've had to try to calm the woman who found him, accommodate your scene of crime team, provide facilities for you, and try to formulate some official statement for the media. I've not had much time to digest what has happened and think rationally about it.'

'I accept that. But you will see that we need an account of exactly what happened last night, as a starting point for an investigation. We shan't declare this a murder until we have the proper confirmation, but the three of us here know already that it is murder that we are dealing with. There must be a strong possibility that it was one of the people who heard Mr Capstick's announcement that he was planning to sell the club who despatched him later in the evening.'

Darren Pearson's taut face had an unhealthy pallor. Tension was a natural enough reaction to the events of his morning, but Peach wondered whether there was also anxiety that he did not give away too much of himself and his own feelings. 'I'll tell it as accurately as I can. Other people may remember it differently.'

'Of course. And the differences may well be entirely innocent. But they will be of interest to us, as we try to find how Capstick died.'

Pearson swallowed hard; it seemed to cost him a consider-able effort to do so. 'If you were at the match, Mr Peach, you'll realize how excited everyone was at the conclusion of it. But it's rather a peculiar atmosphere for the directors and other people who are invited into the hospitality suite afterwards. You have the corresponding dignitaries from the visiting club to entertain, which means you have to control your natural elation.'

'You mustn't appear to crow.'

'Something like that. Very British, no doubt, but it doesn't seem sporting to be too euphoric when the people you are supposed to be entertaining are cast down by defeat. There was a sort of contained excitement, with people not wanting to show their feelings too openly.'

'Whilst you waited patiently for your visitors to leave.'

'Exactly that, yes. No one acknowledged it, but I think that was precisely what we were waiting for.' Pearson allowed himself a small smile, his first for many minutes, in his relief that Peach recognized the situation. 'Fortunately, the visitors don't usually hang around for too long in these situations. Yesterday's was an important defeat for Liverpool, as well as an important victory for us. We do have a repu-tation for good food here – our apple pie is talked of all over the country – but I think our visitors were quite anxious to get away and lick their wounds.'

'And Jim Capstick dropped his bombshell as soon as they had gone?'

'Yes. And bombshell is what it was. Even those who had some idea that a takeover might be a possibility had no idea that things had gone as far as they had. As a matter of fact, even Mrs Capstick seemed to be taken aback by the news. She might have been pretending that she had no prior know-ledge of it, I suppose, but I don't think so. She seemed more surprised by it than some of the rest of us who had an inkling of what was in the offing.'

'Did anyone offer any argument against the sale of the club?'

Pearson smiled fondly at his recollection. 'Edmund Lanchester did. He spoke up strongly against it, tried to point out that a football club shouldn't be treated in exactly

the same way as any other business asset.' Pearson smiled
fondly as he remembered the old man's sturdy opposition.
'He didn't get any change out of Capstick. You wouldn't
have expected him to, if you'd known the man.'

'As you did.'

'Better than most, I suppose.'

'Did you say anything yourself?'

'Yes. I'm not sure why, because I must have known it
would have no effect. Someone – I think it was probably
Debbie Black, our manager's wife – tried to point out that
the football club affected the whole town, not just the people
who owned it. Capstick said that he didn't care about them
and I pointed out that we cared about them every time we
needed their backing, that we expected them to come through
the turnstiles and support our team. I believe I said there
just wouldn't be occasions like the memorable victory over
Liverpool we'd just enjoyed without the people of the area
coming into the ground to support us.'

'And what was his reaction?'

'It was in effect a threat to me. He said that he'd have to
take account of my attitude when he considered whether to
recommend the existing staff to the new owner.' Pearson
watched Lucy Blake's ball-pen speeding over her notebook
and said wryly, 'I've just given myself a motive, haven't I?'

'Much better to be honest, I assure you, Mr Pearson,' said
Peach breezily. 'No doubt someone else would have reported
these things to us, if you had concealed them. And it seems
to me that most people listening to Jim Capstick's announcement had a motive. I don't suppose the prospect of a change
of ownership was welcomed by many people.'

'That is correct. Even the team manager, Robbie Black,
spoke up against it. He's a Scotsman who usually thinks
carefully before he chooses to speak. But he was pretty
bitter about how much connection with football the new
owners might have – how much knowledge of the game or
what it meant to the people of Brunton. I suppose he felt
threatened, like the rest of us.'

'Can you recall anyone else reacting strongly to the news?'

Pearson thought for a moment before shaking his head.

'No. There was a hubbub of noise, and more confusion than I've indicated. But I can't recall any more of what was said. Edward Lanchester was pretty vehement, but that's what you'd expect. He's got a lot of respect and standing in the town, having been around for such a long time and been chairman himself in a different era. And unlike most of the rest of us, he also had nothing to lose by speaking up forcefully.'

'So who do you think it was who went up there and garrotted Capstick?'

The sudden rawness of the challenge made Darren Pearson gasp. He wondered if it was a CID tactic or just a characteristic of Peach to be so forthright. He said as firmly as he could, 'I've no idea. I've told you all I can.'

'For which we thank you, Mr Pearson. If anything else, however trivial, occurs to you, please get in touch immediately.' DCI Peach stood up and placed his card on the desk Pearson had chosen not to use. 'Thank you for providing us with a useful beginning. We shall no doubt need to have further words with you in due course.'

He made the routine conclusion sound like a warning.

FOURTEEN

It had been a long, hard winter, the worst for twenty years. But Spring had now definitely arrived. The crocus had finished, the daffodils were in full bloom, the tulips were in bud. It was a perfect early April day in north-east Lancashire. The clouds flew swift and high against blue sky over Pendle Hill and the greater heights of Ingleborough and Pen-y-Ghent away to the north. On the golf courses, the fairways had been mown and there was the first faint whiff of new-mown grass and summer promise in the air.

Percy Peach wondered whether his chief's colourful dress was an attempt to herald the spring or a reaction against the more sober colours he felt were demanded of him at Brunton police station. Either way, it was a mistake.

Thomas Bulstrode Tucker was a parakeet among the dull crows of the Lancashire landscape. Indeed, a large crow was regarding the chief superintendent with some distaste when Percy located him on the twelfth hole of Brunton Golf Course at eleven o'clock on Sunday morning. Tucker wore a sweater which was the colour of bright mustard and plus twos in the brightest scarlet Peach had witnessed. The knee-length stockings which were obligatory with plus twos were in a shade of lemon which was a pale shadow of the sweater above it. They had a spectacular spattering of mud which testified to the wearer's erratic progress on the eleven holes so far completed.

Peach watched his leader's club hit the ground two inches behind his ball and dispatch it a disappointing thirty yards nearer to the green. The effort soiled further the player's muddied calves. 'Bad luck, sir,' Percy called sympathetically, as Tucker removed the worst deposits of mud from his person and slammed his club violently back into his golf bag. 'Our fairways will be a bit drier at the North Lancs, I imagine.'

It was a source of continuing frustration to Tucker that his applications to join the more prestigious and demanding North Lancashire Golf Club had been repeatedly rejected on the grounds of his lowly prowess in the game, whilst Peach's application had been immediately successful. He whirled upon this unexpected interruption of his game. 'What the hell do you want, Peach?'

'And a good morning to you too, sir,' returned his chief inspector cheerfully. 'Supporting Watford are we this year, sir?'

'Watford?' Tucker assumed the air of blank incomprehension which Percy always found appealing.

'The colours, sir. Very near to Watford football team's distinctive strip, I'd say. They're struggling a little in the Championship this year, I believe.'

'Say what you've come to say and stop spoiling my day!' ordered Tucker as he glared with parallel malevolence first at Peach and then at his ball, which they were rapidly approaching.

'We have a murder, sir. A suspicious death, at the moment. But the SOCO officer and I are both satisfied that this is a homicide, though we await the official confirmation.'

'We are treating the death as suspicious,' Tucker muttered, rehearsing his official reply to all press and media enquiries. Then, with controlled aggression, 'Why are you interrupting my weekend with this?'

'Because you demanded that you should be informed immediately of all high-profile crime on our patch, sir,' said Peach, with equally controlled reasonableness.

Tucker aimed a desperate lunge at his golf ball, with predictable results: the ball sliced high and right and disappeared into a hawthorn hedge at the edge of the course. He wheeled on Peach with predictable fury. 'What the hell do you expect me to do about it?'

'Well, you could try turning your shoulders rather more and swinging more slowly,' said Peach thoughtfully.

'Not the bloody golf ball, you fool, the suspicious death!' shouted Tucker, exciting the interest of a four-ball match on the adjoining fairway. 'Some Saturday night brawl outside a pub, was it?'

'Very perceptive about the time, sir. Yet to be firmly established, but the SOCO officer and I are already quite certain
that the death took place last night, sir. I expect it's your
well-known overview of the crime scene which gives you
these insights.' Tucker was now risking further damage to
his lurid apparel by thrashing a club desperately within the
hawthorns in search of his ball. Peach watched with interest
before saying sympathetically, 'You might have to mount a
full-scale CID operation to hunt down that one, I'd say, sir.'

'Look, you've done what you came here for. Informed
me of some low-profile death and ruined my game into the
bargain! I think it's high time you were on your way, Peach.'

Percy pursed his lips and shook his head slowly. 'Not
low-profile, this one, sir. Not in my opinion. It's the chairman
and owner of Brunton Rovers, sir. One James Capstick.
Thought you ought to know, sir. By the way, your ball is
three yards right of where you're looking and in the ditch,
sir.'

It was a very grand modern house, with a service flat attached
and what looked like more accommodation over the garage.
It had an acre of immaculately tended garden. Daffodils in
full bloom flanked the winding drive to the front of the house,
and the first double red blooms were opening on the camellias which climbed on each side of the door.

Rather to their surprise, it was a man who opened the
door to DCI Peach and DS Blake. He was a powerful figure,
with broad shoulders and watchful, deep-set eyes in a square
face. He recognized them as police before they could
announce themselves and said, 'I'm Walter Boyd, Mr
Capstick's chauffeur. Mrs Capstick is waiting for you in the
drawing room.'

It was a long, elegant room, with two large windows
which looked across a sweep of lawn to the budding azaleas
and laburnums in the border at the end of it. There was a
grand piano in the corner of the room and what looked like
a very expensive hi-fi system alongside it. The chaise longue
at the other end of the room looked highly elegant but
extremely uncomfortable; Lucy Blake guessed that people

rarely sat upon it. There was ample and more comfortable-looking furniture in the easy chairs and sofas which sat upon a huge Persian carpet and occupied most of the rest of the room. The CID officers took two of the easy chairs at the invitation of the woman who had risen to greet them. She did not ask them if they wished for refreshment, but a moment later, a middle-aged maid brought in a silver tray with tea and cakes upon it.

Percy Peach made his customary apologies for intruding upon a grieving widow so soon after her husband's death, but he felt rather as though he was uttering stage lines in a comedy of manners. The air of artificiality was increased by the fact that the central figure in the scene did not seem to be devastated with grief. She poured the tea into the china cups with a steady hand and set them upon small tables beside each chair, then offered them plates and cakes. In all this time, they could not begin the questioning which was the occasion of their visit. It seemed that Helen Capstick and not Peach was dictating the pace of the action.

Eventually, Peach said grimly, 'Mr Capstick appears to have been a man with a number of formidable enemies.'

Helen Capstick didn't hurry her reply, even after the delay her hospitality had ensured. Her hair was an unusual colour, a bronze which shone as if it had been burnished; it was so beautifully cut and set that it was difficult to tell whether the colour was natural to her or not. She had bright blue eyes, which studied her visitors as keenly as if they and not she were the subject of investigation. She said, 'I would expect anyone with Jim's business ventures and successes to have enemies. I have no doubt that he fished in some fairly murky ponds at times, but I took care to know as little as possible about his businesses. He preferred it that way and I was happy to accept it.'

'You're saying that you can't imagine who could possibly have killed him last night.' Peach let a little of his irritation show even as he took his first sip of the tea provided for him.

'No. You're saying that Jim was murdered, then?' She did not seem to be outraged or even surprised by the word.

She seemed almost as if she was joining in a game with
them, for amusement played about her lips.

Peach said stiffly, 'We are treating this as a suspicious
death. That means that the possibility of murder must be
investigated.'

'Or even the probability. Mr Peach, let's not waste any
more time. I think that someone killed Jim last night. The
place where he died and the people who were there suggest
to me that it was almost certainly someone with a connection with Brunton Rovers Football Club who killed him.'
The language was formal, but as Helen Capstick became
more animated, there was just a trace of a Birmingham
accent, which came surprisingly from these sophisticated
lips.

'There are other possibilities. As you have declared yourself, a successful man in the areas where Mr Capstick
operated makes enemies. It is entirely possible that one
such enemy might have employed a contract killer to kill
him at Grafton Park, precisely because that environment
would divert suspicion from the real source of this attack.'

'It is entirely possible, as you say. I had not considered
such an explanation before, because of the announcement
which preceded Jim's death last night. But I am sure that
Wally Boyd, the man my husband chose to employ as a
chauffeur, also operated as his bodyguard. He was not with
him last night, of course.'

She could not prevent her dislike for the man coming out
in the way she spoke, so that Peach was emboldened to add,
'And no doubt Mr Boyd acted as a general factotum and
gatherer of information for Mr Capstick.'

'Possibly. I haven't bothered to speculate about Wally
Boyd's duties: I doubt whether you would find all of them
in his job description.' Again her coolness, even contempt,
for the man edged through the calm phrases. Peach did not
expect that Mr Boyd would remain much longer on the
Capstick staff; he moved him a little higher on his mental
list of people to be interviewed.

'Mrs Capstick, you have just indicated that you think
your husband's death was probably a direct result of an

announcement he made last night. Please now give us your account of that announcement and the reaction of yourself and other people to it.'

She accorded him the measured, patronizing smile he had already seen. 'I'm sure Mr Pearson has already given you his account of that.'

The manner of speech can be as revealing as the content: Peach divined in that moment that this woman had no great liking for Darren Pearson as well as Wally Boyd. 'He has indeed, Mrs Capstick. Quite a vivid account, as a matter of fact. But now we should like to hear how you heard and saw the scene.'

She made a real effort to control her irritation and retain her coolness, well aware that this was necessary if she wanted to give as little as possible away. 'It wasn't the right time to do it, but Jim said that it had to be done then and he was probably right. The newspapers were on to him and were preparing their headlines; it was better that the people concerned got the news from him than from them. Everyone was full of excitement in the hospitality suite, especially after the Liverpool board members had gone and we could let our hair down a bit. It was when the noise was at its height that Jim stopped things and told us that he was planning to sell the club.'

'Did you know about what he was going to say beforehand?'

'No. That may seem strange to you, but it wouldn't if you'd known Jim Capstick. My husband always played his cards very close to his chest. He was probably right to do so. The fewer people who know about these things before they have to, the better, he thought, and I'm sure he was right.'

'I'm surprised that you didn't know, though. I'd have thought that with you there alongside him supporting the team, he'd have given you at least a hint of what he was going to say in the evening.'

'Well, he didn't. And I think I'm happy that he didn't. I'd have felt a hypocrite sitting through the match with people like Debbie Black and Edward Lanchester if I'd known that Jim was planning to sell the club.'

'So how did these people and the others there receive the news when Mr Capstick eventually announced it?'

She paused again, measuring her reply. Peach and Blake could not tell from her manner whether she was merely considering the question or planning to conceal something from them. 'I think the predominant feeling was one of shock. One or two people, like Darren Pearson, must have had some notion that Jim was considering a sale, but I think even they were surprised by the speed at which things had moved on.'

'What did you say when you heard the news?'

'I don't remember saying anything. Oh, yes I do. I listened to several other people like Edward Lanchester and Darren Pearson voicing their concerns about the takeover. Then I asked if we could know who it was who was going to be the new owner of our club.'

'Why did you ask that?'

Again there was the irksome little pause as she gathered her thoughts. 'To be honest, I'm not quite sure. It wasn't going to make a lot of difference to me. In that I was sure Jim would be selling at a profit and making a shrewd business decision, this was probably in my best interests. But we'd had a heady afternoon and a famous Brunton Rovers victory and I felt close to the people in the room. To be quite honest, I think I wanted them to be aware that I had known nothing of Jim's decision until it was announced a few minutes earlier. It sounds stupid and immature, but I think that was why I asked my question. I was as shocked as everyone else, and I wanted everyone in the room to know that.'

'So who do you think killed Mr Capstick?'

For the first time, she lost some of her coolness. 'I've no bloody idea!' She transferred her glittering gaze from Peach to Lucy Blake and her ball-pen poised over her notebook. 'And for your records, young lady, I loved Jim and I want you to arrest the person who did this as quickly as possible.'

Peach spoke more quietly. 'Mrs Capstick, I spoke earlier of contract killers and the possibility that one of them might have been hired in this instance. I was reminding myself as well as you that we have to consider all possibilities. It is a highly unlikely possibility in this case. It is neither the usual method nor a typical setting for such a killing. Hit men prefer the bullet and the anonymity of city streets. Moreover, it would be a huge coincidence if such a man chose the very moment when his victim had made an unpopular announcement and given him a collection of alternative suspects. The probability is that the person who killed Mr Capstick was someone who was in the room with you when you heard about the sale of Brunton Rovers.'

Helen Capstick too was quieter as she replied to him. She suddenly looked as drawn and strained as they would have expected at the outset. 'I had worked out as much for myself.'

'You knew the victim better than anyone else in that room last night. Which of them do you think it was who killed him?'

A small, weary smile. 'I've been asking myself that since I heard the news from Mr Pearson this morning. I knew all about my husband, as you say. But most of the people in that room I hardly knew. I've been through them: they're a varied bunch, but I can't imagine any of them committing murder.'

Peach stared steadily at her, looking for further fissures in the carapace of her composure. 'We need an account of your movements last night. We shall be asking everyone else for a similar account.'

'And one of them will tell you lies.'

'Perhaps more than one. They will be most unwise to do so. Secrets rarely survive a murder investigation.'

She looked at him sharply. 'Jim left the hospitality suite shortly after his announcement. He said he was going up to his office and he obviously did that. There was a lot of discussion of the takeover and what it would mean to the present employees of the club. I felt embarrassed because I didn't believe that I should be part of that. I tried to convince them that I'd had as little warning as they'd had of the news. But after that, I left as quickly as I decently could. I didn't look at the clock, but I'd guess that was about half an hour after Jim.'

Lucy Blake said gently, 'We need the details of your movements during the rest of the evening, Mrs Capstick.'

She looked at the younger woman with distaste, then deliberately away from her and past her to summon concentration. 'I went out to my car and drove home. I stayed there for the rest of the evening.'

Peach studied her carefully and without embarrassment. 'You didn't come to the ground with your husband?'

'No. I used my own car.' A small, mirthless smile. 'We rarely travelled together. We usually seemed to have different agendas. This occasion was patently no exception to that.'

'You didn't go out again during the evening?'

'No. I've just told you I didn't.'

'Can anyone confirm this for us?'

'I don't think so. The domestic staff come in during the day rather than occupy the service flat. I prefer it that way.'

'You mentioned a chauffeur. I think he was the man who let us in today.'

'Yes. Wally Boyd. He's my husband's man. He has his own self-contained flat over the garage. I doubt whether he'll be able to vouch for me. I don't even know whether he was in or out last night. It was Jim who told him when he was required and when he could have time off.'

'I need you to think again about the people you were with in the hospitality suite at Grafton Park. Do you recall any reaction, anything said, which now seems significant in view of what happened to your husband later?'

'No. I'll go on thinking and let you know if I do.'

She saw them off the premises personally, remaining at the door of the big house until their car disappeared, as if it was important to her to confirm that they had really left.

FIFTEEN

'We can't stay long, Mum.'
'That's a fine way to introduce yourselves!' said Agnes Blake with dignity.

Lucy led the two men of such contrasting appearance into the cottage behind her and gestured to Percy Peach to take over. 'I'm afraid she's right, Mrs B,' said Percy regretfully. 'We've a murder on our patch and it's all CID hands to the pumps at the moment. Well, apart from the hands of Tommy Bloody Tucker, anyway.'

'I heard about it on the news. The owner of Brunton Rovers. This man Capstick who bought the club three years ago. They said three years on the news. It hardly seems that long ago to me.'

'This is Clyde Northcott, Mum,' said Lucy Blake rather desperately.

The DC held himself very erect, so that he looked even taller than his six feet three in the low-ceilinged cottage. He was wearing a polo-necked white shirt, which set off his blackness and made it even more uncompromising. His hair was cut very short, seeming to emphasize the lack of flesh on his features and make his high cheek bones even more prominent. He bent a little from the waist and offered his hand to his hostess, so that Lucy was reminded ridiculously for a moment of Jane Austen and Regency bucks in the pump room at Bath.

Clyde said, in his deep voice, with its traces of the Lancashire where he had lived the whole of his life, 'Delighted to meet you, Mrs Blake. Lucy has told me lots about you.'

'And I'm delighted to see you at last, young man.' She held his big hand in her small ones and shook it vigorously.

'Clyde Northcott is the man to have beside you if you get into a pub fight,' explained Percy Peach helpfully. 'That's his function in our team, you see. He's what we call a hard bastard. Excuse my language, Mrs B, but that's a technical police term. Clyde will be very useful if we have any punch-ups at the reception after the wedding.'

'Go on with you, Percy Peach!' Agnes giggled delightedly. 'I expect he's a good boss to you, isn't he?' she asked Northcott.

It was the first time Lucy Blake had ever seen her junior colleague embarrassed. He looked at every face in the room in turn, then bent his head low towards the old lady's ear. 'I might be on the other side of the law without him, Mrs Blake. I was keeping bad company when he first knew me.'

'And we can't have hard bastards on the wrong side, you see, Mrs B,' said Percy breezily.

'Better to have him in your tent pissing out than outside pissing in? I believe that's the expression. Pardon my language, but I believe it was some American President – they don't have our standards, you know.'

There were three seconds of shocked silence which delighted Agnes Blake. Then Clyde Northcott said with a dazzling smile, 'I think you and me's going to get along just fine, Mrs Blake!'

'Oh, I do hope so, Clyde. We'll need to keep these two lovebirds in order on their big day, you see. They'll be billing and cooing all over the place. It will be up to us to keep things moving along on schedule.'

The notion of Percy Peach billing and cooing was an appealing one to Clyde Northcott, but he took care not to catch his DCI's eye. Instead, he nodded seriously at his diminutive new friend. 'I've already gathered one or two interesting stories about the bridegroom for my speech. I might like to run them past you in private some time in the next week or two.'

'And I can give you one or two embarrassing episodes from the bride's childhood, if you need a few cheap laughs.' Agnes giggled again, this time in delighted anticipation.

'Mother, you're not to—'

'Time we were on our way, I'm afraid,' said Peach hastily. 'We have a murder to attend to, as I said.'

'What about next Thursday night, Clyde?' said Agnes. She looked with some disdain at the daughter and putative son-in-law who had thought she might be dismayed to have this impressive black figure as the best man. 'I work at the supermarket until eight, but you could meet me there. I'd like to introduce you to a few of my friends.'

'Thursday's good, Mrs Blake. I could perhaps take you to the pub and sort out the details of the young people's big day.' Clyde Northcott, who was five years younger than Lucy and fifteen years younger than Percy, gazed over their heads with impressive maturity.

Agnes Blake looked up at the smooth features of her new black Adonis. 'You don't play cricket, do you, Clyde?'

Monday morning. The phone rang almost incessantly in Darren Pearson's office, as journalists and broadcasters sought desperately for a quote on the sensational demise of the colourful chairman-owner of Brunton Rovers. 'Colourful' was the most popular epithet in the days after his passing, when death demanded a certain circumspection. James Capstick would revert again to 'controversial' in a week or so.

In the room Pearson had allocated to the police investigators, the club's football manager, Robbie Black, was being interviewed by Peach and Blake.

He was nervous. They noted it, but did not as yet attach any particular significance to it. People involved in the investigation of murder were anxious for all sorts of reasons, many of them entirely innocent and understandable. Black was a man who relied for his reputation and his work principally upon his physical prowess and coaching ability rather than any facility with words. He had become a household name and an international footballer through his skills in controlling and manipulating a football. As a manager and coach, his principal duties were to perceive and develop those skills in the men within his charge. Men like Robbie Black often felt at a disadvantage under questioning, feeling rightly or wrongly that their ability to frame replies did not match the questioning of experienced interviewers.

They took him through the events of the previous Saturday. He was eloquent about the game itself and the way it had evolved, still excited despite himself by his players, especially Ashley Greenhalgh, by the team's success and his own role in achieving it. When they moved forward to Jim Capstick's announcement in the hospitality suite and the reactions to it, he was immediately less forthcoming, more suspicious of where the CID questioning might be leading him.

'I didna get up there until quite late, ye ken. I like to stay with my team while they wind down, whilst they shower and dress. I usually stay until most of them leave.' He gave a grim little smile as he allowed them into an area he usually protected from the public. 'When we've lost, there can be arguments, even punch-ups if you don't control things. People think we're all buddies together, but it's like any other job – we don't always get on with those we have to work with.'

'But you didn't have to deal with any of that on Saturday.'

'No. Things are usually fine when we've won. And Saturday was our best win of the season.' Again the professional pride in the achievement burst through the jacket of caution he had adopted.

'So what time did you go up to the hospitality suite?'

This was what he had been expecting and he had his answers ready. 'Quarter past six. The lads had left by then and I thought the Liverpool directors would be either gone or about to go.'

'You didn't want to speak to them?'

A rueful grin as he recognized a situation familiar to him but foreign to the CID pair. 'I don't like to get involved with the other team's supporters more than I have to. They often want to talk about referees' decisions and key points in the match.'

'And you don't like discussing these things with amateurs.'

Again that doleful smile. 'It's no because they're amateurs. I've had some pretty fierce moments with the professionals – other managers and their assistants. We're all at the mercy of our results. We're better paid than we used to be, but it's an even more precarious business. When there's so much at stake, you don't often see things the same way as the opposition, whether you're professionals or amateurs.' He felt himself being lured on to familiar but dangerous ground. 'What's this got to do with the death of Jim Capstick?'

Peach smiled, not at all put out by the challenge. 'Time will tell. Maybe nothing. But it's my belief as it's probably yours that someone in that hospitality suite on Saturday night killed Mr Capstick later in the evening. As CID officers, we come to this situation knowing nothing about the people involved in it, Mr Black. The more we can find about the way those people think and behave, the nearer we may be to perceiving how a man died. A lot of what we learn will be completely irrelevant, as you imply. But the feelings you took into that room are part of the picture, as are the very different feelings which other people took there. Tell us what happened after you arrived at six fifteen.'

'The Liverpool people had gone. Jim Capstick had obviously been waiting for that. There was a lot of noise and a lot of pleasure over our victory. Capstick soon put a stop to that.' Black paused, obviously waiting for a reaction, but neither Peach nor Blake spoke and he had to go on. 'He told us he was selling the club. That put a stop to all the laughter.'

Peach gave him a curt nod. 'I expect it did. We now need your account of people's reactions to that news.'

'General consternation. Mrs Capstick said she'd known nothing about it. Well, I can't remember exactly what words she used, but that was what she wanted us to hear.'

'Did you believe her?'

'No. Well, I'm not sure whether I did or I didn't, but it didn't seem likely that she'd have no notion what her husband was up to. But I was more concerned with how it was going to affect me.'

'So you spoke up against it?'

'No. My mind was reeling.'

'But this wasn't a surprise to you. You'd known that men were in this building examining the club's books at the beginning of the week.'

Black looked thoroughly uncomfortable at the challenge. 'That's true. I knew something was going on. But nothing definite. And I hadn't realized things had moved as far as they had. I thought we'd get the chance to say what we thought if anything definite was proposed. I was expecting there would be weeks, perhaps months, before any decisions were made.'

'I think Mr Capstick knew there was going to be speculation about a takeover in the Sunday papers. He felt he had to give you the news then so that you got it from him and not from others spreading rumours and uncertainty.'

'So he said. It might be so, but I don't pretend to understand these things. I'm a football man dealing with football players. I don't believe Capstick suited anyone but himself.'

Robbie Black's lips set in a sullen line which said that it wasn't part of his brief to see the owner's problems in timing his announcement. He obviously didn't want to make any allowances for a man he had never liked. Peach let that thought hang unspoken for a moment before he suggested with a deceptively open countenance, 'So you spoke up and let him know how you felt.'

'No. It was Mr Lanchester who spoke up and said what we were feeling. He's a good man, Edward Lanchester.'

'So you remember what he said on your behalf.'

'He said what most of us were thinking. That this might be in Jim Capstick's best interests but not in the interests of the club.'

'By which he meant?'

'He meant that he thought the land which the club owns around the ground and in Brunton was of more interest than a football club with a hundred and thirty years of history. I think he said that people all over the world were interested in buying Premiership clubs either as mere status symbols or for their land assets rather than their future as football clubs.'

'Did you speak yourself?'

'No. There wasna any need to.' As usual when he was animated or uncertain, he heard his speech becoming more Scottish.

'Who else spoke?'

'Darren Pearson asked some sort of question, I canna remember what. He received a threat about his future for his pains. Capstick told him he wouldn't be able to recommend his services to the new owners if he didn't toe the line. That was meant as a threat for all of us who work at the club.'

Lucy Blake looked up from her notes. 'Didn't you say anything, Mr Black? It seems other people think that you did.'

He smiled bitterly. 'You trying to trip me up? I didn't kill Jim Capstick, though I admit I felt like doing something violent to him on Saturday night.'

Peach said grimly, 'It was almost certainly someone who felt much as you did who ended Mr Capstick's life. You will understand that at this stage we can't take anyone's word at face value, Mr Black. If you are now telling us that you said nothing to Mr Capstick after his announcement, that is what we shall record. You may eventually be asked to sign a written statement to that effect.'

He was silent for a moment; whether he was genuinely reviewing those fateful minutes or merely deciding what he would reveal to them was not clear from the sallow, frowning face. 'I did speak. I didn't say much, but I spoke my piece. And much good it did me. Much good it did for all of us, for that matter. The man's mind was made up.'

Lucy Blake said quietly, 'What was it you said, Mr Black?'

Unexpectedly, as he recollected the moment he smiled and the dark eyes brightened in the grave, determined face. 'I think I knew it was hopeless. Mr Lanchester had said everything that needed to be said and got no change out of Capstick. I only spoke up to support Debbie.'

'And what had your wife said?'

'I don't recall her exact words. Something about a football club being more than a business. About its importance to a town that was already suffering in this recession. We weren't told this at the time, but I think we all knew that it must be some Middle Eastern oil billionaire who was buying Capstick out. I think I said it wouldn't be anyone with any knowledge of football or feel for what it meant to

the town. Capstick said he didn't give a bugger about that.'
Black shook his head and the very dark hair moved a little
with the movement. 'I don't recall his exact words, but that
was certainly what he meant.'

'And you left it at that?'

'There wasn't any point in saying anything else. Capstick
had already threatened Darren Pearson's future. He made it
plain that the new man would probably be bringing in his own
team, so we might all be looking for jobs. Then he buggered
off up to his office to carry on with the deal.'

Peach's eyes looked even darker than Black's, their hue
probably accentuated by the whiteness of the bald pate
above them. He said slowly, 'Capstick told you this at
the time, did he?'

Again that frown of concentration wrinkled the forehead
above the strong-featured face. It was easy to see why this
man had the reputation of a disciplinarian in an era when
most managers had grown used to accommodating the whims
of their millionaire players. 'I don't think he said that in so
many words, but I for one wasn't left in any doubt. I think
he said something about having important phone calls to
make.' He paused, then added, as if the thought had come
to him for the first time. 'I suppose that might have been
just bluff, to rub salt in our wounds. I think by that time he
was quite happy doing that.'

Peach nodded thoughtfully. It was through the
Scotsman's words that he had gathered for the first time
some of the electric atmosphere in the hospitality suite in
the minutes after Capstick's announcement. 'You told us
a few minutes ago that you didn't kill James Capstick.
We're certain that he was killed in his office on Saturday
night. Who do you think murdered him?'

The manager didn't flinch at the first mention of the word,
as people often did. He didn't look like a man who would
flinch at anything. 'I don't know. You'll have quite a few
candidates.' The grim smile said more eloquently than words
that the thought gave him considerable satisfaction.

Blake said unemotionally, 'You will understand that we
need an account of your movements in those hours.'

'Aye. We stayed together in the hospitality suite after Capstick had left, discussing what he'd said and what it meant for us.'

'All of you?'

'I can't be certain of that. And I can't tell you who left and when. We were all shattered by what we'd heard.' He paused. 'I think Mrs Capstick left pretty quickly after him. You'd expect that, wouldn't you?'

Lucy Blake didn't respond to that. Robbie thought how composed her face looked beneath the chestnut hair. When she looked up from her notes, her eyes were a remarkable dark green, seeming to him for a moment of fantasy to be able to see further into him than eyes of a more normal colour. She said softly, 'When did you leave yourself, Mr Black?'

'I don't know how long it was after Capstick had gone. I wasn't checking at the time. Perhaps twenty minutes, but I've really no idea.'

'Did your wife leave with you?'

'No. We always go to the ground in separate cars, because I have to be with the players hours before kick-off time. She didn't have to rush away, though. The au pair was looking after the children and seeing them into their beds.'

It was the first time he had spoken of this exotic new addition to their household: he wondered if it sounded boastful. Apparently not, for Blake said without looking up, 'And the rest of the evening?'

'I made a phone call on my mobile. Arranged to meet Jack Cox.'

Peach nodded. 'A fellow manager.'

'Retired now. But a wily old bird, with lots of experience. I was assistant to Jack at Sheffield United when I stopped playing and took my coaching badges. I wanted to discuss what Capstick had said with someone like him. I arranged to meet Jack at his house at nine thirty. He suggested a pub, but I wanted somewhere more private.' He grinned fondly at the memory of the exchange. 'Jack Cox told me to keep my head down and await developments. Not to resign, whatever I felt. If they sack you, they have to pay up your contract.'

'So you arrived home at what time?'

'Probably eleven o'clock or so. Debbie might be able to tell you. She was waiting up for me.' He looked at them with the sort of aggression he had once brought to the football field. 'We spent another hour discussing what we'd heard from Capstick.'

SIXTEEN

The post-mortem examination report on James Capstick told the investigators little that they had not known or deduced already.

He had been strangled by means of a cord or cable. This had been dropped over his head and tightened by twisting from behind. In addition to the deep and fatal wound at the throat, the area at the back of the neck showed bruising that had been caused by the twisting of the murder implement behind the deceased's head. Beneath the technical language and the Latinized vocabulary lay the stark truth: someone, probably taking him by surprise, had stood behind Capstick and garrotted him, twisting the life out of him within seconds.

Most of this the CID team had already deduced. The disappointment for them was the news that no great strength had been required for the killing. The supplementary information about the absence of fibres in the deep wound to the neck indicated that the most probable death instrument was some sort of electric cable. Once this had been applied to the neck, it could have been twisted and tightened from behind by the hands of a woman as easily as a man. The prospect of eliminating some of the candidates for this crime on the grounds of the brute physical strength required had disappeared.

There was no sign of the murder weapon at the scene, and little prospect of its being discovered now. It was probably a very common type of electrical cable, available to anyone. Indeed, a skip adjacent to the ground, containing the detritus from rewiring work being currently conducted there, held short lengths of this type of cable; it was quite possible but by no means certain that the murder weapon had been picked up from there.

Because the time when the last food eaten by the dead man could be pinpointed to between five and six in the

hospitality suite at Grafton Park, the pathologist was able
to be unusually precise in his estimate of the time of death.
The degree of digestion of the food indicated that death had
taken place between ninety and one hundred and fifty
minutes after its consumption.

'Between seven thirty and eight thirty,' said DCI Peach
sourly, as he surveyed the report with his team. 'Thanks for
telling us what we already bloody knew.'

'At least we know that he died relatively early in the
evening,' said DC Brendan Murphy brightly. The big, fresh-
faced Lancastrian with the entirely Irish name was given to
unthinking optimism.

Peach released his frustration in a look of molten
contempt. 'Which merely brings a lot more people into this
as suspects. If he hadn't died until eleven, we could have
presumed that a lone figure, probably someone who knew
that labyrinth of a place intimately like Darren Pearson, had
hung around until everything was quiet, then dispatched our
man with no one around.'

Murphy was not at all put out. 'Or that someone who had
left the ground much earlier had stolen back to the place to
see off Capstick. You wouldn't have allowed us to rule out
that possibility.'

DS Blake smiled at the male stags locking horns. 'Capstick
being killed later in the evening is an unlikely scenario
anyway. Whoever wanted to get at him couldn't rely on him
being around for much longer than an hour after he'd dropped
his bombshell of news and left his audience aghast in the
hospitality suite. I know he said he had phone calls to make,
but if I'd been planning to get rid of him, I would have felt
I had to do it pretty quickly if I was to be certain of finding
him in his office.'

DC Clyde Northcott was studying the last paragraph on
the stomach contents. 'He'd had a drink or two not long
before he died, it says here, some time after the food he'd
consumed. Not a lot, because he'd still have been just under
the limit for driving. Is it possible that he'd been drinking
with the person who killed him? That would strengthen the
possibility that his killer was someone who knew him well,

someone that Capstick might have happy to sit and drink with.'

Peach pictured the scene of crime he had visited twenty-four hours earlier. 'It was Capstick's whisky. Only one glass was found. Forensic found only Capstick's prints on both bottle and glass.'

Northcott nodded. 'Which makes sense, since no doubt he was doing the pouring. But his visitor might well have removed any second glass, which would have had his finger-prints all over it. He'd have been silly not to do that.'

'Or *she* would have been silly,' pointed out Lucy Blake, in an inverted assertion of sexual equality. 'We can't even be absolutely certain that it was Capstick's announcement that he was selling the club which provoked his murder. We're already finding that he was a man with plenty of enemies. The news of the takeover would have been a wonderful smokescreen for someone who already had a personal grudge against Capstick. Someone who already hated him enough to kill him could well have seen the chance of involving a lot of other suspects.'

DCI Percy Peach looked round his team dolefully. 'You lot really know how to cheer a bloke up.'

Debbie Black wished now that she'd told them to come to the house immediately.

When the cool, matter-of-fact voice had told her that senior CID officers wanted to talk to her in connection with the death of James Capstick on the previous Saturday, her first thought had been to give herself time to think, to prepare her replies to some of the questions she regarded as inevitable. She had arranged for them to come to see her at two o'clock, which would give her three hours to compose herself and think of the bland, straightforward answers which would send these as yet faceless people away convinced that she had nothing interesting to offer them.

It proved to be three hours of increasing tension rather than confident preparation. The children were safely at school. She gave the au pair the rest of the day off and encouraged her to go into the town centre shops: she was

still not used to the luxury of employing staff and
it seemed a good idea to have the place to herself whilst
she prepared for the two o'clock meeting. But the empty
house seemed only to increase her edginess and crank up
her apprehension about what was to come in the afternoon.
At twelve fifteen, she made herself a sandwich for lunch.
At one o'clock, she threw more than half of it into the waste
bin and took a big beaker of tea into the sitting room, which
looked even bigger than usual as she curled her legs beneath
her upon a sofa and fixed her nervous hands around the
china. Her normally cool brain refused to take any heed of
her injunctions: she could not think about the questions and
what her replies to them would be. She could not remember
when her concentration had last been so poor.

For the third time, she checked her appearance in the
mirror. For twenty years and more, she had been used to
presenting herself at her best for interviews. During her days
as a tennis star and a model, it had become second nature
to glance into a mirror for no more than a few seconds,
confirming that all was as she wanted it to be before she
presented herself to her public. Now, all she noticed was
that her dark brown hair seemed stiff, forced into place
rather than falling naturally about her face, that her cheeks
were surely paler than when she had last looked at them
half an hour earlier.

There were only two of them when they came, a short
man with a bald head and a black moustache and a woman
with striking red-brown hair, aquamarine eyes and just a
suggestion of freckles, which made her look younger and
more innocent than her job demanded. Yet both of them
seemed to Debbie Black to be studying her more intensely,
to be more aware of her face and anything it betrayed, than
any television or newspaper camera had been in the past.

It was the woman who introduced them: she said she was
DS Blake and the man with her was Detective Chief Inspector
Peach, who was in charge of the case. He looked round the
room, taking in the excellent modern furnishings and the prints
she had taken so much trouble selecting, whilst his colleague
explained the routine of an investigation like this one.

Debbie said nervously, 'You must think I'm very important, if I warrant the attentions of the man in charge and his detective sergeant!' Immediately she wished that she hadn't essayed this feeble levity.

Peach gave her a grave smile. 'You were one of the last people to see the victim alive, Mrs Black. Such people always warrant full investigation.'

'I saw him with a lot of other people. I'm sure you've already been told about the announcement he made.'

'Indeed we have. But now we'd like your account of it.'

Debbie wondered why that sounded so much like a threat. 'There isn't much to tell. We were all full of the famous victory over Liverpool – me more than anyone amongst the women I think, because my husband is the manager and I felt he'd engineered it. By the time of this announcement, the Liverpool party had left and joy was unconfined and increasingly noisy.' That was a sentence she had prepared beforehand. It sounded exactly like that to her as she delivered it, but she pressed on. 'At first I think we all thought that Jim Capstick was there purely to join in the general exultation. We weren't allowed to keep that illusion for very long.'

'How did Mr Capstick seem at this time? Remember, please, that we have to build up a picture of a man we never knew and now never will know through the accounts of other people.'

She welcomed this. It was a question she had not anticipated, an opportunity to move away from the phrases which she had worked on beforehand but which she now felt were too obviously prepared. A chance also to convey to them the bastard Jim Capstick had been, when he was not presenting his public mask of affability to the world. 'He seemed at first a little embarrassed. He said he was sorry to break up the party but that he had something to say which he had rather we heard from him than from the gossip-mongers in the Sunday papers.'

'I expect you had some sympathy with that, as a person who has suffered in the past from such people.'

Debbie hadn't expected the personal slant. She wondered

if it was designed to throw her off track, to shake her composure a little. 'I have indeed. But not for a long time, I'm pleased to say. Not since the days when I was Debbie Palmer, tennis player and model, and they linked me with a string of different men and a string of outrageous and largely imaginary escapades. Jim Capstick was made of sterner stuff than me. I expect tabloid journalists worried him a lot less.' She allowed herself a little smile at the comparison. 'He said that he knew that this wasn't an ideal moment, but there was no alternative. He then told us that he was planning to sell the club. It was a complete bombshell.'

'Not to everyone, Mrs Black. Some people had suspected that something of this nature was in the offing.'

She was beginning to dislike the man and his cool, almost pedantic, persistence. 'And in that "some people" you include my husband, I presume. Well then, let me tell you that it was a bombshell to me. I know now that Robbie knew that accountants had been in the place examining the books and that he was worried about something like this. But he hadn't told me anything about that before Saturday.'

'And why was that, do you think? Wouldn't you have expected him to say something about it?'

'That's between us. It has nothing to do with this death.'

'I'm sorry to probe into areas which would normally remain private, but murder is a crime which removes the normal barriers. It may well be irrelevant to this crime, but you must let us be the judges of that.'

'Very well, though I still can't see why it should be of interest to you. Robbie was aware that there was interest in the club from an outside source. He was even worried about it, as you would expect. But often such interest comes to nothing, particularly when it is a smaller club like Brunton Rovers which is involved. He wasn't expecting events to move on at anything like the speed they did. And he didn't tell me because he knew it would upset me. He knows I've grown very attached to this house and this area. I love the people here and the life we're building up among them. Robbie thought – and I'm sure he hoped – that it would all come to nothing and that he and I and the children would carry on as before.'

'Thank you. I can accept that the news was as you say a bombshell to the majority of the people in the hospitality suite at Grafton Park on Saturday night. Did anyone seem more shaken, perhaps more outraged, than anyone else?'

It was an opportunity, almost an invitation from him, to throw suspicion on to someone else other than her and Robbie, and she was tempted by it. But she was wary of this man now, wary of the pretty woman beside him on the sofa, who sat so quietly in her house and made detailed notes of her replies. They would have listened to others as well as her; she must take care not to contradict the story others had told of these feverish minutes two days earlier. 'If there was anyone like that, I was too excited myself to notice it. Old Mr Lanchester spoke up. You'd expect that: he's a good man, Mr Lanchester. He used to be chairman of Brunton Rovers himself, a long time ago.'

Peach smiled. 'Before even my time, Mrs Black. And I've supported them since I was eight.'

'The more you see of old Mr Lanchester, the more you admire him. He's not afraid of anyone. He stood up to Jim Capstick immediately.'

'Perhaps he had less to lose than others.'

Debbie Black paused, thinking furiously, wondering why he raised this. He was interested in how she saw other people in relation to Capstick, perhaps. That meant that he would be sounding other people about how they felt about her, about whether her feelings were strong enough for her to be a candidate for murder. They would be asking them about Robbie and how he had felt. Peach had already spoken to Robbie this morning: she wished now that she had asked for a more complete account of that meeting when he had rung her at lunch time. The thought of this emotionless man and his team going coolly about the business of undermining her life here was a chilling one.

Defending a man she had always liked seemed in these circumstances the safest option. 'It's true that Edward Lanchester has on the face of it less to lose than others. But he's seventy-five: the easiest option for him would have been to sit back and say nothing – perhaps to tell us later and more privately just what he thought of Jim Capstick. But Edward's a man of greater integrity than that. Perhaps it was because he knew that others had more to lose that he was the first one to speak up and voice what most of us were thinking.'

'Which was what?'

'Well, I think Capstick had said that it was in his own interests and that of the club to sell out now. As far as I can remember, Edward said that it might well be in Capstick's interests, but he very much doubted whether it was in the club's interests to sell out to people in the Middle East.'

Peach nodded. 'I believe you also spoke up yourself.'

She tried not to be disconcerted by how much he already knew about this. It was a reminder to her to be careful not to embroider what she said – it was possible, indeed, that he intended it as that. 'Yes. I remember being surprised to find myself speaking. I think it was the fact that Edward had been so forthright that encouraged me to say what I thought. And others too, I should think. I said that it wasn't like an ordinary business deal, that when Brunton Rovers changed hands, the whole town was involved.'

'And how did Mr Capstick react to that?'

She hesitated, trying to think of the best word. 'He was truculent. He said he saw no reason to do anything except make the best possible deal for himself. I think once he'd made the initial announcement, he quite enjoyed himself.'

'That seems a little odd, doesn't it? Wouldn't it have been more natural to take the view that he had to take what he saw as a good offer, but he regretted that it should be neces-sary to do that?'

Debbie Black's broad, attractive mouth set into a grim line. 'You didn't know Jim Capstick.'

'No, we didn't. As I pointed out earlier, we have to get to know him through the descriptions of people like you who did.'

'He enjoyed power. He enjoyed other people being power-less. When Capstick felt he was in control, he loved it.

He liked to rub other people's noses in the knowledge that he and not they controlled their destiny.' She felt the passion of her dislike for the man surging into her words, but at this moment she didn't care about that.

Peach studied her without embarrassment for a moment. 'You seem very confident about this assessment, Mrs Black. You couldn't have known Mr Capstick very well, surely?'

'Well enough. You're right of course – I don't suppose I met him more than half a dozen times, and always with a group of other people. But I'm telling you how he was on Saturday night and the sort of man he was. I've met a few like him, in the past.'

'I expect you have, yes. Do you think other people who were in the hospitality suite on Saturday would agree with your assessment?'

'Yes. They might not have seen him exulting in his power as clearly as I did, but I don't think anyone liked his manner – probably not even his wife.' She added the last thought as if it had only just struck her.

'Did other people support what you had said?'

She suspected that he already knew that they had, that he was testing her. 'Darren Pearson pointed out that Capstick was happy enough to invoke the people of Brunton, to pretend that they mattered to him, when he wanted their money at the turnstiles and their bums on his seats. My Robbie said that in his view the new owners wouldn't be football men, with any sense of the history of the club and this area.'

'And what was Mr Capstick's reaction to those views?'

'I've told you. He didn't bother to reply. He didn't bother to disguise the fact that any considerations other than money meant nothing to him. In fact, he rather enjoyed asserting just that to all of us. That's what I meant when I said he was a man who enjoyed power. It brought out the bully in him. He warned Darren Pearson that he wouldn't be able to recommend him as chief executive to the new owners if he didn't toe the line. I expect he'd have said as much to Robbie, if he'd persisted with his protest.'

Peach watched Blake scribbling furiously. Only when she

stopped did he say to Debbie Black, 'You've given most people you mention a motive for killing James Capstick. Which of you do you think it was who choked the life out of him in the hour which followed?'

She gave a little gasp at the directness of it, but was otherwise not visibly shaken. It was what she had expected, she told herself. She resisted the temptation to say waspishly that it was their business and not hers to answer that: this was not a man to antagonize with glib rejoinders. 'I don't know. It might not have been someone who spoke. Capstick was a man who almost invited people to become his enemies: you could see that from the way he handled this announcement of the takeover which was going to affect all our lives. Someone might have had quite other reasons to kill him than the change of ownership of Brunton Rovers. Saturday night would have provided him or her with a wonderful opportunity.'

Unexpectedly, Peach smiled at her. 'Perhaps you should have become a detective when you gave up tennis, Mrs Black. One of the things we have to remind ourselves of constantly is that there might be other explanations as well as the obvious ones. Do you know of anyone with a personal grudge against the deceased of the kind you suggest?'

'No. But I'm sure the extensive research you are no doubt conducting will throw up some possibilities.'

'Are you, indeed? What time did you leave the hospitality suite, Mrs Black?'

She was studiously unruffled and unhurried. 'I can't be precise. I didn't know it mattered at the time. We discussed the news among ourselves after Capstick had left us to it. Everyone was pretty excited. I should think it was about twenty minutes after Capstick went up to his office – if that is indeed what he did.'

'Did you leave alone?'

'Yes. My au pair had arranged to take the children home and get them to bed, so I wasn't tied to any particular time, because I knew beforehand that I would be required in the hospitality suite after the game to help entertain our visitors. I went out to the reserved car park to get my car at around half past seven, I should think. But it may have been earlier or later, I couldn't be sure.'

'Did anyone see you leave?'

Again she gave thought to a question which could have provided her with a valuable witness before she said, 'Not that I'm aware of, no. But I know that I was home by eight, because I went to see the children in bed. I didn't leave the house again.'

'I now have to ask you again whether you have any idea who killed James Capstick.'

She smiled her acknowledgement that the interview was coming to an end, that she thought she had handled it well enough. 'Beyond the fact that it wasn't me, I've no idea, Detective Chief Inspector Peach.'

SEVENTEEN

The day had clouded over. The first spots of rain pimpled the big window on the turn of the stairs as Peach climbed the staircase to Thomas Bulstrode Tucker's penthouse office at Brunton police station. The low cloud had already shut out the line of the hills and left only an ever-diminishing view of the grimy roofs of the old cotton town. A suitable obfuscation for a Tucker exchange, in Percy's not altogether unbiased view.

'It's taken you a long time to come and report to me,' said Tommy Bloody Tucker tetchily.

'On the contrary, I took the first opportunity to apprise you of the case yesterday,' his DCI pointed out firmly.

'In an attempt to ruin my weekend relaxation!' said Tucker unreasonably.

'Your golf seemed to be doing that quite effectively without my contribution,' said Peach thoughtfully. 'Golf seems to be that sort of game, don't you think, sir? You set out to unwind and find yourself knotted up with frustration in no time. Still, I'm quite new to it. I haven't yet acquired your philosophical acceptance of misfortune and formidable powers of self-control.'

'What is it you're here to say, Peach? I'm far too busy to waste my time with your fripperies.'

Peach reviewed the square metres of empty desk in front of his chief. 'I thought you said you were impatient for my report, sir. Well, the good news is that we've already interviewed the victim's wife, his chief executive at Brunton Rovers FC, his football manager, and his football manager's wife. None of them appear very enthusiastic about the late James Capstick – not even his wife, in my view.'

'Very interesting, I'm sure,' said Tucker with all the sarcasm he could muster. 'Are you now going to tell me who killed him?'

Peach smiled benignly, not at all put out: chief superintend-
ents, his expression said, must be allowed these harmless
sallies. 'Afraid not, sir. You wouldn't wish me to leap to conclu-
sions, I'm sure. Your overview would tell you that haste is the
last thing the CID can afford in a high-profile case like this
one.' He brightened as if struck by an original thought. 'I think
you might tell the press officer that enquiries are proceeding
satisfactorily and that the public are co-operating with us, but
that no arrest is imminent.'

Tucker, who had already directed that a statement including
just these anodyne phrases should be issued, glared fiercely
at his acolyte. 'We're under pressure here, Peach. The nationals
and the radio and the television are pressing us, in view of
the high-profile victim. We need a result, and a quick result.'

Peach considered whether he should invite the man to
take direct responsibility for the case he was nominally
directing, the most reliable method of deflating him. Instead,
he said tersely, 'As soon as I've anything tangible to report,
I shall do that, sir. In the meantime, I advise against one of
your media-briefing conferences; it could be a trifle embarrassing with so little to reveal to the jackals. I wish to broach
another and more personal subject with you, sir.'

'Personal?' Tucker did his goldfish impression, as if this
was some exotic foreign word which he could not be
expected to understand.

Percy took a deep breath. 'I'm getting married, sir.'

'Married?' More bemusement.

'Yes, sir. I always thought it was to be a case of "once
bitten, twice shy" in my case – you are no doubt aware that
I had a brief and not altogether happy experience of matrimony many years ago, sir. When I was in my green and
salad days, as the Egyptian queen memorably expressed it.'

'Salad?'

Percy thought that Tucker had now mastered perplexity
and should move on to some other reaction. 'I suppose that
beholding the deep and unbroken contentment which char-
acterizes your own marriage might have had a subconscious
effect upon me, sir.'

The vision of Brunhilde Barbara finally broke through

Tucker's bemusement. Alarm burst suddenly into his florid features. 'Now look here, Peach, I don't know what you're implying, but—'

'So I thought I would take the plunge again into the uncertain seas of commitment, sir. I am to be married at the beginning of May. In view of the fact that it is my second voyage on these perilous seas, we thought a quiet ceremony would be advisable, sir. I hope you will understand that in such circumstances I thought it advisable not to issue an invitation to you and your wonderful wife, sir.'

'No. I mean, you're quite right there, Peach.' The thought of his spouse's Wagnerian rejection of a wedding invitation from Peach induced an uncharacteristic decisiveness in her husband. Barbara Tucker, who had no conception of how completely her husband's reputation depended upon Percy Peach, could not understand why he tolerated the insufferable man. 'Keep the gathering small, as you say. Much the best policy.' Tucker waved a wide arm vaguely at nothing in particular to signify his approval. 'I expect I shall have the opportunity to meet the lady at some future date.'

'Actually, sir, you already know her.'

'Already know her?' Welcome return of goldfish.

'She's a police officer, sir. To be precise, she is Detective Sergeant Blake.'

'Detective Sergeant Blake?'

'A member of your CID team, sir.'

'I am aware who Detective Sergeant Blake is, Peach! Kindly credit me with a little knowledge, will you?' A fact surfaced unexpectedly from the primeval swamp which was Tucker's memory. 'DS Blake is the woman you thought it would be impossible to work with when I assigned her to you.'

Percy smiled in fond recognition of that moment four years earlier. 'Indeed, sir. It shows how far your enlightened attitudes have pervaded your staff, doesn't it? There was I thinking that I'd be unable to work with a woman and you with your wider perceptions saw that you were offering me happiness beyond the realms of detection.' He beamed what he hoped was the appropriate romantic-novel bliss at the corner of Tucker's ceiling. 'Well, I am now able to tell you that your projection of your bedroom happiness with Barbara into other lives has borne fruit, sir.'

The linking of bedroom with Barbara rang loud alarm bells in Tucker's racing brain. He said sternly, 'You shouldn't be working with the woman, Peach, if there's a relationship. Against all the codes of the service, that is.'

After all this time, the bloody idiot is still so out of touch that he didn't know we had a thing going, thought Percy. Tommy Bloody Tucker, top Brunton CID brain. God help us. He said sternly, 'A whirlwind romance has overtaken us, sir. But you are right, as always. At the conclusion of the present Capstick case, DS Blake and I will reluctantly sever our working relationship. And shortly afterwards, we shall be united in holy matrimony.'

'That will be in order.'

'Thank you, sir.'

'Is there anything else. I'm really very busy at the moment.'

Peach surveyed the shiningly vacant desk again. 'No, sir. I shall get back to solving this business at Grafton Park now.'

'Do that, please.' His relief at seeing the back of his DCI was shaken by a belated thought of team management. 'And Peach.'

Percy turned wearily with his hand on the door handle. 'Sir?'

'Do convey my congratulations to the lady in question. To DS Blake. To . . .'

Percy took pity on him. 'It's Lucy, sir.'

'Of course it is, yes. Well, tell her that I hope she will be very happy. Oh, and you, too, of course.'

Tucker shook his head in bewilderment as the door finally closed and he was left alone. Someone wanted to marry Percy Peach – an attractive girl, too, if he'd got the right one. The world got stranger every day.

'Do come in. I've been expecting to speak to you ever since this happened.'

Edward Lanchester took the pair through the high Edwardian hall and into a comfortably furnished sitting room, where the flames of an open fire danced unexpectedly and cheerfully.

'The central heating is perfectly adequate, but I'm of the generation which still likes to see a real fire in the evenings. I can
remember us digging ourselves out of many feet of snow in
1947, though I was still a boy at the grammar school then.
And everything seemed to freeze up in 1963 – that was the
last year in which I remember there being burst pipes all over
the town. I think we'll draw the curtains and shut out the rain
and the miserable evening, shall we?'

Lucy Blake wondered if he talked so much because he
was nervous, like so many of the people they spoke to in
murder enquiries. Within a few minutes, she had settled for
another explanation: like many people who lived alone, the
old man was lonely, whether he realized it or not, and his
reaction to visitors was to talk rather more than was necessary. She said, because some response seemed to be called
for and Peach was still studying their host, 'I like your
curtains. This is a very pleasant room, isn't it?'

'I think it is, though it's probably a little old-fashioned for
your taste. I can't claim any credit for the curtains, or for
anything else in here, for that matter. My wife chose everything. Practically everything in the house was her taste. I
suppose that's the way it was when we were young, the man
was the breadwinner and the woman made the home. Eleanor
died two years ago.'

'You must miss her very much.'

'I do, I'm afraid.' He thought suddenly of the daughters
he saw so rarely, of the sympathy and support they might
have offered him if they'd been closer. It was pathetic that
he should be so grateful for such a small moment of warmth
from this pretty young woman with the dark red hair, who
had never known Eleanor. 'But I'm forgetting my manners.
Can I offer you some sort of refreshment?'

'No need for that, sir. But thank you for the thought.'
Peach had been studying Lanchester, as his junior had
expected. But Lucy Blake had missed noticing the thing
which had really kept him silent: Percy had for a totally
uncharacteristic moment been in awe of someone. Edward
Lanchester had only just ceased to be the chairman of
Brunton Rovers when the diminutive Denis Charles Scott

Peach had begun supporting them as a small boy. Such a figure surely merited a moment of respect, even from the grown man who was now the senior policeman Percy Peach.

Only a moment, though: Percy hastily reasserted his professional persona. 'We need to speak to you about the murder of James Capstick.'

Lanchester nodded his smiling acceptance of that. 'As I say, I've been expecting you ever since the news broke yesterday.'

'We've already spoken to a number of other people, sir. We haven't been idle.'

'Oh, I wasn't implying anything like that. But I expect I shall now be a disappointment to you. I don't suppose I shall be able to add anything useful to what you already know about the events of Saturday night.'

'We speak to everyone who was close to the incident. It's part of the routine of a murder enquiry.' Peach found himself unusually ill at ease in the presence of this alert and well-groomed elderly man. It could only be because of Lanchester's eminence at the football club during his formative years, he decided. He determined to assert himself. 'You didn't like James Capstick, did you?'

The white-haired man was not at all put out by the abruptness of this. He'd always liked men who came straight to the point, who didn't defer to his real or imagined eminence. 'I don't think many people liked James Capstick, Chief Inspector. I expect you've already discovered that. But to answer your question, no, I didn't like him at all. He was a necessary evil, in the modern football world, but that did not mean I had to like him.'

'A necessary evil?'

Lanchester sighed. 'You can't run a Premiership football club, especially in a small town like Brunton, without having a lot of money behind you. Not nowadays. I chaired the club for many years, and I hope ran it prudently and efficiently. That was what was expected of a chairman in the sixties and seventies. Nowadays, unless the club is a public company, the chairman usually owns it and is expected to finance it. Jim Capstick had a lot of business interests and a lot of money.'

'So he was necessary. But you called him a necessary evil.'

Lanchester considered his reply. He was used to being cautious, after many years of being badgered by journalists. But this was a different and more serious situation. 'Capstick was involved in some pretty dubious enterprises and had some very dubious associates: I know enough about the way he made his money to say that. I suspect the police in the Midlands know more than I do, though there have never been any criminal proceedings against him.'

'Reliable evidence to mount a case is hard to come by, when people are in a position to threaten witnesses and many of the people involved have criminal records themselves.' Peach had spent an hour on the phone and the police computers himself, enlarging his knowledge of James Capstick.

'He wasn't the man I wanted to see buying Brunton Rovers three years ago. But there weren't many other candidates. To be frank, there weren't any. But when I said that I regarded him as a necessary evil, I meant that I was never convinced that he had the interests of the club at heart. I felt that he was at best an asset-stripper – that he'd sell what property and what playing assets we have and leave the club in a sorry state. I stayed on the board in the hope that I could prevent that, but I was well aware that I was pretty well powerless. The most I could do was to expose any of his moves for exactly what they were rather than allow him to put the gloss he wanted on them. I would have done that in this case, but I couldn't have prevented the sale of the club.'

'Do you think this deal will still go through?'

Lanchester shrugged his well-suited shoulders. 'Who knows? The radio suggested at lunch time that the sheikh who was planning to buy the club is no longer interested. We shall see.'

'Tell us exactly what happened on Saturday night, please.'

Edward wrenched himself away from his contemplation of the future of his beloved Rovers. 'We were all full of excitement at the victory over Liverpool. I can remember the fifties, when they were in the old second division with us and we were more or less equals. Those were the days! But a victory over one of the top teams now is a bigger and rarer event than ever it was then, so we were all very excited and happy. Until Capstick breezed in and told us he was selling the club!'

'I can see what a damper that must have put on things. I understand that you were the first person to react to it.'

'I expect I was, yes. I suppose I usually spoke up first when someone had to oppose Capstick, if you want the truth. But then I had less to lose than most other people who were around, hadn't I? He could always chuck me off the board, if I went too far, but he wanted me there, as a representative of the town and the old days. And I suppose I had a certain respectability, didn't I? I suspect that men like Jim Capstick crave respectability, in spite of themselves.'

'You're probably right. And he probably expected you to oppose him. Did you offer him any sort of threat?'

Edward Lanchester smiled. 'I'm sorry. I don't mean to treat this lightly – a man has died, after all, even if he is a man I couldn't respect. It's just that the idea of me threatening a man like Capstick is slightly ludicrous, you see. I'm sure I'd have threatened him with whatever I could which was legal, but I had no weapons at my disposal. Capstick held all the cards: he owned the club and could do with it as he thought fit. He took a great delight in telling me just that in front of the assembled company.' A little tic of pain twitched his cheek, and they had a glimpse of the proud man he had been and perhaps still was.

'Wasn't Mr Capstick at all apologetic about his news?'

'Capstick wasn't an apologetic man. Arrogance was more his forte. He said he was sorry to have to interrupt the merry-making with his news. That much was probably true. But once he'd announced the takeover, he positively enjoyed emphasizing the fact that there was nothing any of us could do about it, that the decision was his and his alone. He was one of those men who liked to assert his power openly rather than go quietly about things.'

Peach looked at him steadily for a moment. 'There was something you could do and one of you probably did. You could remove him from the scene. That might stop this deal going through.'

Lanchester smiled ruefully. 'As I said, the media, and especially our wonderful sporting press, are speculating that this might already have happened. The mysterious sheikh has apparently reserved his position. I suppose there is some chance that whoever inherits James Capstick's assets – Helen Capstick, I presume – will not be as enthusiastic to dispose of the club as he was. There has even been a local report in the *Evening Telegraph* that I will be asked to take over the chairmanship. I wouldn't do that, even on a temporary basis. My time has gone.'

Peach waited for a moment to see if he would elaborate on this, but the silver-haired man said nothing more. The DCI asked quietly, 'Who do you think killed James Capstick, Mr Lanchester?'

Another smile. Edward was not shaken by a question he had anticipated, which also signified to him that the interview was almost over. 'I don't know. I'd tell you if I did, despite the feelings about him that I've just expressed to you. If this were crime fiction, I suppose I'd be yelling hysterically that I don't know and I wouldn't tell you if I did. But this is real life, and the law must be upheld.'

It was Peach's turn to smile. 'So in real life, you probably think some of the people in that room on Saturday night are more likely candidates for murder than others.'

'No. I've thought about it over the last forty-eight hours, of course, but I really have no idea. Our chief executive and our manager had been told they were likely to lose their jobs. I noticed that Debbie Black was also very animated at the time. I scarcely know Helen Capstick, but for all I know, she might have other and more personal reasons to be rid of her husband. I presume she will be a very rich woman as a result of this death. But speculation is useless, because I find it impossible to suspect any of these people of killing anyone. I don't envy you your task, Detective Chief Inspector.' He paused, and this time his smile was ironic. 'I suppose that even an ageing ex-chairman who sees his beloved club being destroyed might be a candidate for you.'

'Indeed. When did you leave the club on Saturday night?'

Lanchester looked as if he was enjoying playing out this

little charade. 'I suppose it would be about an hour after Capstick said he was going up to his office. I can remember that when he left I immediately sat down in the corner of the room. I suppose I must have been more shaken by the news than I'd cared to show to Jim Capstick. I appreciate that it would simplify your task if I could tell you that I'd garrotted the man in his office before leaving, but I cannot do that.'

'Did anyone see you leave?'

'One of our stewards had been locking all the doors in the players' section. Harry's been around for years – he must be as old as I am. I said good night to him. I then drove here and didn't go out again, but there are no witnesses to that.'

His sad face gave a glimpse of his loneliness. Peach nodded. 'You know this club better than anyone, Mr Lanchester. If anything occurs to you which might be even marginally relevant, please ring the CID section at Brunton immediately.'

At nine o'clock, the drizzle had set in for the night. Darren Pearson's windscreen wipers flapped steadily as he drove to his wife's flat. There were pools of water now in the gutters; in one stretch in the lower part of the town, a drain was clogged and the water stretched dark and sinister across the road, so that cars waited cautiously to crawl along the middle in low gear.

He sat in the Vectra for a moment before he went into the block of flats, but as usual the thoughts which he found so easy to marshal in a working context refused to be forced into a logical sequence when he was beset by emotions. By the time he knocked tremulously on the plain wooden modern door, he was not even sure that he was doing the right thing, whereas he had been quite certain that he was before he set out.

Margaret Pearson must have divined his confusion from his face. She made him accept the offer of tea and sit in the big armchair she had brought to the flat from their old home. She set a beaker he had not seen before in front of him and said, 'Everyone's talking about that death at Grafton Park. You must have had a busy day.'

He smiled weakly, his face grey and drained. 'It was murder, Meg.'

'I guessed that. "Suspicious death", the police said. They don't give much away, do they?'

'I don't think they know much, yet. But you're right, they wouldn't tell us if they did. I've been trying to calm everyone down and carry on as if nothing has happened, but it isn't easy. All anyone wants to talk about is Capstick's murder.'

'Well, that's natural enough, I suppose. But I can see it must make things difficult for you.'

He smiled at her, grateful for even this conventional, meaningless sympathy. 'It complicates things, being a murder suspect yourself. You wonder all the time what other people are saying about you when you're not there.'

'But surely the police can't think you had anything to do with it?'

Her surprise and concern were genuine and instinctive, and again he was ridiculously pleased. 'It isn't just me, Meg. It's everyone who was in the hospitality suite on Saturday night when Capstick announced he was selling the club. Well, all those who stood to be losers by it, anyway.'

'I've never been close to a murder enquiry – never even had to think about it.'

'It's an odd feeling. You can't believe that it's really happening to you. And according to the papers today, the takeover might now be off. I might keep my job, as a result of this killing.'

Both of them were silent for a moment. Then she found herself voicing the thought she had told herself she would not raise. 'How are you getting on otherwise?'

He gave her an acrid smile. She wouldn't even name his vice openly, as if the very word might bring its own curse with it. At one time he would have lied to her. He had determined before he came here that he would lie to her no more. 'I'm fighting the urge to bet. Gamblers Anonymous are a great help.'

'Fighting but not winning?' She had been over this ground too often to deceive herself.

'I went back to my old betting shop last week. They refused

to take the bet.' When they had lived together, he would never have admitted either the visit or the refusal. Now he was ashamed, but the confession brought also a kind of relief.

'Because of the debt you're in. Because of what you already owe them.'

'Yes. They rendered me a sort of service didn't they? It didn't feel like it at the time – all I felt was humiliation.' He stared straight ahead of him, not daring to look at her. 'It's the only time I've lapsed, Meg. And they protected me from myself. I told them all about it at Gamblers Anonymous. We're a strange, disparate bunch there, but we help each other. Their support is a strength to me. You said it would be.'

'I didn't know that. I just knew that you needed every ounce of support you could get.'

'Yes. I need you, Meg. I need your support, if I'm to beat this.'

There was a long pause, with neither of them looking at the other. Then she said bleakly, 'I've heard that too often before, Darren.'

'I know. This time it's true, but how can I expect you to believe that?' He turned suddenly to her, his face frighteningly close, so that she could see the deepening lines round his mouth, the desperation in his grey, haunted eyes. 'I need you to come back home, Meg. I can beat it, with you to help me.'

'I've been making a life of my own here, a new life.' It didn't sound convincing, even to her.

'There's no one else though. No other man who really matters.'

'There isn't, but that doesn't mean that you can presume—'

'I'm not presuming anything, Meg. I'm asking. Pleading, if I'm honest. I can beat the gambling this time, but only if I have you to help me.'

'That's blackmail.' But she knew as she said it that it was but a ritual protest.

'Maybe it is. I didn't mean it to be that. But I know that it's true.'

'You're saying that the rest of your life is in my hands. That's not fair, Darren.'

'I've gone beyond what's fair, Meg. But I do know what's true. I know that if I have you to help me I can do it. I've learned my lesson at last, but I need you at my side to win this war.'

He wanted to say more, but he sensed he shouldn't. He could feel their two wills wrestling with each other, almost as if it were a physical contest. Eventually she said, 'The rent on this place is paid in advance until the end of May,' and they both knew in that moment that she was going to give in. 'I'm reserving the right to come back here at any time in the next few weeks, if you let me down.'

'And so you should. But I won't let you down.' He took her into his arms and kissed her, softly but at great length. 'When will you come, Meg?'

'No point in delay, once we've made a decision, is there? Tomorrow. When I've stopped the milk and the papers.'

Both of them smiled at this sudden descent from high emotion into practicality. He could think of nothing to say, so he said, 'The neighbours will be glad to see you back,' and both of them smiled at the welcome banality of it. He was at once overjoyed and suddenly exhausted, and he left shortly afterwards.

Meg Pearson sat for a long time after he had left, staring at the blank and silent screen of the television. She would have expected a turmoil of emotions, but she felt instead quite numb. She had no idea whether she was right to accept Darren's assurances of reform, when he had let her down so many times in the past.

At the back of her mind, subdued but insistent, was the thought that she might just have agreed to move back into the house of a murderer.

EIGHTEEN

'I want to make it clear that I'm here under protest.' The chauffeur of the late James Capstick sat bolt upright on the hard interview room chair and spoke the words they had heard so often before.

DCI Peach smiled the wide smile of a shark presented with an easy meal. 'On the contrary, Mr Boyd, you are here in a voluntary capacity. You came willingly into the station to help the police with their enquiries into a serious crime, as every good citizen would wish to do.'

'I said that I was willing to talk to you. I didn't say that I expected to be shut in an interview room with you and another policeman and treated as a criminal.' Wally Boyd glared without effect first at the amused face of Peach and then at the totally unamused and unflinching ebony features of Clyde Northcott.

Peach shrugged his broad shoulders with elaborate incomprehension. 'You agreed that it would not be a good idea from your point of view to interview you in your flat in the Capstick mansion. Indeed, I think that notion came from you. Once you had agreed to come into the station, an interview room was the only suitable place for us to talk. It offers a proper privacy for what you have to say to us.' He looked round the small, windowless cube of a room with as much approval as Wally Boyd had accorded it dislike.

'I don't like these places.'

'You have previous experience of them, then?' Peach's eyebrows lifted elaborately towards the baldness above them.

'You bloody know I have.'

'Ah! Thank you for respecting our attention to detail, Mr Boyd. Not everyone is so complimentary about our efficiency.'

'You know about my past.'

'We know about some of it, don't we, DC Northcott? The

criminal bits, to be precise. The rest of your life isn't our business, unless you choose to enlighten us with interesting snippets of it.'

'I know the way you people operate.'

'Really? Well, that's gratifying. It means I don't need to remind you that you are not under oath and that you are giving us willing assistance with our investigation into a serious crime – the most serious of all, indeed. Your familiarity with our methods also ensures that it won't surprise you if I suggest that this conversation be recorded. It's surprising how often people remember things differently, we find.' Peach gave him another beam as he switched on the cassette recorder and announced to it that Mr Walter Boyd was being interviewed by Detective Chief Inspector Peach and Detective Constable Northcott and that the interview was beginning at nine forty on the morning of Tuesday the seventh of April.

Wally Boyd felt even more uneasy. This was the procedure which had preceded charges against him in the past. Surely they couldn't suspect him of murder? He said a little desperately, 'Mr Capstick was a good employer to me. Why would I want him dead?'

'No one here has suggested that you might, as far as I am aware, Mr Boyd. Have you heard anyone accusing this gentleman of murder, DC Northcott?'

Clyde hadn't worked with Percy for two years without learning his role in turning the screw. 'No, sir. Not yet. I'm keeping an entirely open mind on the matter.'

'As you should, DC Northcott, as you should. I don't want any of that old police business of "once a villain always a villain" on my patch. Innocent until proved guilty, people should be, in my view. Just because Mr Boyd was proved guilty once, we shouldn't hold it against him now.'

Boyd attempted desperately to interrupt this bizarre double act. 'I was never guilty of anything like murder.'

'And you aren't now, Mr Boyd, I'm sure. Well, not absolutely sure, perhaps. I have to keep an open mind, as DC Northcott has just reminded me.'

'Bit of violence, that's all it was!' grumbled Wally Boyd, as much to himself as to his tormentors.

'Grievous Bodily Harm, I believe,' said Peach with a cheerful smile. 'And violence often escalates into greater violence, the psychologists and the sociologists tell us. And you know how we policemen love psychologists and sociologists.'

'I was nowhere near the scene of this killing!'

Peach decided by the desperation in the tone that his man was now thoroughly unnerved and unlikely to conceal anything. 'Let's presume that's correct, for the moment, shall we? Tell us who you think killed the man who employed you.'

'I don't know, do I?' Boyd abandoned his indignation as if taking off a garment. He stared at the scratched table between them and said sullenly, 'It could have been his wife.'

'It could, couldn't it? She certainly had the opportunity. And now you're about to give us the motive.'

Wally Boyd glared at the cheerful, expectant face which was within three feet of his and watching him intently. He had a fair experience of policemen over the years, but this one seemed already to know far too much about him, about even the way he thought. 'I'm not saying she did it. I–I don't much like the woman, that's all.'

'Which you think is ample reason for you to accuse her of murder. I expect you'll be looking for new employment very soon now, won't you?' As Boyd flashed him a look of hatred, Peach's tone hardened. 'Let's have it, Mr Boyd. Let's have the information we all know you want us to have.'

'I'm not accusing her of murder. I'm telling you things you might not know, that's all. Things she might not have told you. It's up to you to decide whether they've anything to do with this killing.' His voice rose as he made the protest which even surprised himself. 'Mr Capstick was a good employer to me. Treated me fair and looked after me well. I want you to get his killer, whoever it might be!'

Clyde Northcott leaned forward, his spare, uncompromising features even nearer to his man. 'So tell us all about Helen Capstick, Mr Boyd.'

'She was cheating on him. She's got another man, I'm sure of that.'

Peach was deliberately low-key now, almost casual. 'How sure, Wally?'

'I can't give you a name and address. I can get you a phone number.'

'In Brunton, is he?'

'No. Greater Manchester, somewhere. I've checked the mileage on her car, and it tallies.'

'Proper little detective, aren't you? Among your other duties.'

'My loyalty was to Mr Capstick. It was my duty to find these things out. If she was playing away when he wasn't at home, he'd have wanted to know, wouldn't he?'

'I think he very probably would, yes. So did you tell him?'

'No. I–I didn't know for certain, did I? I think he suspected something was going on, But I wanted to be sure of my facts before I went upsetting Mr Capstick.'

'You mean you saw the possibility of blackmail, of getting a hold over Mrs Capstick. Well, knowledge is power, isn't it, Wally? Francis Bacon said that four hundred years ago. A man with whom I'm sure you have much in common.'

Clyde Northcott was almost as unnerved by the mention of Bacon as Boyd. Not for the first time, he wondered exactly what Percy Peach's background before the police service might be. Francis Bacon was not a common figure in police canteen discussions. He took refuge in an even more menacing attitude to the burly man on the other side of the table. 'James Capstick had some very dubious business associates and some very nasty enemies, Mr Boyd. And you were his bodyguard as well as his chauffeur. Do you think any of them might have done this?'

'No. People like that would have used a contract killer. I don't see how one could have got in there, with all those people around. Anyway, they wouldn't have done it there, on his own patch. And they'd more than likely have used bullets.'

Peach gave him the beam he found even more unnerving than the black man's glower. 'You've plainly given the matter some thought, Mr Boyd. For which we thank you. How much more do you know about Helen Capstick?'

'Nothing. I know what I've given you's a bit vague. I just thought you should know.'

'You mean that you don't like her and she doesn't trust you. That you thought you'd get your retaliation in first by dishing the dirt to us. Well, in the circumstances, we have to welcome that. Don't tell her you've spoken to us. Let us follow it up. We don't reveal our sources, so there's no reason why she should know this has come from you. In return, if you have any further thoughts or any further interesting discoveries, you should contact me immediately.

He offered Boyd a card, but the man said, 'I don't want to carry that, DCI Peach, in the circles I move in. I shan't forget the name and I know the number.'

Tucker was on the phone. He waved a hand towards the chair in front of his desk in an appropriately tycoon gesture and Percy Peach sat down carefully upon it.

'I'm very busy, as you can see and hear,' said Thomas Bulstrode Tucker grandly as he set down the phone. He opened his diary, stared at it with a frown for a moment, then shut it and put it back in front of the ornamental inkstand. 'This had better not take too long.'

'It needn't do that, sir,' Peach assured him modestly. 'I just want to plant a thought and let it fester.' He wondered for a moment whether that was the right process for Tucker's brain, then shrugged and went on. 'We shall need a new Detective Sergeant to replace DS Blake when she moves out of my team, sir.'

'DS Blake?'

'Lucy Blake, sir. The woman I am planning to marry.'

'Ah! I wish you would always make yourself so clear, Peach. I have many other concerns, you know.' His gesture with his hand towards the window of his penthouse office presumably indicated the wide world outside and all the criminal dangers it contained. 'I don't suppose there is anyone we could promote from within?'

Tommy Bloody Tucker always went for the easiest solution. Peach had relied upon that. 'I believe there is, sir. There are several candidates, in fact.' He watched panic suffuse his chief's

face as his ignorance of the officers who served him flooded
into his brain. 'I am prepared to make a recommendation,
if you wish it.'

Tucker tried not to sound too eager. 'Any recommendation you care to make would be subjected to a rigorous
examination from me, of course.'

'Goes without saying, that, sir. The candidate, like everything else in our working world, would be subjected to
your rigorous overview, your grasp of the wider criminal
environment in which we all exist. Anyone becoming a
detective sergeant would have the satisfaction of knowing
that his or her credentials had undergone the pitiless survey
of the informed professional expert.'

'Eh? Oh, quite. Well, who is it you wish to recommend?
I haven't got all day.'

'DC Clyde Northcott, sir.'

There was such a long pause that Peach felt sure that he
could hear Tucker's brain ticking. Then the chief superintendent said, 'DC Northcott is black, Peach.'

'Yes, sir. I had noticed that. I work with him quite a lot.'

Even Tommy Bloody Tucker was aware that there were
some prejudices you shouldn't voice. Institutional racialism,
they called it nowadays. He contented himself with a heavy,
'Are you sure about this, Peach?'

'Quite sure, sir. Clyde Northcott is in my view the best
of two or three promising detective constables in my team.
I have no doubt DC Brendan Murphy will become a DS in
due course, but in my view Northcott has the strongest
present claim.' He waited for Tucker to bridle at Murphy's
Irish name, but mercifully it passed him by. 'It would do
us a bit of good with the ethnic lobby, don't you think?'

Tucker brightened for a moment: you had to pay lip
service to these modern trends, whenever you could. Then
his noble brow clouded visibly. 'He was a drug-dealer,
Peach. You seem to have forgotten that.'

Peach sighed the patient sigh of the teacher of slow
learners. Perhaps it was the lobby for slow learners which
had secured Tucker his CID promotions. 'I haven't forgotten
it, sir. He was also a murder suspect: that is how our paths

crossed in the first instance. But he was guiltless, sir. Just as he has long since dispensed with any connection with the illegal drugs industry. DC Northcott still rides a powerful motorbike in his leisure hours, sir, in case you wish to take that into account.'

Peach thought he could forecast most of Tommy Bloody Tucker's reactions by now. But even he was surprised when his leader said, 'I think I may discuss this with my wife, Peach. Get an outside view.' Then catching his junior's surprise and hastening to appease him, he added, 'Barbara will be glad it isn't another woman.'

Even Peach was astonished by this new evidence of Tucker's unpredictability. He said weakly, 'Mrs Tucker isn't a feminist, then? Believes that the woman's place is in the home, with the man taking all decisions?'

'Well, no.' Not for the first time, the director of Brunton's CID section was struck by the contrast between Barbara's insistence upon total female domination in domestic affairs and her reactionary attitude to everything else in life. 'I'd just like to run the idea of promotion for a black officer within my team past her, that's all. Get the outside view.'

'There are issues of confidentiality here, sir.'

'Quite. You don't need to remind me of such things, Peach,' said Tucker huffily. 'I shall take your views into account when making my recommendation.'

'Thank you, sir. I'm sure you will. It wouldn't do to be seen as being in any way prejudiced against a coloured officer, would it?'

'Indeed it wouldn't, Peach! I'm glad to see that you are for once aware of modern trends in police work.'

As usual, this negative argument thrust home with Tommy Bloody Tucker much more easily than the positive ones. Peach went back down the stairs confident that Clyde Northcott's promotion was almost in the bag.

The window was open in Wally Boyd's flat above the big triple garage when Peach and Blake drove up the drive of the complex of modern buildings which the late James Capstick had owned. The dead man's chauffeur and minder was probably well aware of their arrival, but they saw nothing of him.

Helen Capstick let them into the big house herself. The polished bronze hair was perfectly in place; the hard blue eyes studied her visitors carefully; the smile was careful, formal, with no real hint of welcome. There was no means of telling whether she knew that Wally Boyd had been to see them, whether she suspected that they had come here with more information than when they visited her two days earlier. She said merely, 'You come exactly at three thirty, as we arranged. I've always found that it is busy people who seem to be most punctual.'

Tea and what appeared to be home-made biscuits were laid out on the long low table in the lounge. As they sank back into the soft leather of the sofa, she poured tea from the silver teapot, her hand perfectly steady. Lucy Blake produced her notebook whilst Peach let a short silence develop, waiting for any hint of nervousness from Helen Capstick, who seemed determined to act the part of hostess on this bright spring afternoon. There was something ludicrous in the cameo, with a woman who must know she was a murder suspect behaving as if she were in an English comedy of manners.

It was Peach who had to speak first; he was beginning to feel that if he didn't some bright young man in white shorts would appear at the French windows and ask if there was anyone for tennis. He said, 'We now know considerably more than when we spoke to you on Sunday, Mrs Capstick.'

She offered him a biscuit and said brightly, 'I would expect that. I am grateful for your efforts. Are you near to an arrest?'

It was his turn to be lightly amused. 'You would not expect us to answer that if we were. We have a list of people who had the opportunity to commit this crime. A rather longer list than we would wish to have.'

'And a list of motives, no doubt.'

'Motives are not always immediately obvious. We prefer to establish facts first. Several people, including your good self, had the opportunity to climb the steps to your husband's office and kill him. That is fact.'

His briskness did not disconcert her. She said reasonably, 'I can think of motives which are equally factual. All the people who felt their jobs threatened by the sale of Brunton Rovers FC obviously had a motive to be rid of the man who was engineering that sale.'

'Indeed.' Peach finished his biscuit before he said, 'Other motives are less obvious, but perhaps even more powerful. When emotions are aroused, the strongest motive is often a matter of conjecture. But whenever people are less than fully honest with us during a murder investigation, that inevitably interests us.'

Her measured phrases dropped suddenly away from her. Her face hardened and she said, 'You're accusing me of that.'

'I am. I think you should have told us that you were conducting a liaison with another man at the time of this death.'

'It was irrelevant.'

'In that case we shall dismiss it. But we shall need to check it for ourselves before we do that.'

'You've been talking to Wally Boyd.'

'I know it's a cliché, but we don't reveal our sources, Mrs Capstick.'

'That bloody man!' For the first time, her composure was shaken and the blue eyes flashed real anger. Peach didn't envy Boyd's position, but he was no doubt a man used to taking care of himself. 'Boyd's making mischief, nothing more. It's what I'd have expected of him.'

'Mrs Capstick, I take it your husband did not know of this affair.'

For a moment, he thought she would dispute his use of that term. But all she said was a terse, 'No.'

'And what do you think your husband's reaction would have been if he had discovered these meetings of yours?'

'DCI Peach, I'm a woman of forty-seven and my husband was ten years older than me. We'd both been round the block a few times, but we were genuinely fond of each other. So what do you want me to say? Jim wouldn't have been pleased, I'll admit that. All right, he'd have been bloody annoyed.' She paused, her face at once pained and furious. 'This is that man Boyd, isn't it? He has his nose into everything.'

'Perhaps he saw it as his duty to protect his employer's interests, Mrs Capstick.'

'He did that all right. But most men wouldn't have seen spying on their boss's wife as part of their duties.'

Lucy Blake looked up from her record, noting the slightest of nods from Peach. She tried not to be intimidated by this sophisticated woman whose dress and shoes would represent a year's clothing budget for her. She tried not to imagine what Helen Capstick had experienced when she claimed to have 'been round the block a few times'. She said as boldly as she could, 'We have to investigate every avenue in a murder enquiry, Mrs Capstick. Are you a major financial beneficiary as a result of this death?'

Helen resented the woman's youth and looks. DS Blake was not as young as she had thought at first – late twenties, perhaps – but she had that light colouring and lustrous dark red hair which no beautician's art could ever reproduce, and the vigour and openness to experience which the older woman had lost and could never recapture. Helen sighed, more to give herself a moment to frame her reply than in disapproval of the question. 'I imagine that I shall be a major beneficiary of Jim's will, yes.' She gave Blake a humourless smile. 'I am so confident of that that I haven't yet bothered to check the details.'

She watched Blake make a note, and was startled when Peach broke into the silence. 'Your expectations of wealth might have been severely affected if Mr Capstick had learned from Mr Boyd or anyone else that you were being unfaithful to him. You've already admitted as much.'

This time she did not attempt to control her anger and frustration. 'Yes! What the hell do you want me to say? That I walked up the stairs and killed Jim so that he wouldn't disinherit me?'

'It's a possibility we have to consider.'

'Then go away and consider it. I've nothing more to say to you.'

'And no idea of who might have committed this crime you say wasn't down to you?'

'Oh, for God's sake, Peach! Robbie Black or his wife, I should think – they're both capable of it, if you ask me. Or Pearson: he looked pretty sick to me when he heard his job was in danger. Or even old man Lanchester. He never liked Jim and he didn't bother to hide it. You'd better get on with it. You probably know them all better than I do, by now.'

That was correct, thought Peach, as he sat in the passenger seat of the police Mondeo whilst Blake drove it slowly back down the long drive. The gardener on his ride-on mower was giving the first cut to the sweeping north-facing lawn by the drive. The window had shut now in Wally Boyd's flat. He didn't envy the chauffeur his next meeting with the mistress of the house.

NINETEEN

The children were in bed and asleep. The au pair was watching television in her own quarters; the canned laughter from an American sit-com spilled occasionally into the silence which filled the rest of the house. Debbie and Robbie Black had tried to release their tensions through separate sessions in the gym they had built on to the back of the house. At nine o'clock, they were sitting with drinks in their hands and trying to relax.

They talked about the children's school, about Brunton Rovers' prospects in their away match at Newcastle on Saturday, about the children's charity for which Debbie, using her tennis fame and continuing celebrity status, had raised over a million pounds in the last two years. None of these subjects had occupied them for than two or three desultory sentences.

Eventually Debbie said abruptly, 'Did the police speak to you again today?'

'No. There were coppers about, taking statements from cleaners and secretarial staff and even the players. I didn't see that aggressive little chief inspector or the detective sergeant woman who seems to be his sidekick.'

'Are they any nearer to an arrest?'

'I don't know, do I? You'd need to ask them.' He realized he'd spoken sharply, but couldn't think how to put it right, whereas normally contact would have been automatic and unthinking. 'How are your Open University studies going?'

She smiled at his deliberate, clumsy attempt to take them away from the subject which filled their thoughts. 'I got a good grade and some complimentary remarks on that last assignment. I'm considering whether to make Philosophy one of my final options. We've got a good group going and two or three of the others are going to do Philosophy. What do you think?'

Normally Robbie would have made a joke about how little he knew of the subject and they would have had a laugh about it. Now there was silence and she knew he hadn't even registered what she had said about her study choices. It seemed a long time before he said, 'Are they coming to see you again?'

'The police? I don't know. They said they might do, but I don't see the point. There's nothing more I can tell them.'

He nodded and they left it at that. Each of them fell silent, unable to voice the one thought which preoccupied them. What was the possibility, however remote, that you were sharing your bed and your children with a killer?

Darren Pearson put the phone down and stared at it as if it had a baleful power of its own. 'They're coming here,' he said. 'You've only been back in the house for three hours and they're coming here.'

'They don't know that, do they?' said his wife. 'There's no reason why you should tell them that we've been separated, if you don't want to. It's probably better that you don't.'

'They probably know it already. They seem to get to know everything. Maybe I told them last time we spoke. I can't remember.'

'Well, there's no need to tell them anything about us, unless they raise it. But don't lie about it. It wouldn't do to be caught lying.' She was obscurely glad that the CID were visiting him at nine o'clock in the evening. She hadn't been looking forward to the awkward intimacies of a sexual reconciliation, to the preliminary fencing more appropriate to a first night together. Neither of them was much good at negotiating these things. They would have something else to talk about once the police had been. With luck, they would be able to fall into bed together preoccupied with the menace of outside agencies, to resume married life as a welcome afterthought to other, more urgent, external threats.

Darren said suddenly, 'Why are they coming round here at this time of night? What is it that can't wait until the morning?'

'I don't know, do I? Perhaps they want you to be alarmed about their visit in exactly the way you seem to be. I think I've read somewhere that the more time that elapses after a crime, the harder it is to solve. Perhaps they just don't wish to waste any time. You've nothing to hide, have you?'

Darren didn't like her framing that as a question rather than a statement. He grinned bleakly at her and said, 'I'll be better with you here, Meg. I know that much.'

Margaret Pearson said firmly, 'You'll be neither better nor worse, Darren. You'll just be yourself, and that will be enough to satisfy them.'

'I don't want to tell them someone else did this, when I don't think they did.'

That was a strange thing to say, thought Meg Pearson. She glanced at the clock. 'They'll be here in a minute. Just be yourself and let them be the judge of what things mean. Don't try to conceal anything.' She felt that as if she were instructing an inexperienced teenager, not the efficient chief executive of a company with a turnover of millions of pounds. She saw with searing clarity what he had been aware of for many months: the contrast between the public life which was all quiet efficiency and the private life which was on the edge of chaos. She was back where she had been for years, hating the gambling vice which threatened to destroy what had been a good and reliable man.

It was at that moment that they caught the sudden brief blaze of the car's headlamps as it turned into the drive. He squeezed her arm and said, 'I'm glad you're here, Meg!' It was a small, ridiculous gesture of love.

If the CID pair were surprised to see Margaret Pearson here, they gave no sign of it, nodding amiably at her as she opened the front door to them and directed them to the dining room where Darren had said he would talk to them. Peach said briskly to Pearson, 'This shouldn't take too long. There are one or two things we'd like to clear up as quickly as possible.' He shut the door firmly upon the hall and the woman whom Darren saw as his chief means of support.

They sat on each side of the dark surface of the table with the light directly above them, as if about to embark on a game of cards. Peach gave his man the wide smile which suddenly seemed menacing rather than affable. 'We now know considerably more about the people who benefit by this death than when we spoke to you on Sunday, Mr Pearson. Not conclusive stuff, by any means, but very interesting in several cases, including your own.'

Darren licked his lips and tried to answer the smile. 'I can't really think what you could discover about me which pertains to this crime.'

'Can't you? That seems to show a certain lack of imagination.'

Darren gathered his resources and prepared to resist. 'I'm a practical person. Being the chief executive of a Premiership football club calls for hard work and a combination of abilities, like handling figures and dealing with people from a variety of backgrounds. It doesn't need a lot of imagination.'

'I see. Well, DS Blake and I will help you along, then. Perhaps you should put yourself in our position for a moment. Thanks to your prompt action, we are called to the football ground at Grafton Park on Sunday morning to a suspicious death. We quickly establish that this is murder and that it has taken place on the previous evening. Within an hour or two, we know that a gathering of people in the hospitality suite at Brunton Rovers on the previous evening had access to the deceased after he had left the gathering and isolated himself in his office. Agreed so far?'

'Yes. Several people had the opportunity.'

'Indeed they did. And I will take you into my confidence and tell you that so far we have been able to eliminate very few of them. As far as the major suspects go, I'm afraid I would have to say none of them.'

'Major suspects?' Pearson uttered the phrase unwillingly, like a moth drawn to Peach's flickering candle.

'Our major suspects are all people who stood to gain by Capstick's death, whether positively or negatively.' He waited for this phrase to be questioned, but this time the grey eyes were watchful and the mouth in the prematurely lined face remained shut. 'Mrs Capstick is obviously going to be a very rich woman as a result of this death.'

'One presumes so. But it isn't certain, is it? Capstick was
a ruthless man. He was quite capable of cutting Helen out
of his will if he felt that way.'

Peach wondered how much Pearson knew about Helen
Capstick and her relationship with her husband. But he
smiled and said, 'As you would expect, Mrs Capstick is a
major financial gainer by this death. That was confirmed to
us by her husband's solicitor this afternoon. Murder sometimes compels the disclosure of these things. Other people
have more negative gains. Edward Lanchester now has
reason to hope that his beloved Brunton Rovers will not fall
into foreign and insensitive hands.'

'You can't think that Edward Lanchester would do a thing
like this.'

'I may think it unlikely, but at this stage I cannot rule it
out. He cannot prove that he did not climb the stairs to that
room and see off a man that he makes no secret of disliking.'

'You don't kill a man because you dislike him.'

'The sentiment does you credit, Mr Pearson. Let us say
that I have to take into account that dislike can quicken
into hatred when a man's passion is threatened. Let us agree
that Mr Lanchester is an unlikely rather than an impossible
candidate.'

Darren felt himself being drawn into a dangerous game,
whose rules he did not understand. He shook his head, trying
to clear it. 'Your killer won't be Edward.'

Peach was apparently at his most benign. 'Others who
feared the developing situation and who seem much happier
after this death are Robbie Black, your football manager,
and his wife Debbie.' He waited for Pearson to intervene
on their behalf as he had done for Lanchester, but this time
he said nothing. 'Black would in all probability have lost
his job when the new Middle Eastern owners moved in,
wouldn't he?'

'It's not certain, but probable, I suppose. These people
usually like to put in their own people and establish their
control over all aspects of a club.'

'Black's fortunes obviously affect those of his wife
Debbie. Apart from a natural commitment to her husband

and his career, she seems genuinely attached to this area and its people.'

'I've noticed that, yes.' Pearson looked as if he was about to say more, but he checked himself and looked at the table with a series of little nervous nods.

'Which brings us to your own situation, Mr Pearson. Perhaps the most perilous of all.'

Darren hadn't expected anything as head-on as this. He said rather feebly, 'Oh, I'd hardly say that!'

'Wouldn't you? You've just indicated that the new owners would probably have wanted to replace you with their own appointment. If that were to happen, I'd say that a chief executive with a serious gambling problem wouldn't find it easy to obtain a similar post elsewhere.'

In the agonized silence which followed, Lucy Blake concentrated on her notes, whilst Pearson stared aghast at Peach, who returned his stare steadily and unblinkingly, until the man dropped his eyes to the table and said hoarsely, 'My gambling has nothing to do with this murder.'

'That may be so, Mr Pearson, but you can hardly expect us to accept your word on that. I should tell you that we know the state of your personal finances and the amount of your personal debt. Very little can be kept private, once a murder investigation is under way.'

Pearson did not look up from the table as he said in a voice which was barely audible, 'It's under control.'

Peach, who enjoyed bouncing ruffians much more than he enjoyed bouncing men like this, felt suddenly very sorry for Pearson, who seemed from what he had seen to be a model administrator, with consideration for even the humblest of his staff. He was too professional to let the thought affect his probing of the man and his motives. 'Forgive me for saying so, but there is very little evidence that your debt is under control. Your bank has repeatedly requested you to reduce your overdraft, with nil effect.'

'I've joined Gamblers' Anonymous. They're going to be a great support to me, the group there. And Meg's come home. She's going to help me get through this.' He showed his first signs of animation in many minutes with this assertion;

his grey eyes were moist and wide, pleading with them to believe him.

'Let's accept your good intentions, Mr Pearson. At the moment they are no more than that. There is precious little evidence of your reform.'

Darren wanted to say that Meg was evidence, that she'd left him because of his problem, but had now come back to him because she believed in him. Couldn't they see that that was the best evidence of all? He shook his head hopelessly. 'All that I can say is that if you come back in a year you'll find I've beaten this.'

'I see. But in the meantime, do you agree that you wouldn't find it easy to get another job with the same salary if you lost your post at Grafton Park?'

'That is probably so. I haven't given the matter much thought.' That sounded so unlikely that he tried to qualify it. 'The gambling monster has loomed so large for me lately that I've thought only of vanquishing that. I haven't really thought much about losing the post at Grafton Park.'

Lucy Blake, receiving the now familiar little nod from Peach, said quietly, 'Is that because you removed the man who might have ensured your dismissal on Saturday night?'

'No.' He looked aghast at the open, enquiring face beneath the striking chestnut hair. He had almost forgotten her presence in the intensity of his confrontation with Peach. Now the openness and innocence of that face seemed like an invitation to confess and be finished with this. 'I agree that from your point of view it looks bad. I agree that I never particularly took to James Capstick as an employer. I worked for him and he paid me handsomely enough, but I never quite trusted him – I always felt that he was prepared to sell out to the highest bidder, irrespective of what it meant to the club and the town. But I didn't kill him. And I don't really know who did.'

Blake let that last phrase hang in the air between them for a moment. Then she delivered it back to him. 'You say you don't *really* know, Mr Pearson. That implies that you know a little more than you've told us, doesn't it?'

'What I'm telling you is that I didn't kill him. Nothing more.'

The chief inquisitor was back in quickly on this. Peach said with a world-weary air. 'Let's have it, Mr Pearson. It's been a long day for all of us.'

'I saw someone, that's all. It may mean nothing.'

'Indeed? Well, you'd better let us be the judges of that, hadn't you?'

Darren Pearson could not meet the DCI's dark, intense eyes. He stared at the table as he said in a monotone, 'As I went out to my car in the reserved car park, I saw a movement in the street and realized that someone was going back into the building. I was naturally curious to see who it was.'

'So you watched and identified this person. Who was it, Mr Pearson?'

'Debbie Black.'

'You're certain of that?'

'Yes. She was still wearing the boots and the coat she had worn earlier.'

'And did you wait until she came out again?'

'No. I drove away immediately. I'd no reason to do anything else. I didn't know until the next morning that Capstick had been killed, did I?'

'Didn't you, Mr Pearson? Hadn't you already despatched him at this point? And aren't you now desperately trying to offer us other candidates for your murder?'

'No. I'm telling you what I saw.'

'So why didn't you offer us this titbit earlier?'

'I don't know. It didn't seem as important at first as it does now. And I like Debbie Black. She feels the same way that I do about this town and its people. I suppose I didn't want to implicate her. I still don't, but I'm telling you now, aren't I?'

'You are indeed, however belatedly. And for whatever reasons. Please don't leave the area without informing us about your intended movements, Mr Pearson. Good night to you.'

Peach swept out as briskly as he had arrived, leaving DS Blake to take their leave of the man he had questioned. Darren Pearson was immensely relieved that Meg was back, so that he was not left alone with his thoughts.

*   *   *

'Rubenesque,' said Percy Peach dreamily from beneath the bedclothes.

Lucy Blake jumped as if a dart had been shot into her. 'A girl can't even get undressed in peace.'

'Prancing about in your underwear. Trying to get a man over-excited at the end of a long and trying day.'

'I didn't know you were there. I didn't know a man could get undressed and into bed so quickly.'

'It's a talent you develop. Practice makes perfect, as with so many things.'

'And I'm not sure "Rubenesque" is flattering. Didn't his women have big thighs and round bellies?' Lucy inspected the parts in question in the full-length mirror of her wardrobe, prompting a groan of agonized pleasure from her paramour.

'Ample,' Percy offered, when he was again capable of speech. 'Curvaceous. And as for his bottoms, Aaaaaaah!'

His loss of control was occasioned by his bride-to-be's discarding her last garment. As she stepped demurely from her pale blue pants, he forsook all attempts at speech and applauded vigorously, prompting a blush which made Lucy in his view even more pinkly Rubenesque.

Actions spoke louder than words in the ensuing twenty minutes, but Lucy did manage to interject, 'I don't know how you can find so much energy after a twelve-hour day!' which her lover took as a compliment.

When she lay back and gradually resumed her normal rate of breathing, she said reflectively, 'I'll be Mrs Peach in a fortnight, and then you'll lose interest.'

Percy had his eyes closed and his head flat on the pillow. He wore the most blissful and relaxed of his vast range of smiles. 'Rubenesque!' he murmured softly.

Lucy stared at the invisible ceiling. 'I sometimes think it was better in the old days, when people waited until they were married to sleep together for the first time. A wedding must have been more of an occasion then.'

'Pink and rounded and Rubenesque,' muttered Percy in his dream-like haze.

She poked him in the side with the elbow which he claimed was her only sharp contour. 'I'm talking to you,

Percy Peach! Giving you my philosophical ramblings on marriage.'

'I always enjoy rambling with you, my love,' he said dreamily. He suited the action to the words and began unhurried exploration of her stomach with his right hand. Then, to show he had been listening, he said, 'There must have been a lot of fumbling bridegrooms who didn't know quite what to do in those days.'

'And fumbling brides who weren't able to help them out,' said Lucy, arresting his hand at the point of no return with practised ease. 'I don't think we'll have those sorts of problems.'

Percy Peach stirred himself dutifully into action. 'Practice makes perfect, Lucy. Better be on the safe side.'

TWENTY

Edward Lanchester was alert, well-dressed, beautifully shaved. Every hair of the still plentiful white hair on his venerable head was in place. At seventy-five, he was no longer accustomed to conducting meetings at nine o'clock in the morning, but that was no reason to let anyone think that his standards had slipped. He checked his appearance in the hall mirror and decided that Eleanor would have been proud of him. As was now his habit, he addressed a few silent words to his dead wife. Then he opened the door to the CID officers.

Peach was dapper as usual in well-cut grey suit and tie. He was glad of that when he saw Lanchester's elegant blue suit and tie and spotless white shirt. He wouldn't have wanted to let himself down in the presence of a former chairman of Brunton Rovers; the deferences we acquire in childhood are the hardest of all to relinquish. He said, 'Good morning, sir. Thank you for your time. There are just a few things we need to clear up.'

Lanchester led them into the same comfortable sitting room where he had spoken to them on Monday night. There was no fire burning in the grate this morning, but wood and coal were set ready for when one was next required. The curtains which Lucy Blake had admired were open now, revealing a mature, well-tended garden, which dropped away from the window across a lawn to where an early rhododendron was beginning to glow rich red with bloom. A comfortable, slightly old-fashioned house, this, with an occupant who she sensed was desperately lonely beneath his spruce exterior.

She opened her notebook and began the exchanges, as she had agreed with Peach before they entered the house. 'The steward you mentioned, Harry Barnard, has confirmed that you left the football ground at around seven thirty on Saturday, as you told us he would.'

'Thank you. He's a reliable man, Harry. He seems to like being employed for a few hours at Grafton Park, though he's at least as old as me. He doesn't need to be supervised – if he says he'll do a job, you know it will be done. He's – well, I won't say any more.'

'You were going to say he has the standards of an older generation.'

Edward looked at this bright young woman with a new respect for her prescience. 'I was going to say something like that, I suppose. But that would be less than fair to you and others like you. I'm sure there are people around today who are just as capable and just as reliable as they were in my day.'

She smiled at him, half-mocking, half affectionate, and he thought again of the daughters he saw so rarely and how he would have loved one of them to tease him gently like this. Or much more robustly, for that matter. He didn't need to be treated with kid gloves, but there were times when he felt it would be nice to receive any sort of attention at all. 'Perhaps the modern worker just needs a little more direction and supervision than people like Harry.'

She smiled at him again. 'Let's agree on that, shall we? We've now put together a list of people who had the opportunity to commit this murder. We wondered if you'd had any further thoughts on the people who might have also had the motive and the nerve to kill James Capstick. We think you know them better as a group of people than anyone else who was around at the time.'

'I don't know Helen Capstick well.' Edward was playing for time, telling himself not to be too easily swayed by this attractive young face which seemed so friendly and accommodating.

Lucy smiled. 'But you've formed an impression, as we have. It would be interesting to have your view, in confidence.'

He'd given a lot of thought to Helen Capstick since the events of Saturday night. It surely couldn't do him any harm to say what he thought about her. 'Helen is a woman of the modern world. She knows how to look after herself. She'd been married before, as Capstick had. I would imagine she's had other relationships as well. Women like her don't reach their late forties without learning how to look after themselves. That doesn't mean that I think she killed her husband – it's a long step from keeping a beady eye on your interests to murder.'

Except that if Helen Capstick thought her husband was about to discover her affair and disinherit her, she might think drastic action was needed, thought Lucy Blake. She gave Lanchester a winsome smile and said, 'You said you didn't know Mrs Capstick well. That implies that you knew some of the other people involved considerably better than you knew her.'

Edward gave her an answering smile, meant to convey that he understood what she was about and would help her as much as he thought appropriate. 'I know Darren Pearson quite well. I helped to appoint him. I'm happy to say that because he's been an excellent secretary to the club – or chief executive, as we now have to call him.'

'Despite personal problems.' She nodded understandingly, making it a statement rather than a query.

Lanchester glanced at her sharply, then said rather stiffly, 'I know that his wife has left him. I'm sorry about that. I liked Meg.'

'Then you'll be happy to hear that they're back together at present. Perhaps I should tell you that we know about Mr Pearson's problems with gambling.'

'The gambling thing has never affected his work. He's always been efficient at the club and always been there when he was needed.'

'But he must have felt threatened when he heard about the sale of the club. He wouldn't easily get another job, with the problems in his private life.'

'You would need to discuss that with him. I reiterate that as far as I'm concerned – and I'm sure as far as someone much more demanding like Capstick was concerned – Darren Pearson was a model employee.'

The barriers were going up. Sensing that his DS had got as far as she was going to get, Peach said sharply, 'And what about Robbie Black and Debbie Black?'

Edward turned unhurriedly to face the dark eyes and challenging face of the man directing this investigation. 'As a football manager, Robbie is highly successful. For a club the size of Brunton Rovers, success consists of keeping us in the Premiership. That's a fact of life we have to accept in the modern football world.'

'And as a man?'

'He's a disciplinarian. There aren't too many of those among modern managers, now that they have to deal with millionaire prima donnas.' For a moment, his nostalgia for an older and simpler era which he knew was gone forever misted his eyes. Then he recalled himself sternly to the matter in hand. 'Robbie Black learned to look after himself in one of the toughest areas of Glasgow and he hasn't forgotten it.'

The three of them were silent for a moment, thinking of the implications of this for the crime committed five days earlier. Then Peach said, 'What about Mrs Black?'

'Debbie's devoted to her husband and her family.'

'You like her.'

'It would be difficult not to like Debbie. She was a tennis star and a successful model, but she seems to have relinquished the celebrity spotlight without a qualm to become a loyal wife and a devoted mother. She loves Brunton and she's building a life for herself and her family here. I believe she'd do anything for Robbie.'

'Even murder?'

He smiled at Peach's intensity. 'No, not murder. Anything within reason. Murder isn't within reason, is it?'

Peach relaxed a little, answering Lanchester's smile while still studying him relentlessly. 'The trouble is that, at the time of the death, murderers sometimes see killing as exactly that, Mr Lanchester. As the only reasonable way out of a particular situation. Have you any further thoughts to offer us?'

Edward Lanchester looked at him curiously for a moment, wondering exactly how much Peach knew about these people, before he said firmly, 'No. Nothing at present.'

'Then we shall be on our way. Thank you for your help.' Peach stood looking out of the window for a moment, as

if taking in the full glory of the scarlet rhododendron, and
then left without looking at Lanchester again.

The Blacks' au pair was Swedish. She was tall, blonde, and
competent, and like most young Swedes she spoke excellent English. She had completed her degree and was spending
a year acquiring work experience before she committed
herself to a career. She was sure now what she wanted to
do, partly as a result of her experiences in Brunton. Sixteen
months from now, after another year of training, she would
become a primary school teacher.

Hilde Svendson was also a soccer enthusiast who had
followed the results in the English Premiership diligently
in her home country. One of the attractions of this post for
her had been involvement with the children of a football
manager in the Premiership and the connection, however
tenuous, with the glamour of big-time soccer. She supported
Liverpool: she felt that she was the only person living in
the Brunton area who had been dismayed by last Saturday's
result.

At ten o'clock on Wednesday morning, the children were
at school and the spacious modern house felt curiously quiet
and empty. Hilde was sorting through the children's discarded
toys with Mrs Black, gathering together a considerable array
of highly coloured wood and plastic which would be taken
first to the local play group and then, after being been sifted
there, to the charity shop.

'We should have got rid of most of these a year or
more ago,' said Debbie Black, handling a wheeled wooden
horse with a touch of nostalgia. 'It's having plenty of
storage space that does it. In our last house I'd have had
to be much more ruthless because we needed the room.
Look how much clutter we've gathered! And it's all stuff
they'll never touch again.' She looked at the formidable
array with a moment of regret for the years of infancy which
would not come again. 'We've almost finished now. We'll
have a cup of coffee and then you can have the gym to
yourself for an hour if you like.'

Hilde was enthusiastic about fitness, and delighted with

the array of exercise machines in the private gym at the back of the house. Debbie had noted her Junoesque figure and the fact that she was an enthusiastic trainer, and thus wore very little in that room. She trusted Robbie implicitly, of course, but there was no use thrusting temptation under a man's nose. Vigorous men of forty-four should be protected from the sensations generated by a panting and scantily clad Hilde Svendson, for their own and everyone else's sake. You tended to be a little more cautious about these things when you had yourself reached forty-three.

The bedroom was at the back of the house, so that neither of them heard the car coming up the drive. It was not until the doorbell rang that Debbie went and looked through the window of the front bedroom and realized who the visitors were. 'It's the police,' she told Hilde, as she watched DCI Peach climb out of the passenger seat of the Mondeo and look up at the house. 'Do you think you could stow these things into my car and take them to the play centre?'

Hilde hesitated. 'What is "stow"?'

'Sorry. I just meant pack them into the back of the car and dispose of them for us. The police will probably want to speak to me on my own, you see.'

If Hilde was disappointed to be cut off from the drama of detection, she hid it well. She hadn't been a qualified driver for very long and she appreciated being trusted with her employer's car. By the time Debbie Black had prepared coffee and biscuits for Peach and Blake, she had packed the toys into the car and was easing it carefully past the police vehicle.

This time it was Peach who began the questioning. 'We asked you to go on thinking about Saturday's killing and the people who were around at the time, Mrs Black.'

'I've done that. It's difficult not to, when you've been close to something horrific like that. I haven't managed to come up with anything which seems significant.'

'Really?' Peach's eyebrows arched impossibly high towards the baldness above them. They seemed to Debbie Black the most expressive black arcs she had ever seen. 'Have you reviewed your own story? Are you happy that you've told us what the courts used to call the whole truth and nothing but the truth?'

Debbie felt the skin on her face suddenly very warm. She fought for calmness as she pretended to review what she had said to them on Monday. 'I think I told you everything. James Capstick dropped his bombshell and shocked us all – even his wife, as far as I could see. Several people, including me, spoke up against the sale of the club to people who knew nothing about this area, but Capstick made it clear that none of us had any say in the matter. Then he left us and we indulged in a collective bout of righteous indignation. It was clear to me pretty quickly that we weren't achieving anything more than letting off steam, so I left and drove back here. I couldn't be certain of the time I left, but it was probably around half an hour after Capstick had told us he was going up to his office.'

'You didn't go out again?'

'No. I was here for the rest of the evening. Robbie rang and told me that he was going to see his old friend and fellow-manager Jack Cox about the implications of the takeover for him. I think he got in at about eleven and we then spent another hour discussing what was going to happen to us.'

'You didn't go back to the football ground after you'd left?'

'No. I just told you. I didn't go out at all for the rest of the evening after I'd returned here.'

'That isn't quite what I asked you, Mrs Black. I asked if you returned to Grafton Park at any time after you'd left.'

'Then I'm telling you again that I didn't.'

He looked at her steadily for what was probably a few seconds but what seemed to Debbie a very long time. She stared steadily, fixedly, back at him, trying to thrust away the thought that her cheeks must be reddening. Then, almost reluctantly it seemed, Peach said, 'Our information is that you did in fact return to the football ground on Saturday night, not long after you had left the private car park.'

Her first instinct was to hold stubbornly to her denial, as if she had been a child caught in some minor transgression.

But they must have a witness, possibly more than one. She wouldn't drop her eyes, but she couldn't meet Peach's gimlet stare for any longer. She transferred her gaze to the woman who sat with her eyes on her notebook as she said dully. 'I did go back. But I didn't kill Capstick.'

Peach was quieter, less challenging now after her admission. He said softly. 'You had better give us a full and exact account of your movements.'

'Yes.' But there was a long moment before she spoke again, whilst she fought to stop her mind from racing. 'I left as I told you, perhaps half an hour after Capstick had left us in the hospitality suite, perhaps a little less than that. But I didn't come straight back here. About a mile away from the ground, I turned into a lay-by and stopped to collect my thoughts. Eventually I decided to go back and speak to Capstick. To plead with him, if you like.'

'From your description of the man and his reactions in the hospitality lounge a little earlier, you couldn't have expected him to be very receptive.'

'I don't suppose I did. But Robbie's future was at stake. Our whole life in Brunton was at stake. I was prepared to try anything to save those things.'

'Even murder.'

'No. Not murder. I wasn't thinking of that.'

'So what exactly did you do?'

'I sat in the lay-by for ten minutes, perhaps fifteen. Then I drove slowly back to the ground. I had to make myself do it, because I didn't really think Capstick was going to take much notice of me. But I've persuaded a few men to change their decisions in the past.' A private, unconscious smile relaxed her taut features for a moment. 'Anyway, I had to try, because there was so much at stake for us.'

'Did you see anyone else when you went back?'

'No. It was very quiet around the entrance by then. I parked in a side street, not in the private car park. I didn't think anyone had seen me.'

She looked interrogatively at Peach, but she knew he wasn't going to reveal the identity of his witness. 'Go on, please. Try not to miss anything out.'

'I slipped through the single wooden door which was the only one which was open and went quickly up the stairs to the chairman's office. I'd never been up there before, so I wasn't even sure which room was his at first, but the door was clearly labelled. I knocked and there was no reply, so I pushed the door open cautiously and went in. I got a terrible shock. I think I might even have given a little scream, but I'm not sure of that.'

She was silent then, recalling the scene, thinking for a moment that they already knew what she was going to say. It was Lucy Blake who prompted her with the obvious question. 'So why were you so shocked, Mrs Black?'

An involuntary shudder shook the slim body opposite them. If the woman was acting this, she was doing it very well. 'The man I'd come to plead with was dead. He was slumped forward over his desk and I didn't realize what had happened, until I saw that awful mark around his neck, as if something had cut right into it.'

TWENTY-ONE

An hour later, DCI Peach sat with his head in his hands at his desk, pondering his next move. That was determined for him when his internal phone informed him that Chief Superintendent Tucker needed to see him urgently.

He climbed the stairs dutifully, then watched Tucker shuffle papers self-importantly into a file before he could afford his DCI his full attention. 'It's time you were getting results in this James Capstick case,' Tucker said portentously.

'We've made progress, sir.'

'That isn't enough, as you know. The press are implying that we're baffled.'

'Yes, sir. It's a favourite word of theirs, isn't it? I think we are quite near to an arrest. I would appreciate your guidance.'

Tucker glanced at him suspiciously, but there was no hint of irony in the round and expressionless face. 'You're welcome to my advice.'

'Thank you. Proof may be the difficulty, sir. I think I know who did this, but I have no proof worthy of the name and I don't see it presenting itself easily.'

Tucker, who had been preparing to browbeat his DCI, was thrown off balance. He couldn't remember when his advice had last been sought. 'You'd better tell me what you've found about the people involved in the case, if you want my views.'

'Yes, sir. The wife is Helen Capstick. She is a major gainer by this death – however dubious the sources of his wealth, Capstick was a rich man. She was conducting an affair at the time of his death. Capstick was ignorant of this, though he may have had his suspicions. Helen knew that his chauffeur was about to put him in the picture.'

Tucker pursed his lips, stared at the ceiling for a moment,

and said with an air of revelation, 'The widow could be the one, in my view. Did she have opportunity as well as motive?'

'Indeed she did, sir. Alongside several other people, of course.'

Tucker looked disappointed. 'We shall bear her in mind. What about this chief executive you mentioned in your notes?'

'Darren Pearson. Another man with motive and opportunity, sir. He seems to be an effective administrator, but his private life is in turmoil, as a result of a serious gambling problem. He would probably have lost his highly paid post had Brunton Rovers FC been sold. He admits he would find it difficult to obtain a similar post elsewhere.'

'That makes him a strong candidate for this crime, you know.'

Peach reflected for a moment on Tommy Bloody Tucker's continuing talent for the blindin' bleedin' obvious. 'Yes, sir, I thought that. He knows the labyrinth of passages and rooms beneath the stand at Grafton Park better than anyone, which makes him on the face of it the most likely person to have followed Capstick up to the chairman's office. Apart, perhaps, from the man who had been chairman himself in a previous era.'

'Edward Lanchester? I don't think you should entertain Edward as even a possibility. He's been a prominent figure in the town for forty years now. A very successful businessman, in his day, and still a highly respected local figure.'

'Yes, sir.' Percy held his peace and forbore to remind Tucker that respected local figures and even successful businessmen were not immune from temptation. 'There's the Blacks. Robbie and Debbie.' He glanced at Tucker's uncomprehending face. 'The football manager at Brunton Rovers might also be out of work after a Middle Eastern takeover. His wife is not only a determined supporter of her husband but much attached to this town and its people.'

Recognition dawned on the head of Brunton's CID. 'The tennis player. Nice girl, that. Hardly strikes me as a killer.'

'Some time since she was a tennis star, sir. Debbie Black is forty-three now. A very determined woman when her family's interests are threatened, I would say. Also, she returned to Grafton Park after leaving on Saturday night. A visit which she initially concealed from us.'

Had he expected a compliment on his diligence in discovering this, Percy would have been disappointed. Tucker said ponderously, 'And how did the woman seek to explain this?'

'She says she went to try to reason with Capstick. She claims he was already dead when she entered his office.'

Tucker rocked back on his chair, then leant forward decisively. 'No doubt you're taking that story with a large pinch of salt, Peach. That would certainly be my advice.'

'Yes, sir. I thought it might. Would you like to know who I think did this and how I think we might extract a confession?'

Chief Superintendent Tucker did his usual impression of a particularly obtuse goldfish, and Peach hastened to take him into his confidence. It was always as well to have the hierarchy behind you when you played a hunch, in case you were totally mistaken and the proverbial hit the fan.

The April afternoon was bright with the promise of summer as Lucy Blake turned the police Mondeo between the now familiar high gateposts of Edward Lanchester's substantial Edwardian villa.

'This will be a bluff,' said Percy Peach.

Lucy thought she had never seen him look so nervous. 'You're good at bluff,' she said firmly.

Lanchester was standing on the top step with the big blue front door open behind him before they got out of the car. 'You look as if you have news for me,' he said breezily. He glanced up at the clouds racing across the spring sky before he took them into the sitting room with the long window which looked out across the garden to the big scarlet rhododendron.

'They announced on the radio at one o'clock that the takeover was definitely off,' he told them with satisfaction.

'You'll be pleased about that,' said DS Blake. She knew that he liked her by now, so that it seemed natural to her to respond to his news.

'We think we are very close to an arrest,' said Peach, who had not taken his eyes off the handsome, ageing face since they had come into the room.

'That's good.' Edward waited for a moment. Then, when neither of them offered anything, he added, 'I think I said to you on Monday that whilst I didn't like Capstick, I couldn't really condone murder.'

'Indeed you did. It was something which Darren Pearson told us which led us towards the solution of this particular mystery.' Peach was fencing with the man with his own weapons, offering phrases couched in politeness rather than anything more direct.

'That implies that your man is not Pearson. I'm glad about that. I think I told you on Monday that Pearson has been an excellent servant to Brunton Rovers. I also happen to like him.' He nodded his satisfaction two or three times, as if they had been talking about some minor piece of good fortune for the chief executive.

'Darren Pearson told us, you see, that he had seen someone returning to the club after they had apparently left on Saturday night. Someone who had neglected to tell us anything at all about this episode.'

'Who was this?'

The directness was startling after the previous leisurely phrases. For the first time in their three meetings, Lanchester looked both animated and disturbed. Peach took his time, but he still stared unblinkingly, disconcertingly, at his man. 'It was Debbie Black.'

'Debbie Black couldn't commit murder. She isn't that sort of person.'

'Isn't she? Your reaction does you credit, but I'm afraid you must leave us to be the judges of that, Mr Lanchester.'

'But didn't you listen to what she had to say? She must have given you some explanation for her actions.'

'Oh, she says that she went back to try to reason with James Capstick, though she agrees that he wasn't the sort of man who would have listened to reason.'

'But surely that's possible? It was clear when the man made his announcement that Debbie and Robbie Black were

most upset about it. I think it's quite possible that she went
back to plead with him.'

'Shouldn't you be asking me what sort of reaction she
got from Capstick?'

The well-groomed elderly man looked thoroughly uncomfortable. 'I suppose I presumed that she got no satisfaction
from him. I think you implied that. What did in fact happen?'

'Nothing at all, according to Mrs Black. She claims, you
see, that when she climbed the stairs and entered that office
Mr Capstick was already dead.'

'Well, isn't that quite possibly what happened? Debbie
Black may well be telling you the truth.'

Peach shrugged his broad shoulders elaborately. The
expression on his face said that he couldn't believe that
anyone could be so gullible. 'You learn to be cynical, in
this job, Mr Lanchester. Mrs Black concealed the whole
of this episode from us, when we interviewed her on
Monday. That seems significant, to me. It certainly won't
count in her favour when she is in court, facing a charge
of murder.'

The old man rose from his chair with startling agility. 'I
think we need a drink.'

'Not for me,' said Peach promptly. Blake shook her head
when Lanchester gestured towards her with the whisky
bottle. He poured himself a measure, looked for a moment
in silence across the long stretch of weedless lawn to the
border beyond, and sat down again, sipping the spirit neat,
whilst his brain raced furiously towards a decision.

'Debbie Black's a good woman and in my view an honest
one. That will surely count in her favour.'

Peach noted the desperation in his tone with satisfaction
and allowed himself another, less elaborate, shrug. 'The
judge will direct any jury to consider the facts of the matter.
Debbie Black will not be able to deny motive – both she
and her husband had a lot to lose with the proposed change
of ownership. She will have to admit that she went to the
room where murder was committed and that she lied about
it afterwards.' Peach knew that the Crown Prosecution
Service would never take so thin a case to court, but believed

that Lanchester like most members of the public would have only the sketchiest knowledge of their procedures.

Edward Lanchester took another substantial sip of his whisky, felt the warmth of it coursing through his throat and his chest. 'You must have other candidates for this crime. I felt the atmosphere in the hospitality suite on Saturday night when Capstick was telling us all that whatever we said, whatever we felt, wouldn't make a jot of difference to him. When he was positively enjoying telling us that we were completely powerless in the matter, there was real hostility to the man.'

'I accept that. Everyone who was there seems to be agreed upon it. But only one of them had the nerve to take action.'

Perhaps it was the implied admiration for the boldness of the action that finally swayed him. Edward had already decided that he couldn't allow a woman he liked and admired to be charged with a crime she had not committed. But the final, logical step to removing her from the spotlight was an admission. He downed the last of his whisky with a decisive swallow, then said with devastating simplicity, 'I killed Jim Capstick.'

If he had expected astonishment in his audience, he was disappointed. The young woman he had increasingly regarded as a substitute daughter rose silently, moved across the room to him, and quietly and unemotionally voiced the words of his arrest. He looked up at her, fancied he caught in her vivid blue-green eyes the sympathy she had so carefully excluded from the formal phrases of the arrest. He said dully to Peach, 'You knew, didn't you?'

'I thought I knew. We needed a confession. Neither of us thought you'd allow someone else to be charged with a crime you knew you'd committed.'

Edward gave a small, sad smile at this oblique tribute to his integrity. 'How did you know?'

'Something you said on Monday evening when we first talked to you. Something I hardly noticed myself at the time. When we asked you if you'd any idea who might have committed this killing, you said that of course you'd been thinking about that "over the last forty-eight hours". That was too precise for your own good. You'd only been told of the murder by Darren Pearson on Sunday morning: officially you'd known about it for less than thirty-six hours. Only the person who'd committed the crime had known about it for forty-eight hours and more.'

Edward Lanchester nodded. The details of his error seemed only a matter of curiosity to him now. He felt he'd always known that he was going to confess. He even felt a curious relief in acknowledging his guilt. 'I couldn't let that man destroy Brunton Rovers. The football club's been a central theme in my life. People say it's only a game, but it's always been a lot more than that for me.'

Peach said with a reluctance which was real, not simulated. 'We'll have to take you to the station. You'll be formally charged there and put in a cell overnight.'

Edward said with a belated touch of pride. 'I've made my dispositions. Settled my money and my property upon my daughters. That was well before I disposed of James Capstick. It was as if I was getting ready for this.'

They took him outside to where the second police vehicle was waiting as arranged behind the one Lucy Blake had parked. Lanchester took a last look at the handsome elevations of the house where he had lived for half a century. He dropped back into the dialect of his boyhood as he said to no one in particular, 'My Eleanor was nobbut a lass when we moved in here.'

DC Clyde Northcott was waiting with two uniformed officers to take their man to the station. Peach said on impulse, 'Let DS Blake sit in the car with Mr Lanchester. He isn't going to give us any trouble.'

If Northcott was surprised, he knew better than to show it. He slid into the driving seat of the Mondeo, adjusted it for his long legs, and drove Peach back in silence to the station. In the car ahead of them, they could see Edward Lanchester between a uniformed constable and Lucy Blake, turned slightly towards her, voicing the occasional words to this woman with whom he seemed to have formed the lightest and most intangible of bonds.

Peach rode in silence, wondering exactly what was passing

between this odd couple. As they approached the station, he realized that his driver had been smiling for some minutes. It was an unusual lightening of the normally stern black features. He said, 'What is it you find so amusing, DC Northcott? That's a decent man we're about to lock up for the rest of his life.'

'It's not that, sir. I wasn't thinking about Edward Lanchester. I was just revising a few anecdotes about you for my best man's speech at the wedding.'